Tales at the Top

First edition, 2024

Book Design by Nuno Moreira, NMDESIGN

ISBN 978-1-965178-00-3 (paperback)

Tales at the Top

The Beeze Series Book #02

David Lee Luedtke

To my children,
Matthew, Hannah, Valentino, Callahan, and Margaux

PREFACE

Many paths lead concurrently to the same destination.

*

"As soon as I can, I'm going to ride my motorcycle away from here and out of this marriage," Jay Baumers declared, sitting in a Green Bay, Wisconsin coffee shop, after signing the documents that made his divorce from his childhood sweetheart official.

*

"Why would I ever need to know how to design semiconductor chips?" Brian Lomax said to his roommate while pulling an all-nighter cramming for his Electric Circuits Design course at the University of Wisconsin.

*

"I must be at the epicenter of technology," Daniel Kim said when he left his Korean family restaurant in Vancouver to take his technology degree to San Francisco where Stanford University accepted him into the MBA program.

*

All three people arrived in Silicon Valley in 1984 for various reasons. At the time, Silicon Valley had previously morphed from a defense industry location in the 1950s to become the leading semiconductor center by 1984.

In the 1950s, Silicon Valley was primarily known as an area dominated by the defense industry, home to several major defense contractors and research institutions. The defense industry bloomed by its proximity to prestigious universities and a skilled workforce. The region's natural beauty and temperate climate also served as an attraction for scientists and engineers.

During this time, the transformation to what became Silicon Valley took place with seeds from the defense industry. In the late 1950s, two Stanford University professors, William Shockley and Frederick Terman, played crucial roles in shaping the future of the region. Shockley, one of the inventors of the transistor, established his own semiconductor company, Shockley Semiconductor Laboratory, in the area. However, internal turmoil and clashes with his employees led to a group of eight talented engineers leaving and forming a new company called Fairchild Semiconductor. History later called them "The Traitorous Eight."

This event marked a turning point. Fairchild Semiconductor became one of the first successful commercial semiconductor manufacturers, introducing groundbreaking technologies. The company's success not only established Silicon Valley as a hub for semiconductors but also laid the foundation for future high-tech industries.

The 1960s saw the birth of several iconic technology companies that further propelled Silicon Valley's growth. One of the most notable was Intel, founded in 1968 by Gordon Moore and Robert Noyce, former employees of Fairchild Semiconductor. Intel's development of the microprocessor revolutionized computing and set the stage for the personal computer era.

Simultaneously, Stanford University played a crucial role in fostering an entrepreneurial environment. Frederick Terman, often referred to as the "Father of Silicon Valley," encouraged Stanford's faculty and students to start their own companies, which helped bridge the gap between academia and industry. Terman's support led to the founding of companies such as Cisco Systems and Sun Microsystems.

By the 1980s, Silicon Valley became established as a center of technological innovation. The region was home to a myriad of startups and established technology companies, working in various areas such as semiconductors, computer hardware, software, and networking. In 1984, Apple Inc., founded by Steve Jobs and Steve Wozniak, launched the Macintosh computer, solidifying its position as a pioneer in the personal computing industry.

Silicon Valley's transformation from a defense industry location to a global technology powerhouse within a few decades was the result of multiple factors. The collaboration between academia and industry, the entrepreneurial spirit, the availability of venture capital, and the concentration of skilled minds all contributed to this remarkable evolution. Today, Silicon Valley remains at the forefront of innovation, shaping the world through advancements in technology and driving the digital revolution.

The origins of artificial intelligence, autonomous driving, the internet of things, and algorithms began in garages and warehouses by a bunch of nerds doing cool things. Some of them dropped out of college to work on their great ideas. Some of them took cautious routes that eventual led to other risk-takers making their mark on the industry instead. Some of them worked at companies that turned them into millionaires in spite of their lack of abilities. And some used knowledge gained at one company, spun off to another company and became wealthy that way.

"There's gold in them thar hills," is how one person supposedly declared.

CHAPTER 1

At tunnel's peak, where paths converge and blend,
A mix of old and new, delights extend.

Many paths lead simultaneously to the same destination, although some paths are more difficult than others. Daniel Kim toiled up a winding and steep staircase from the street below in order to get a clear view of the sign that beckoned him to the Top of the Tunnel bar. He paused at the top of the tunnel for an opportunity to catch his breath, but could not help but stare at the view before him. Looking off to the south, he saw the path he took from the Financial District, the area of the city representing all things new in the world. Below him and northward through the tunnel underneath him lay Chinatown, the oldest and most traditional part of the area. Behind him at the top of the tunnel lay the scene of wealth, the Ritz Carlton Hotel. An eastward and downhill trek to the waterfront led to shipping and industry. And to the west, the road climbed uphill to rows of residences along with bars and eateries. Daniel stood at the junction of all these worlds and also in front of a new bar after a long day of work.

The vibrant feel of the streets of San Francisco is a triumph of city planners and architects gone before. The big problem to overcome was that the grid-based urban map superimposed over the steep and hilly region surrounded by an irregular bay of water does not fit well with straight lines. Hundreds of small, winding alleys, walkways, lanes, courts, stairways, plazas and paths traverse the crooked landscape. There are even some tunnels. It seemed like an impossible task, trying to stretch this square map across the back of an armadillo.

Daniel Kim had used his college degree to take a chance at success.

Finally, after years of waiting around in Vancouver, the Stanford business school offered a full-ride scholarship which he later converted into a job in Menlo Park, the nucleus of venture capital operations for Silicon Valley. Each night, he sluggishly made his way north to San Francisco on the train, feeling lucky to have a steady income. This evening, he took a different path home from the train station to his family's apartment and discovered a bar called Top of the Tunnel.

Daniel arrived at Top of the Tunnel wearing a blue sport coat over a neat white dress shirt and black tie, with blue jeans and spotless Nike shoes as was the standard attire among executives in Silicon Valley in 1984. His idol, Steve Jobs, topped off the ensemble with a black turtleneck instead of the shirt and tie that Daniel sported.

Daniel headed toward the front door of the bar, noticing its grand Italian canopy overhead and checkered tiles on the entryway below. The bar was noisy, but all conversation ceased as everyone looked up when Daniel walked in. Some people raised their eyebrows and then quickly diverted their gazes. An elderly white-haired man behind the counter, Frank Renado, waved at Daniel cheerfully and beckoned him over to a barstool in front of the recently wiped bar top. He introduced himself and suggested a beer.

Daniel examined the bar top and then scanned up and down the long wooden bar and across the long, narrow tavern, taking in every detail of the rustic place. Two men sat at a side table wearing black suits, sipping from glasses filled with scotch. A Chinese man seated at the bar watched a golf outing broadcast on television while two Black men seated at the far end of the bar laughed boisterously at a recent joke. An attractive woman with raven hair and sapphire eyes carried drinks to two young women seated at a side table. Further back, several older Italian gentlemen enjoyed an intense game of cards beneath a lone overhead light. The din and odor of the place caused Daniel to smile as if he had found a new home.

Saloon doors banged open at the side of the bar, and a tall, dark-haired man entered carrying a tray of focaccia sandwiches and fries for delivery to the two ladies at the side table.

"Welcome to Top of the Tunnel," Frank said from behind the bar and motioned with one hand for his new customer to sit down. Frank set a paper menu in front of Daniel, who then looked at the row of tap spigots for the numerous beers on tap instead of reading them from the menu.

"What lagers do you have?" Daniel asked and selected one after hearing the detailed explanations about each beer from Frank.

Daniel settled in while staring up at the rows of glasses stacked gracefully in rows in an overhead wooden racking system seemingly for every type of drinking glass ever made, with dust settling on some of the more ornate glasses on side racks. Two large mirrors flanked the center of the wide, finely crafted back bar. The scrolling along the entire bar looked as if handmade a hundred years ago. Rows of liquor lined every nook and cranny of the polished wood surface, reflecting light from gleaming brass spigots mounted on small whiskey barrels on the back bar. A massive wooden door led to an old walk-in cooler at the end.

Daniel rotated on his seat and studied all the framed photographs taped to the back walls opposite the bar. Scenes from parties and gatherings covering decades filled line upon line around him, from past sports teams and numerous championships to local professional teams. Prominently displayed above rows of photos were pieces of autographed memorabilia from sports legends and a fairly new one signed by Joe Montana himself commemorating the quarterback's 1982 Super Bowl win.

More and more people poured in, and the busy young waitress spread the guests out amongst the side tables and barstools. The older Chinese man down the bar mumbled something to Daniel about golf but Daniel said he had not swung a club in years. Daniel glanced at the other TVs in sight and took notice of the basketball games playing on the other ones instead.

Daniel felt a tap on his shoulder that awakened him from watching the beautiful scenery displayed on the golf channel. He stiffened his shoulders as he wheeled around slowly to see a tall and powerful-looking Black man standing beside him.

"Pardon me, sir," the gentleman inquired with politeness. "Do you mind if we switch this TV to watch the Warriors and Knicks game?"

Daniel shifted his perspective before flashing a smile. "I'd love to see that game. Sleepy Floyd is back from his injury tonight, right?"

The gentleman let out a laugh and patted Daniel's shoulder as they both shared some details about the star on the team, Sleepy Floyd, coming off his injury. The man introduced himself to Daniel as Charles Kang.

Daniel studied Charles, a towering figure with muscles bulging under his work shirt. The man looked like one of those fire dancers in a Polynesian dance at a Hawaiian resort. Charles revealed his mother was from Korea and his father was a Vietnam vet and that he worked on one of San Francisco's iconic cable cars. Charles's storytelling had Daniel engrossed, who asked numerous questions about how Charles managed the large lever in the center of the cable car to grip onto the cables beneath the streets.

Charles looked at the television and back at Daniel. He said jokingly, "When I saw you watching the golf channel, I thought you were just another rich guy who wanted to watch golf instead of basketball."

He waved over to Frank, the bartender, to change the channel, and Frank rushed over with a remote control ready in hand. After briefly scrolling through channels, the screen eventually displayed the Warriors game as the starting lineup ran onto the court.

Charles waved over his friend seated at the end of the bar who then came over and took the last remaining seat next to Daniel and Charles. They all watched the screen and eagerly awaited Sleepy Floyd's entrance. Charles introduced his friend, Jorge Freeman, a small and stocky Black man with long dreadlocks cascading past his shoulders. Jorge was a cable repairman on the cable car system. He worked late into the night repairing the underground cables damaged by heavily-weighted cars that clamped too tightly onto the cables as they made their way up steep hillsides with cars overloaded with tourists and locals.

The roar of the crowd on the television grew intensely as they caught sight of their much-loved star emerging from the locker room area. For two hours, Daniel and his new companions watched the game unfold before their eyes; yet another loss for Golden State Warriors against the New York Knicks. Jorge made his leave in the third quarter due to an upcoming shift at the repair yard.

As the bar began emptying, with Daniel and Charles still talking about basketball, the other bartender took over for Frank and introduced himself as Jimmy Baumers, the bartender for the late-night shift. Jimmy was tall and relatively handsome, with a nicely trimmed mustache and long sideburns. He explained that Frank, the owner, did the lunch through evening hours, and Jimmy came on to manage the evening and usually closed around 3:00 a.m., seven days a week.

After noticing raised eyes from Daniel about the long hours required at the bar, Jimmy explained while polishing a beer glass that, "My brother Jay is here now to help out, so I should be able to get some nights off finally."

Daniel acknowledged the discussion of the long hours. "I know the feeling. I worked at my family's restaurant for three years up in Vancouver. The hours are long."

"What brought you here?" Charles asked.

"My engineering degree from the Korea University of Technology, and then I got into Stanford for an MBA," Daniel explained as he set his empty beer bottle off to the side. "I didn't plan on working in a bar in Vancouver my whole life."

Jimmy stopped wiping the glass and looked at Daniel with surprise. "Me either," he said quietly, a hint of determination in his voice.

Daniel opened his mouth to apologize but Jimmy cut him off, offering a smile to show that he took no offense. "But this is too good to be true," Jimmy continued, leaning into the bar to speak more privately to Charles and Daniel. He grinned broadly now as he declared, "I am going to own this place in a few years. Frank and I struck a deal."

From behind them, a pleasant voice from a young woman passing by on her way out added to the secret conversation. "And I'm going to teach him some finance skills so he can actually keep the place open."

The men turned toward the voice and saw Jiewen Li walking past, her business suit hugging her slender curves and her skirt meeting regulations for modesty yet still accentuating her confident stride and shapely legs.

Jimmy raised an eyebrow in response to her comment and called out after her while waving for her to pause. He spoke proudly to Daniel and Charles as he introduced the woman. He pronounced her name the way she instructed, so the name came out as "Jay When." Jimmy added, "Let me introduce you to my financial advisor."

Jiewen flashed a warm smile back over her shoulder before replying, "Hi boys," as she placed her hands on Charles and Daniel's shoulders. Her eyes twinkled mischievously as she announced her departure: "I have a busy day at the office tomorrow, so I have to run. See you next time."

Jimmy said goodbye to Jiewen and slowly moved down the bar to check on other patrons with eyes flitting over the those seated around its circumference. Daniel with his beer and Charles clutching a whiskey sour, deep in conversation, spoke of jobs and life. Jimmy heard snippets of their discussion as he approached them. He paused in front of the two men and asked, "What do you do now?"

Daniel took a quick sip from his beer before replying. "I work at a venture capital company reviewing proposals for investments."

"Any software companies?" Charles inquired, taking another gulp of his drink and then continuing confidently. "That's where the real money is these days."

The question threw Daniel off for a second, but he could not really disclose specific details about his work at Sequoia Capital. Daniel simply replied, "Everything with technology. Hard drives, electronic circuits, software, bit-tech, fin-tech. Really just about anything that comes out of Xerox Park."

Jimmy leaned forward, intrigued by the mention of Xerox Park. "What's that place all about, anyway?"

Daniel directed his answer to Jimmy: "Xerox Park is a big think-tank. They do a lot of research projects for the Defense Advanced Research Projects Agency," he replied with a sly grin on his face.

Charles burst out laughing at Daniel's explanation. "You invest in DARPA projects? Aren't they the ones who tried to make a robot elephant?"

Daniel chuckled, and Jimmy looked puzzled but chuckled along. After the laughter had died down and a few more examples of strange projects that DARPA tried developing, Daniel revealed one investment that paid off. "But there is this one company called Apple Computers that I'm really interested in."

"Apple?" Charles responded incredulously.

"They are entering the PC market and challenging IBM," Daniel continued.

Jimmy frowned as he did not understand much of what Daniel and Charles talked about.

Charles jumped in with enthusiasm. "Did you see that Superbowl ad with that sexy lady throwing a hammer at the screen? So cool! Very Orwellian."

"This is only the beginning," Daniel replied, surprised that Charles was aware of such things. "Their product pipeline for thirty years from now includes tech that doesn't even exist yet."

"I bought a Macintosh computer the very next day after seeing that commercial," Charles said. "What an incredible bit of advertising."

Daniel looked astounded and turned to Charles. "You bought an Apple computer?"

"What? Did you think I couldn't read or something?" Charles chuckled and raised his drink for a clinking toast and then added, "I won't be driving cable cars my whole life."

The glasses above the bar began making a tinkling sound as they rattled against each other like wind chimes, causing everyone to look up simultaneously at the source of the sound. A quick rolling earthquake sent tremors across the floor and Jimmy instinctively placed both hands on the bar top for stability. "Earthquake," he cautioned as patrons struggled to keep their balance.

Charles shrugged it off nonchalantly. "That's nothing, maybe a 4.5 at most." The shaking finally subsided, and an announcement appeared on the television screen—a 4.7 magnitude earthquake had hit San Francisco on the San Andreas fault only minutes ago. People murmured as they all compared their predictions of the magnitude. A couple of people exchanged money based on their bets on the magnitude of the tremor.

The Top of the Tunnel bar had nearly emptied by 2:00 a.m., apart from Daniel and Charles, their heads lolling drunkenly over their drinks. Jimmy continued wiping down the bar as he prepared to close up the place. The lone waitress, Joanne Stoddard, sat on a side table studying her homework. She stood up after checking the clock and tucked her long black hair back into a ponytail before beginning to clear the last table. She set the last glasses back in the kitchen behind the saloon doors and popped out promptly. "That's it, gentlemen," she said with a wink as she swept across the room like a broom. She waved goodbye and slung her purse over one shoulder as she pushed open the large entrance door. The men glanced at her as she went through the door, with their last glimpse of her of her pony tail and purse both swinging with her stride.

Jimmy watched Joanne with concern through the window as she crossed the street then turned to the left toward the path that bypassed Chinatown to head over to the residential area where she lived in North Beach—a hip place to live down by the waterfront. He remained concerned for her walking home by herself at this late hour but knew that somehow Joanne seemed to be fearless and self-reliant.

Jimmy kept watching out the window as various restaurants and bars all closed up and released people onto the streets. He saw several well-dressed people walk by the window on their way back up to the Ritz two blocks up the hill. He also noticed a young Chinese man standing on the street corner, who looked away when he noticed Jimmy looking out the window.

As Daniel and Charles made their way out of the bar, Jimmy double-checked to make sure he extinguished all of the lighted signs and had locked the front door. He went around the bar and flipped off each beer sign in the window one by one and then switched off the lamps atop each table until the only light that remained was from the glowing liquor bottle lights behind the bar. After wiping down the surface of the bar with a damp cloth, he opened the register to count up all of the night's receipts already packed in thick wads of cash. A large vinyl envelope with the name of his bank lay tucked behind the cash drawer to contain the nightly deposits.

To ensure a fair tip distribution among his workers, Jimmy pulled out old envelopes from beneath the countertop and proceeded to split up the contents of the shared tip jar into individual shares for safekeeping.

With everything squared away, he looked outside to scan for any lurkers who could potentially ambush him, then tucked the envelopes containing tips into a hidden drawer. He held the vinyl bag for the bank and stuffed it inside his jacket. He looked out the window one more time and noticed the young man previously standing at the corner seemed to have moved on. Then Jimmy retrieved his telescoping blackjack from behind its secret spot by the front door and quickly slid it up his long sleeve until only its weighted end remained visible beyond his fingers.

Jimmy stepped outside and locked the door behind him while keeping a wary eye on the street. He took off at a rapid pace to the bank to make his deposit before could head uphill to his home, a large three-story Victorian built by his great uncle.

After making the deposit in the night deposit box, Jimmy noticed a figure emerge from the shadows near an alleyway and recognized that it was the same man who had been standing outside the bar earlier. Jimmy raised his blackjack and shouted to the man to stay away.

"No, no, no!" the man exclaimed while raising his hands in surrender. The young man was of average height and build, dressed in blue jeans, sneakers, and an oversized sweater.

Jimmy gradually lowered the weapon but stayed on guard. "What do you want? Why are you following me?"

"My name is Yuze Li. I'm Jiewen's brother," he said.

Jimmy looked perplexed at first but then pulled the blackjack back into his sleeve. "Oh right, I remember you now."

Yuze began talking fast, telling him that he wanted a job and his sister thought Jimmy might need someone who could speak Chinese now that people from Chinatown began frequenting the place. He could work hard and start right away. He was strong and sorry for scaring Jimmy, and he was not sure when would be a good time to ask about employment so he thought he would wait until the bar closed.

Jimmy tried to ease the nervous man's anxiety with questions before finally telling him to go to the bar tomorrow afternoon to see Frank, the owner. With a smile of relief on his face, Yuze thanked Jimmy profusely before practically running away with joy.

At nearly 3:00 a.m., Jimmy walked uphill and stumbled up the long granite stairway leading to the front door of his faded, multi-tenant Victorian. Taking in renters was the only way he could afford to keep the family home. Aunt Betsy would be proud of him for being able to do whatever it takes to keep the house in the family.

A few days later, Yuze came to the bar for his first shift as "Back Bar" bartender. His role was to move dirty dishes back to the dishwasher, wipe down tables and chairs, restock the glasses at the bar, refill the condiments tray, bring prepared food out to the customers, restock the bar refrigerators, and most importantly, keep the walk-in refrigerator stocked and organized.

Jimmy began explaining the bar and the ways they worked. "We have five types of customers here. We got the brainiacs coming from the Financial District down Stockton Street. Most of them head to their homes up here past the bar. Then we got the Italians coming from North Beach and they've been coming here for fifty years some of them. And we got the people of Chinatown now when they cut through the tunnel and up these stairs out here. And we also got the people from the Ritz."

"That's only four," Yuze said while holding up the count on his fingers.

Jimmy looked startled at the comment. "Well, the locals, of course."

Yuze absorbed all of that information as well as many other tips and tricks of the bar. He looked out the window and glanced at the walkway across the top of the tunnel as Jimmy continued his descriptions. He also glanced up the street to the Ritz hotel, surrounded by well-dressed tourists as Jimmy described the rich folks and their behaviors.

Liz Mawbry, a tall and muscular woman dressed in a blue business shirt and blue jeans while clunking her large black boots methodically while surveying the bar, walked in from the kitchen. She wore her hair clipped close and never looked up from her notepad as she walked along the bar to inspect the refrigerators and sinks tucked under the bar top. She gripped a pen tightly in one hand and a notepad in the other, her eyes scouring for cleanliness violations. She added to Jimmy's descriptions as if she heard Jimmy's entire speech about the customers. She looked up at Yuze and said, "And you got building inspectors after they finish their work."

"Hey, Liz. Can we stay open today?" Jimmy asked jokingly.

Frank, looking tired, stepped out of the kitchen. "She shut us down back in 1975, and it took six days to clean up the mess."

Liz handed her checklist with the approval as shown in a large checkmark on the correct box. "Yeah, but Frank, you were cooking food on a hot plate, and your walk-in hadn't been working in two months."

The group chuckled as explanations, threats, funny anecdotes, and laughter held their attention for a while.

Jimmy then stepped forward and made introductions between Liz and Yuze.

Liz paused for a moment, and then realization spread across her face as she recognized Yuze from a meeting at his family's market. She asked, "Li's Market, right?"

Yuze nodded, looking sheepish. "You shut us down a few years ago, too," he added softly.

At first, everyone was silent, and then an uproarious laughter erupted and some good-natured ribbing occurred all around. Liz offered a supportive comment about changes made at the market.

Yuze looked a little frightened but then added, "My grandmother says an ounce of prevention is worth a pound of cure."

"That's true in any language," Frank responded. He laid a hand on Yuze's shoulder and whispered something to him that caused the younger man to nod.

Liz put away her notebook and moved over to the other side of the bar where she ordered a beer and burger before settling in for what would likely be several beers. At one point, Yuze asked if everything was alright and she replied while looking around, "These are good people here. Just like your family."

Yuze met her gaze and said quietly, "I think I'm starting to see."

CHAPTER 2

Paths veer and meet, old college friends in tow,
San Francisco hills steep, car and bike below.

Many paths lay parallel in arriving at the same destination, although some paths are more difficult than others. Although they drifted apart, college friends Brian Lomax and Jay Baumers stepped into the late-night San Francisco air after stopping briefly at the old Victorian house they called home. Brian leaned his tall frame against his completely rebuilt 1967 Camaro parked at the edge of the steep driveway. To the right, he glanced at a little-used motorcycle sitting neglected for a few years. He checked his watch and waited for Jay to walk down the granite staircase from the first floor down to the driveway.

Brian ran his hands along the shiny front fender of his car, recalling the hundreds of hours it took to finish the curved surfaces of the car a few years ago. He completed the work and used the car to move nearly everything he owned packed tightly into the trunk while driving all the way from Wisconsin to California. He remembered the primer gray paint on all four of the Camaro's wheel wells that covered the unstoppable rust from the salted roads of Wisconsin. Jet black paint had covered the remainder of the shapely car that from a distance, looked like an intentional pattern of gray fenders with a black top. Upon closer inspection, the pattern was the product of continuous bodywork after repairing the winter damage every year –three years running.

The dream had been to have the entire car painted a nice shade of metal-flake midnight blue to seal in the metal. The problem was that the weather in Madison, Wisconsin was relentless, and so was the rust that seeped through the bodywork in what seemed like only seconds after spraying on the protective primer coating. But now Brian admired his handy work of the beautifully painted car that shone in the midnight blue like the stars in the sky.

Brian had packed his fishing pole, golf clubs, backpacking equipment, and clothes into the car for a three-week trip across the nation to his new home in California. His friend Jay Baumers also headed west at the same time. His brother Jimmy ran a bar and had a house big enough for a few roommates while they all struggled to find their way in life. The room came at a modest rate if the person also worked in Jimmy's bar two nights each week.

Brian was an electrical engineer looking to break into the burgeoning semiconductor field but had only a few years of relevant experience since graduating from college in 1981. Some recent experience at a college lab that used the same high-tech cleanrooms as those in Silicon Valley was his springboard into the high-technology field in California.

Brian looked inside his Camaro after wiping away some dust on the windshield. The car had a Hertz three-speed transmission that worked well for getting off the line in a race but was terrible for the hills of San Francisco. When arriving a few years before, he recalled how he snubbed the car numerous times while climbing the Mason Street hill that was so steep that the locals called it, "The Mason Wall." After reaching the top of the steep and narrow street, the road went immediately downhill at the same cliff-like slope where he found the street where Jay Baumers now lived.

Jay walked down the stairs above Brian and signaled he was ready. He slipped a black leather jacket over his shoulders and ran each arm through the sleeves while stepping quickly down the stairs. He added a baseball cap and sunglasses to complete the ensemble. Jay had arrived a few years ago also, fresh from a painful divorce from his childhood sweetheart. He arrived on a Kawasaki KZ750 with leather satchels filled to the brim with clothing and a tent and sleeping bag strapped to the front fork. The motorcycle now sat rusting in need of massive repairs on the side of the Victorian. Jay instead used his long legs to walk from the room he rented from his brother to where he worked at the Top of the Tunnel bar two nights per week. He also worked a full-time job with a high-tech construction company. Jay was very handsome and much to his brother's chagrin, often dated women that came into the bar. What Jimmy hated was that then the women later stopped coming into the bar.

Brian and Jay walked downhill and later stumbled into the dimly lit Top of the Tunnel bar, even though it was Jay's day off. The bar had become their de facto living room on most Friday evenings. Yuze worked behind the bar alongside Jimmy on busy nights. Jimmy had enough trust to leave his protégé in charge whilst he took a break and he disappeared through the front door, trying not to attract attention.

Just as Jay ordered another beer from Yuze, he looked out the window and noticed someone crossing the walkway outside above the tunnel. Jimmy emerged from the shadows when a woman approached from across the walkway. Jimmy stopped her halfway across the path and he leaned in for an intense yet playful kiss. The couple stayed together for a moment then separated as the woman walked alone toward the entrance to the bar. As she walked closer, Jay recognized her as one of the other waitresses from the bar. She opened the door and smiled at him before quickly composing herself while stepping into her professional role as if donning a jacket.

Jay glanced at the television and spotted a recent score by the San Francisco Giants, then opened his clunky flip-phone to initiate a call. "Make it a trifecta with the Dodgers and Yankees. Put me down for twenty bucks."

Brian playfully punched Jay on the arm. "Dude, you can't keep gambling like this."

"But it's a sure thing!" Jay replied and felt his arm for soreness. He got up and said his goodbyes. "I'll be at the tables tonight if you're looking for me."

Brian looked twice at Jay. "I thought you had to be on the construction site tomorrow."

"That's not until 8:00 a.m.," Jay replied and walked toward the door, his closely cropped black hair noticeable under the San Francisco Giants hat he tugged from his back pocket and pulled down tightly on his head. "I'll be up a thousand bucks by midnight."

As Jay left the bar, Yuze turned to Brian with a look of admiration and also a look of curiosity. He shook his head. "I don't know how he does it."

Brian nodded in agreement and withdrew his bulky flip-phone from his jeans pocket, feeling the familiar weight in his hand while tucking his golf shirt back into place. He had been one of the first to adopt this Motorola "brick"—the world's first truly portable cell phone with a battery inside. As he clicked open the clamshell and studied the tiny screen for messages, he noticed no one had called since noon. He snapped the phone shut and tucked it away as he slowly sipped his beer, then glanced up to see Joanne Stoddard walking in. She sauntered over confidently, her jeans and high western boots contrasting perfectly with her white shirt and leather jacket. At the newly vacated barstool, she smiled at Brian and said playfully yet provocatively with a wink, "Buy a girl a drink?"

Brian nodded shyly and waved to Yuze, who had also taken notice of beautiful Joanne. The bartender quickly made a rum and coke for her before she could even sit down. "What brings you here on a night off?" Brian asked sheepishly.

"I'm sick of studying," she replied as she accepted the drink and took a sip. She looked around the bar and appeared as if she were going to step in and help the other wait staff, who seemed overwhelmed at the moment. The impulse to help quickly faded, and she looked at Brian.

"Exams coming up?" Brian questioned, trying to fill an awkward silence that felt more noticeable to him than to Joanne. He knew she was smart and was very preoccupied with her studies.

Joanne nodded and met Brian's eyes. "Finals on Monday in my biology class, but I think I know the material."

Brian looked away quickly after studying her beautiful face but then added, "Didn't you say you had an environmental engineering degree?" Brian asked curiously.

Joanne nodded again with a smile. "Yeah. But I couldn't get a job anywhere, so I went back to school," she replied proudly and raised her glass toward him in silent appreciation. She added, "I always wanted to be a nurse. I just pushed it aside for a while."

Daniel Kim swung the front door open and entered the bar wearing a blue jacket over a golf shirt and the usual blue jean/tennis shoes ensemble. He walked over to Brian and Joanne and looked at the two of them sitting together. They all exchanged pleasantries, and Daniel ordered a drink and stood behind them to continue the conversation, although he looked uncomfortable as if he were intruding on a private conversation. Daniel looked over at Brian and commented, "You got a job at National Semiconductor, I hear."

"Yup. It's really good," Brian replied and toasted by clinking glasses around the group. "I'm on a special project and it is pretty cool."

"They got you on 150mm wafers I bet," Daniel said and set his drink down on the bar top nonchalantly while he checked his cell phone.

"How would you know that?" Brian asked incredulously. He looked at Joanne who was very interested in the conversation, seeming to understand what that all meant.

"We followed the DARPA investment and put some funds into National, too," Daniel said as he slipped his cell phone in his pocket and grabbed his drink. "Follow the money is what I say."

Joanne added, "We had a guest speaker in my classes last week from Apple that said the same thing."

"That's the next big opportunity," Daniel said confidently, turning to address Brian specifically. "If I were an engineer like you, Brian, that's where I would be going."

Just then they felt it, a faint rumble beneath their feet causing them to clutch their drinks tightly and glance around warily. Brian rose from his chair and pressed his palms on the window ledge, peering out at a nearby light pole gently swaying after the shock. "Maybe a 3.5 this time," he muttered.

Joanne appeared shaken by the tremors. "I'll never get used to those things," she said with a tight smile of apprehension. Her flat lands of Arizona didn't have earthquakes.

Brian reached for her hand in reassurance. "You know this bar may actually be the best place to be if there was a big one."

Joanne looked at Brian's hand on hers on the edge of the wooden bar. She slowly pulled her hand away and smiled.

"Really? How so?" Daniel asked curiously, with Yuze pausing behind the counter to listen in as well.

Brian pointed at the ground as he answered, "This bar sits on solid rock and has post piles stuck right into the rock in order to hold up the structure."

Yuze listened intently and looked down at the floor as if he could see the tops of the post piles. Other patrons listened, too, while inspired murmurs rippled through the other listeners and then quieted down once more.

Brian looked around at all the faces turned to him. "This building has a hard first-story. That means we have a solid foundation that won't shake. Unlike all those buildings down on the flats that are all built on landfill. That stuff shakes like jelly when a roller hits."

Yuze and the others all looked as if they were thinking about their own homes and where they would be if the big one hit.

Joanne peered up at Brian with wide eyes and whispered softly, "I live down on the flats, you know. My apartment is in Frank's building."

Brian didn't realize what he said might disturb anyone. Least of all Joanne. He clarified, "I'm sorry. I'm sure that building is built tough, too."

Brian wished he could keep conversing with her, but at that moment a handsome man entered the bar and Joanne said her goodbyes. She greeted the man and went out of the bar with him and down the street toward the waterfront. Brian watched them cross the tunnel top and disappear down the hill. Daniel rested his hand on Brian's shoulder in understanding, also recently feeling unrequited love for another.

Brian and Daniel finished the night and closed down the bar at 2:00 a.m. by helping Yuze turn off the lights. Both men staggered home to get up in the morning and do it all over again. Being twenty-something allowed their bodies to recover quickly.

CHAPTER 3

Thinking of creations, only a shell,
Unseen hands craft places for us to dwell.

Brian, still driving his beloved 1967 Camaro a few years later, parked in a wide spot and walked into the building ready to start work on a new project recently assigned to him. He recalled his first days at work when he finally got a job at National Semiconductor Corporation, or "National," as everyone called it. He walked toward one of the aging, gray concrete buildings of the company, which looked like an industrial warehouse, but behind those old slabs of concrete were some of the top designers in the world.

With a swipe of his security badge, he entered the office building through a solid white door. He walked down a long, narrow corridor lined with plaques and photographs of past company presidents. One in particular caught his attention —a congratulatory note from the previous president, dated eight years ago. The note praised the current CEO, Charles Sporck, for leading National Semiconductor to become one of the largest semiconductor companies in the world. Brian had joined the company in 1984, during its peak period of innovation. National was the first company to successfully make 75mm wafers with 50 computer chips on each wafer and then transitioned to even larger 100mm wafers with over 100 chips on each wafer —all at the same cost as the smaller ones. This revolutionary breakthrough drove down costs for the entire industry and solidified National's lead in innovation.

Brian's new project, which he had been working on for months, involved developing a 150 mm wafer. As he excitedly shared his plans with his colleagues, he explained that within two years, they would move up to a

200mm wafer, roughly the size of a person's hands with fingers fully extended. This meant they could produce 1000 chips on each wafer, for just a few cents more than it cost to make 100 chips on a 100mm wafer. The smaller wire and transistor sizes also allowed for exponential growth in computing power. This was a pivotal moment in computer chip development, as now these tiny chips could fit into any device imaginable. The term "Internet of Things," or IoT, became commonplace as people marveled at the possibilities. Others were skeptical, wondering who would need a computer chip in their toaster.

When Brian first stepped into the National Semiconductor office building in the bullpen area where his new boss recently assigned him, he scanned the other hundreds of workers typing away at their desks as he searched for an open desk that would become his own. Each desk had a telephone with a row of clear buttons for the five telephone lines routed to each phone.

Occasionally, one of the workers in a white shirt and black tie rose from their seat to use the mimeograph machine, a rudimentary form of communication that ran on electricity but took about five minutes to read the message, package it into electronic pulses, and then another five minutes to reassemble the message and print it out on another spinning mimeograph at another machine across town. Despite its slow speed, it was still considered cutting-edge technology at the time.

Brian stopped a person at the mimeograph and asked if they had a fax machine too, a scanning machine that could send images almost instantly in just fifteen seconds. The person pointed to another tiny room where Brian found it amusing when he saw an executive make a copy of his original before putting it through the fax machine, as if the machine might actually disassemble and reassemble the paper on the other side.

He walked over to his new boss's desk and noticed an old cash register-style adding machine, which made loud clanging noises as it multiplied numbers using its mechanical addition mechanism, with some multiplications taking up to ten minutes each. Brian followed his boss to the desk assigned to him and Brian blended in quickly to the machine-like production of the designs for the 150mm wafer.

About a month after starting and suffering through the manual methods of work, Brian, the ever-inventor, built an IBM PC from scratch by visiting an engineering supply store to buy the individual parts. He assembled and tested the device at the old Victorian flophouse where he still lived with the Baumers brothers Jimmy and Jay. Building the computer took Brian about a month, all the while under the scrutinizing and disbelieving eyes of his friends. When he brought the PC into the office, his boss immediately came out and disparaged the new machine and wondered how Brian had commandeered an expensive machine from requisitions. Brian explained the PC was his own invention, and from then on, his coworkers watched as Brian outperformed them ten to one with the assistance of his new machine. Within a few months, every worker had their own IBM PC on their desk. None were as powerful as Brian's optimized machine, but the productivity of the reinforced group showed up in the speed of design.

One year had passed since Brian's promotion to manager, and now he stood surrounded by his coworkers at his cubicle. The large monitor on his desk cast a blue hue on their faces as they huddled around, studying the intricate design of the semiconductor chip displayed on the screen. Tiny wires intertwined like a complex spider web, connecting gates, switches, capacitors, and resistors in a dizzying pattern of colors.

"I wish we could print this out," Brian grumbled to one of his coworkers. He longed to see the design laid out on paper so he could trace the pathways more easily. He tapped a pen impatiently against his desk as he studied the intricate design on his computer screen.

"You'd need a wall-sized printer for that," the coworker replied with a chuckle, knowing it would be impossible to print such a massive design.

But Brian couldn't give up. He took a deep breath and dove back into tracing the lines, determined to find the elusive bug causing issues with their latest batch of test wafers. The team's success depended on it, after all.

"Let's add a batch system to capture the results for each one thousand calculations," Brian instructed one of the members of his team. "That way, we can analyze any trends and improve our next set of calculations."

"I don't understand what that would do," the coworker asked, looking confused.

Brian patiently explained, "Every thousand calculations will show a pattern or trend we can follow to make improvements."

The team exchanged glances and began discussing the potential effectiveness of this method. One member even suggested it could be considered a form of artificial intelligence. They all laughed at the thought, but deep down, they knew Brian's idea could lead them to success.

The other members of the team drifted back to their desks in the bullpen when Brian noticed something peculiar in one portion of the drawing. One of the pathways connected differently than all of the others. Brian's heart raced as he realized this might be the missing piece—the answer to their mystery. He quickly called his colleagues over to his side and pointed out the anomaly. They all began discussing possible solutions and theories. After a few minutes, they were all convinced of the problem, but the repair would take a very long time because of the daisy-chain effect one pathway causes on the next, like neurons triggering electronic pulses in the human brain.

Brian imagined working in a sleek, modern office with a view of the city skyline, surrounded by brilliant minds who shared his passion for technology, but instead, he worked at a bunker of a building that lay flat and unattractive in the middle of a parking lot.

But as much as he had longed to work in Silicon Valley and was now here, he knew that he was lucky to have a job at all. Many of his friends had lost their tech jobs during the recent recession, and were struggling to make ends meet while searching for a new job.

As he worked, he could not help but think about the tiny 150 mm diameter wafer, about the size of his hand, that held the key to their entire operation. It was amazing to think that a photolithographic tool laid down all of the complicated patterns on the chip and that toxic gases layered the semiconductor materials onto the wafer. It was a delicate process that required extreme precision and care. And using such strong gases in such concentrated areas was dangerous to the people and the environment. Gases such as arsenide and silane were some of the most poisonous gases on earth.

Despite the challenges, Brian was determined to succeed. He worked tirelessly, his eyes burning and his fingers cramped from hours of typing and clicking. But in the end, his hard work paid off. He fixed the bug and the chip was finally functioning properly.

Brian stepped back and beheld the finished product of weeks of hard work. The computer chip his team designed was a thing of beauty: its tiny transistors, no larger than microscopic particles, could process calculations faster than any human brain and millions at a time. He thought of Moore's Law, which prophesied that the number of transistors on an integrated circuit would double every two years—a prediction that was proving to be accurate from 1975 to 1984, and now National Semiconductor was one of the many companies that planned on fulfilling it into the 1990s. Brian smiled with pride. He had made a difference.

As Brian made his way down the hallway from the bullpen to the manufacturing area, he was in awe of what he saw. Rows and rows of pure white cleanrooms lined the building like large "H" patterns, with one cleanroom leading into the next, robotic machines lining each wall, and people dressed in bunny suits and breathing apparatuses walking among the rooms like astronauts.

The printing machines in the photolithography section were humming with activity as they printed thousands of layers of material onto a 150mm wafer ready to receive the semiconductor circuitry. After each layer, technicians inspected the work to ensure accuracy. Brian watched as a dicing machine then cut out microscopic electronic circuits from the wafer and sent them off to a packaging machine that attached tiny touch points on the circuit to points on the package for connection on a circuit board. He knew the two-month duration from manufacturing of test batches to verification by the labs was worth the wait. Once successful, millions of chips could begin production.

Brian continued walking down the hallway but stopped and stood in awe of the graphics on the wall before him that dramatically depicted the evolution of the semiconductor industry over the last two decades. From the far left of the graphic, he could see the timeline slowly progress from 50mm wafers in 1965 to 100mm and then 125 mm at Fairchild Semiconductor. His eyes stopped as they reached a black space on the wall with a white circle representing 150mm wafer size; only moments ago, Brian had completed the design work for this model.

His gaze shifted to another genealogy tracing back to Charlie Sporck, CEO of National Semiconductor, who had been one of Robert Noyce's "Traitorous Eight" at Fairchild—the group of visionaries and innovators who famously split from Shockley Labs in search of different opportunities. Brian smiled at how their ambition and risks ultimately paid off, each of them forming successful companies within their respective territories.

Brian continued walking down the hall to another display showing the future of the semiconductor world with a highly speculative prognostication. Using Moore's Law of doubling the horsepower of an electronic circuit every two years, images showing wafer sizes stretching to 450mm by the year 2025 with the results of computing size being equal to the human brain by the year 2035. The label below the graphic called it "Artificial Intelligence." The graphic showed an attractive woman wearing all sorts of wearable technology, including a telephone on her watch and a computer screen on her eyeglasses. She rode an electric-powered scooter and studied on a laptop screen mounted to the scooter.

"Makes you think, doesn't it," a voice said from behind Brian.

He glanced back and saw Dr. Philip Burnett, the keynote speaker from the conference he attended at lunchtime. "Hello, Dr. Burnett."

"Please call me Philip. We are working on the same team here." He motioned back at the picture of the young woman on the wall wearing all of the gadgets. "That's going to be us someday."

Brian examined the image again and commented, "I'm not sure we'll ever have enough computing power for that."

Philip stared at him before glancing back at the poster. "We need to find a way to store all this data without having to lug around hard drives like a bunch of astronauts in deep space."

Brian chuckled, reminded that he was addressing the foremost specialist in computer engineering in the world: Philip held the lifetime chair position in DARPAI and led artificial intelligence research as part of his role with the Defense Advanced Research Projects Agency (DARPA). He wondered sometimes if by adding the I at the end of the DARPA acronym, that it may be a play on the acronym for artificial intelligence, AI, instead of simply I for Intelligence. The elongated acronym of DARPAI should actually be DARP-AI then.

"How is work going on those 150mm wafers?" Philip suddenly asked seriously. "I heard the designs were sent for photolithography."

With surprise, Brian replied "How did you know that?" Then he immediately corrected himself. "Sorry, of course you are in the loop on that."

"How long until they're done?"

"Forty-five days," Brian answered. "Unless the design doesn't work."

Philip patted Brian on the back in an encouraging gesture and replied before continuing down the hall, "Right on schedule as usual. Well done."

Brian beamed as he watched Philip walk, a tall gangly man of maybe thirty years old but walking as if he must know everything going on in the world somehow.

Philip suddenly turned and stared coldly at Brian, who flinched slightly under the man's gaze. Philip stated, "I expect your work on the 200mm wafer within two years." Then he turned without waiting for an answer and disappeared around the next corner.

CHAPTER 4

A woman stirs up dreams of times long past,
Regulars, like kin, remind us what will last.

Brian meticulously straightened his black tie in the mirror, adjusting it to sit perfectly under the crisp white collar of his shirt. As he made his way to the Top of the Tunnel bar, where he still worked part-time as a bartender, he felt a sense of nostalgia. He was grateful for his successful job in the technology industry, but seeing Joanne Stoddard waiting tables brought back memories of simpler times and hopes of building on that relationship.

The once familiar faces at the bar had now become more like family, though they didn't gather as often as they used to. But when they did, it was usually for special occasions or to watch sporting events together. Meanwhile in the rest of the valley, the rise of Silicon Valley had only solidified its position as the world leader in semiconductor design, but manufacturing had started to move overseas.

Unwilling to be left behind and instead following the guidance of trusted advisors, Brian took a leap of faith and left National Semiconductor to work on a DARPA-funded project at Apple Computers. His new role required frequent travel to Taiwan, where he worked closely with an equipment company called Applied Materials. Brian spent most of his time in Hsinchu, testing new materials and design tools that would aid in the production of 200mm wafers for semiconductor chips. Despite being thousands of miles away from home, Brian kept in constant contact with his friends and family through email —a revolutionary form of communication recently developed.

When Brian was in town, he occasionally worked a shift at the bar as a favor for his friend Jimmy Baumers, who could take a night off knowing Brian managed things well in his absence. Brian also worked there to see

Joanne Stoddard, who he'd asked out a few times but she preferred to keep their relationship friendly instead. His heart ached as he watched her date other men.

Thursday nights were the only time that Brian worked at the bar because Joanne worked the same night. She always dressed impeccably in black skirts that showed off her slender ankles and calves and a white button-down blouse that fitted her shape perfectly. Brian traditionally wore a cotton-point business shirt and a black tie. Together they gave the place a touch of class each Thursday.

Joanne moved effortlessly among the patrons, her eyes scanning the room for drink orders or any chance to improve someone's experience. She was one of the best waitresses Brian had ever seen, but she also planned on moving on from the bar as soon as she received her nursing degree at next month's commencement ceremony. Three years of hard work finally came to an end for her.

Brian had been trying to make their friendship move beyond platonic for many months now, but she declined all offers of dinner and drinks unless it was with a group of their mutual friends. She joined him if there were others but never alone on an actual date. Although he did notice her lingering near him longer during slow moments at the Top of the Tunnel bar. She had been spending more time in conversation with him than ever before.

At precisely 11:00 p.m. on a Thursday evening, the front door of the bar flew open and a burst of rowdy laughter and shouts entered the room. A group of young men stumbled in, donning blue sports coats and dress slacks that appeared slightly rumpled from a night of revelry. They eagerly passed around a bottle of whiskey, taking swigs and boisterously joking with each other.

Brian glanced up with a knowing look at a couple of his regulars, Charles Kang and Daniel Kim, who sat quietly together at the far end. Upon seeing Brian's subtle nod, Daniel grabbed a telescoping rod from behind the bar counter and held it close to his chest. In his other hand, he firmly grasped a baseball bat that he handed to Charles quietly under the bar. Hopefully this was just a precaution.

Joanne moved toward the group of men to try and usher them to one of the tables, but they brushed by her while looking her over and making some crude remarks about her beauty.

Brian took umbrage with the comments but knew the men outnumbered him five to one, and five very drunk ones at that —drunks tend to feel no pain during a brawl. He moved toward them at the end of the bar and welcomed them to sit down, trying to calm things down before it became more difficult. Brian had become an expert at calming things down in ways that only an experienced bartender would know. He knew tricks of the trade in outsmarting very drunk people and keeping them from harming anyone or harming the bar itself.

"Welcome to the Top of the Tunnel, gentlemen," Brian said to a man appearing to be the leader. That was one of the tricks of keeping things calm was identifying the leader and also identifying the most problematic drunk— like bookends. The leader looked to be slightly older than the other drunken men —probably future groomsmen at a bachelor party by the looks of their similar outfits. The most problematic drunk appeared to be the younger man currently holding the bottle and taking more swigs than the others while staggering around. He kept staring at Joanne and making comments to her.

Brian added, "Listen, you know we cannot allow bringing in outside liquor. We could lose out license. Do you mind putting that away somewhere?"

The younger drunken man said, "What? Are you afraid we're going to cut into your profits?" He burst out laughing and handed the bottle to the leader while doubling over. "Go ahead. Your turn to drink."

The leader took the bottle and took a swig and then stared at Brian and said in a calm voice. He pointed out the window at the lights of the Ritz Hotel. "Don't worry about it. We're going back to the hotel."

Imperceptibly, Charles and Daniel moved a few more stools closer to Brian and the drunks, who began circling around the bottle and Joanne. Charles held the bat behind him out of sight behind his large torso. Daniel held the telescoping weapon behind his wrist. They both moved to the side of the men without moving too quickly.

Brian nodded to Charles and Daniel and held up his hand with a signal of five fingers extended, meaning the fifth chair is where they would meet. Brian then turned to the leader of the drunks holding the bottle. "I'm going to have to ask you to leave then. We can lose our liquor license that way."

The drunks all roared with laughter in response and separated slightly as they slapped each other on the backs and exchanged high fives. The very drunk one put his arm around Joanne and kissed her smack on the lips as she resisted and tried to push him away. Her rejection seemed to fuel him and he became even more clingy and held her around the waste while grabbing her shirt to hold her still. The top buttons of her blouse broke off as she jumped back and then tried to cover herself. She looked very angry as the man moved toward her again.

Brian's muscles tensed as he leapt over the bar and landed inches away from the drunken man. The other patrons scattered in confusion, but Brian stood firm in front of the leader and the very drunk man as time stopped for a moment. The drunk man lunged at Brian.

Brian recoiled as the man tried to grab him but he felt a very strong push from behind that moved him to the side. He turned to see Joanne charge at the very drunk man and trip him from behind, gripping the man's shirt with one hand and shoving him toward the barstools with the other. As the man flailed his arms wildly, Joanne kept him off-balance, forcefully pushing the drunk backward until he tripped.

With expert speed and determination, Joanne pushed the man's chest down into the floor. His back hit the floor with a sickening thud and the wind rushed out of him, leaving him sucking for air. His head hit the footrest, which kept his brains from splattering across the floor. She screamed at him to never touch her again. She stood over him and scolded him even more while the others looked on in shock.

Charles emerged from the side at the same time, his large physique stunning as he swung the bat menacingly toward the other drunks. "One move from you lot, and I'll bash your damn heads in," he growled.

The other drunks cowered in fear and backed away as Brian and the leader of the drunks stared at Joanne who stood with one foot pushed onto the man's chest on the floor. She cursed at him and the warnings she gave seemed to be for everyone who ever harmed her. Her face shone with fury.

Brian stood stunned and confused to the side but studied the situation to make sure that Joanne was safe. He stepped toward the leader of the group, his voice low and deadly serious, "Take your party and go. Now."

The leader surveyed the scene and looked down on his younger brother, the drunk on his back, gasping for air on the floor, surrounded by broken glass and spilled drinks as he tried to get to his feet. The leader moved slowly to help the younger man up and stopped before nodding solemnly at Brian. He grinned in awe of the powerful Joanne.

Brian sensed the tension lowering and saw Charles still waving the bat in front of the others as they slowly backed away. Brian added, "No more trouble, okay?"

The leader helped the younger man up and spoke to his group, "Come on boys. Time to go."

The young drunk looked dazed and confused and could barely stand without help. He looked sheepishly at Joanne, stunned by how fast she moved and how the world spun out of control in his mind. He looked as if he were about to vomit.

The leader ordered the others to grab the dazed man and carry him outside. He stopped as they all left and turned to Joanne. "I'm sorry for his behavior, miss. We've been drinking too much at his bachelor party. That's all. Momma didn't raise us this way. It's just the liquor."

Joanne nodded at the leader and suggested they leave.

Charles slowly lowered his bat and Daniel retracted his weapon while the leader of the drunks watched them. He turned to Brian and grinned. "That's an interesting method you people use here. Mixing extreme violence with a soft landing."

Brian crossed his arms and returned with a deadpan expression, "We wanted to take him out—not kill him."

The leader of the group smiled and turned to the door. He tipped a finger to an imaginary hat when smiling at Joanne and offering apologies. The group began marching up the hill toward the Ritz Hotel, each one quiet aside from their occasional muttered apologies, except for the leader, who threw their last bottle of booze into the bushes before moving on.

Brian thanked Daniel and Charles and bought a round of drinks on the house. Joanne tied a new apron over her torn blouse –her face still red rimmed from adrenalin. She cleared more dishes from a table of people that left right after the brawl, her movements quick and jerky as she explained it was a bachelor party from up at the Ritz and that it didn't happen here very often.

After a while, Brian and Joanne sat together alone and quietly at the end of the bar. Brian looked into his soda and then turned to her while choosing his words carefully, "Do they teach that in nursing school?"

Joanne burst out laughing and rested her hand on Brian's shoulder, practically crying from the drop in adrenalin and then this latest comment. She turned to Brian and said, "I saw your signal to the boys, so I knew what was going to happen. But then I thought, why not me?"

"You scared the shit out of that guy," Brian replied. "And me too!"

Joanne laughed and explained how she had two younger brothers and they used to rough-house all the time. "They taught me how to use my knees and elbows during a fight."

"I bet they regretted that."

Joanne burst out laughing again. "Yeah, I beat up all the boys in class after that. Well, the ones that bullied me anyway."

As the time wound down and they prepared to close, Brian asked Daniel if he would escort Joanne home, who still seemed a little dazed by the attack.

31

She said she would be okay but Brian noticed her arms were shaking slightly as she crossed them in front of herself.

"Joanne, I really don't think it's safe to be walking home alone at one in the morning," he said softly and held his jacket out for her.

She stared at the jacket for a moment before glancing back up into his eyes with hesitation. "You know I'm a big girl."

He nodded but still moved closer to drape one sleeve over her arm, then pulled the other into place before lifting the jacket up over her shoulders from behind. She grabbed his hands still on her shoulders and patted them before releasing them.

"Chivalry is not dead, I see," she said warmly and held his jacket close around her. She quickly leaned forward and kissed him on the cheek, then nodded toward Daniel that she was ready for the walk home. She stopped and smiled at Brian before heading out the door.

The next morning was difficult for Brian with so little sleep after the late-night hours at the bar. Perhaps it was time to stop bartending, but that was the only way he saw Joanne, and he did not want to give that up. Brian nodded off on the train ride south, but awoke with the jostling of the train as it pulled into the Sunnyvale stop where he could catch the shuttle to the Apple building a few miles away. Rumors of a new super Apple campus flew through the ranks, but Brian stuck to business in the older lab near Highway 280. A large image of Einstein, nearly fifty feet high, hung from the roof of the building as an inspiration for those working inside.

Brian glanced at Einstein and entered through a side door that served as a shortcut to the labs. He tapped his badge against the card reader, and as the door opened, he stood face to face with Dr. Philip Burnett from DARPAI.

"Ah, there you are," Philip said and moved backwards to allow Brian through the door. He motioned for a startled Brian to walk with him down the hall.

"Hello, Dr. Burnett," Brian said awkwardly to the brilliant scientist as they walked side by side down the long white corridor. He had not spoken to Dr. Burnett in several years but the man appeared out of nowhere once again.

"Please, call me Philip," he replied and began talking as if this were a regular occurrence. He asked question after question about the progress toward the 200mm wafer size.

Brian answered every question truthfully and without any hesitation even though he was revealing secret details of the project to a non-employee. But he knew that Dr. Burnett somehow knew everything anyway. When they arrived at Brian's lab, Philip used his badge to swipe at the security badge reader, and the door opened. Brian followed Dr. Burnett through the door after swiping his badge through the reader, too.

"Tell me what happened in Taiwan last week," Philip asked as he removed his long jacket and laid it over a bench, then sat down. Philip's hair was a little grayer and a little longer than the previous time Brian had seen him.

"Taiwan Semiconductor used a new recipe we produced with the Applied Materials equipment that cut the defects to below 20 percent," Brian revealed. Brian's jet lag from the previous week's travels had finally subsided a few days ago.

Philip thought for a while, scratched his chin, and replied while standing and grabbing his jacket. "Good work."

"Thank you, sir," Brian replied, knowing his audience was over.

Philip nodded and smiled strangely at Brian. "We should have the 200mm done shortly, and then we start on 300mm right away. Correct?"

"That's right, sir," Brian replied. "We already have some designs in the works."

Philip smiled again and patted Brian on the shoulder before extending his hand to shake. He turned to the exit of the lab and then stopped to look back at Brian. "You know, with the 300mm driving the costs of each chip down to below a dollar, the chips will be used in almost everything."

"Yes, maybe some of those wearable devices will become reality," Brian replied, recalling the last time he ran into Dr. Burnett in the hallway at National Semiconductor.

"Maybe, but I think the next big use of chips will be in the automotive industry. And with electric cars at that," Philip added and started toward the door again while swinging his long coat over his shoulder. "You should think about that, young man. Automobiles are the future of the computing industry."

CHAPTER 5

In sterile rooms where filters guard the air,
And miracles take place with fervent care.

Jay Baumers stepped into the vast construction site, a scene bustling with workers, machines, and with the constant hum of diesel generators. The white noise of industry surrounded him, but he balanced it with a deep sense of calm and reverence for the work accomplished here. Merely a construction site now, this was where the next generation of a revolutionary device would come to life at Apple. And he thought of all that had happened in the past few years since losing his job, getting divorced, and leaving Wisconsin. The move to California turned out pretty well since then.

The cleanrooms were the heart of the new site. Gleaming white and ultra-sterile, they were the heartbeat of the semiconductor industry. Heavy-duty air filters guarded the cleanrooms from foreign particles that could impede the flawless production of the computer devices produced within. For the thousands of workers here, the cleanrooms were almost a holy place, a kind of temple of technology. It was where magic happened.

Jay walked around the site, marveling at the attention to detail that had gone into this project. The designers considered every aspect, thought through every angle, anticipated every potential problem, and mitigated each one with a work-around. This was Apple's way, and it was a marvel to watch in action. There was no doubt in his mind that this project would be a success.

Every morning, Jay walked onto the construction site dressed in a hard hat and safety vest. As an estimator and finance manager for the construction project, he was responsible for ensuring that the construction of this large project—the first 300mm semiconductor wafer manufacturing plant—met all of the necessary requirements of generally acceptable accounting standards. The completed project would work in parallel with TSMC in Taiwan, and Applied Materials in Silicon Valley. This was an important step for Apple to produce their own electronic circuits.

Jay walked through the maze of trailers that served as temporary offices for the construction project. The air was thick with the smell of fresh coffee and the sound of ringing phones echoed throughout the cramped space. He pushed open the door to the executive team's trailer, where he sat shoulder-to-shoulder with top-level executives from Apple.

As a finance manager, Jay played a crucial role in ensuring the project's financial success by managing budgets, controlling costs, mitigating risks, and providing valuable insights for informed decision-making. This was no easy task, but Jay's expertise and knowledge were crucial in aligning the project's financial aspects with Apple's overall corporate strategy and financial goals. His contributions were vital in helping Apple achieve their objectives and stay on track toward completing the project successfully.

Jay effortlessly maneuvered through the construction site, his hard hat slightly askew as he consulted blueprints and made cost estimates in his head. His high school friends used to tease him, saying he could ace exams while listening to classic rock. But it was true; Jay had a natural talent for numbers and problem-solving.

As the finance manager, he meticulously tracked budget expectations and financial data, drawing on skills taught by his ex-wife's father at their Wisconsin construction company. He also oversaw procurement processes and monitored cash flow, always keeping in mind Apple's strict financial goals.

Despite facing challenges and making tough decisions, Jay's vast knowledge and experience enabled him to navigate the project with ease. But deep down, he was bored out of his mind; this job didn't challenge him like it used to.

Stepping through the gates of the construction site, Jay felt a familiar surge of confidence emanating from his intellect with numbers. This same skill set allowed him to play Texas Hold-em at the local card clubs where he made most of his profits from many of the new overly-eager players. The house took a stake, but his winnings were unlimited until the new players discovered his expertise and began leaving any table where he sat down to play. Then, it was off to another card club to strike against newbies there.

As the evening wore on, Jay surveyed his surroundings from his seat in the only illuminated construction trailer. The once bustling site was now eerily quiet, with all of the laborers having gone home for the day. He peered out the window at the busy Montague Expressway, watching as people rushed by in their quest to find something exciting to do on a typical weekend night.

Jay pulled out an envelope filled with crisp one-hundred-dollar bills from his briefcase. These were his winnings from the past month, totaling nearly ten thousand dollars from just one card club. He looked at his watch and debated whether he could make it to the bank before closing time. Deciding to take a chance, he hurried off to the Bank of America where Jiewen worked. She had assisted him in keeping his deposits under the limit that would trigger a report to the IRS for potential drug money.

As he crossed the dusty parking lot to his car, a BMW convertible pulled up filled with four young men with their arms hanging over the doors. He watched them drive to a nearby trailer. A bulky young man, the rich son of the lead foreman on the project, stepped out of a new pickup truck and walked up to the men in the car. Jay watched as the man handed over a small package to the boys in the car and received money in return. The rumors of cocaine distribution were true then—so far, all investigations by the FBI's Bureau of Alcohol, Tobacco, and Firearms had led back to the trade union hall of the plumber's union. Jay ducked behind another truck and waited for them to complete their transaction. The last thing he needed was for some FBI people to catch him near that bunch while carrying all his cash from his poker winnings.

Jay drove his Honda Civic north to San Francisco via a gorgeous and scenic highway along the ridge of the Santa Cruz Mountains. The road led into the western side of the city, where he took side streets to head into the Financial District, in the opposite direction from all those people leaving work for the week. He parked his car in a multi-story lot that had a bridge that went straight into the second floor of the Bank of America building. This was the safest route into the building, knowing that pick-pockets and thugs somehow smelled out a pedestrian carrying valuable objects. Jay brushed his clothes off as he entered the grandiose lobby and went to the private banking section at the rear end. He saw Jiewen finishing up with another customer and he waved to her suggesting he could be next in line for her help. She smiled and motioned to a nearby chair for him to wait.

Jay's turn came next. He hesitated for a moment then stepped forward, his eyes fixed on the ground as if trying to hide something as he approached her desk. His heart was beating rapidly, not only because he had just raced northwards before closing but also because of his growing attraction toward this beautiful banker. With trembling hands, he pulled out an envelope bulging with cash from the pocket of his rumpled suit jacket and laid it on the desk.

He said in a low voice, "Hello, I need to make a deposit again."

Jiewen picked up the envelope and glanced inside before setting it back down. She adjusted her black-rimmed glasses, straightened her form-fitting suit with a matching skirt, and then peered at Jay intently over her desk. She asked in a playful tone, "Jay Baumers, have you been gambling again?"

Jay shushed her and then realized she was only toying with him. He sat down and pushed the envelope toward her while reaching for his deposit slip to write the exact amount. "You should come with me one of these times."

Jiewen replied, "My father would kill me if he found out." She looked up at him while smiling. "And then he would kill you."

Jay chuckled but also knew she was probably right. He contemplated numerous times before about asking her out on a date, but he never found the courage. Today was different. "Would you have dinner with me tomorrow night?"

Jiewen looked as if she ignored the question, paused only briefly, and slowly returned to counting the money she removed from the envelope, her long nails flipping through the bills with precision as she meticulously inspected each divided stack of money. When she finally finished counting, Jiewen examined Jay carefully before responding with a smile. "Yes, Mr. Baumers. I would love to dine with you tomorrow evening." She suggested a location and extended her hand to signal their transaction was complete.

"It's a deal," Jay replied, feeling wonderful that she had accepted the invitation. He felt the soft skin of her hand as they both lingered a moment. He looked into her beautiful brown eyes and somehow felt she was open to him.

As he walked back to the Victorian, a card club caught his eye where he had not played for a while. The light of the neon sign glowed against the dark street and seemed to call him in. He stepped through its front door while his eyes darted around the room with a seasoned practice.

The atmosphere was electric, with tables scattered throughout the room and players intently focused on their cards. After surveying the options, he settled on a table that met most of his criteria and sat at the third-base position. A lovely hostess made her rounds, taking orders for food and drinks from the players. He chose a soft drink, feeling righteous as his opponents indulged in stronger beverages that would impair their judgement over time. His determination to win drove him to tip generously, ensuring that the waitresses would continue bringing refreshments to his opponents and giving him another advantage in the game.

Jay leaned forward in his chair, craning his neck to get a better view as the house dealer expertly shuffled the single deck of cards. He reviewed the rules of Texas Hold'em in his mind—it was an increasingly popular variant of poker that blended skill and luck, perfect for players looking to make money. The house did not directly participate in the gameplay or compete against the players, but instead earned revenue two ways: by taking a small percentage of each pot, capped at a maximum amount, known as the rake; or by charging an hourly fee for using the table.

He glanced around the table at his opponents: two hardened gamblers with stacks of chips in front of them and three newer players with a decreasing pile of smaller chips. One of the newbies had an air of bravado and did not like to back down. As Jay looked across the table, each person seemed to be carefully calculating their odds and deciding what move to make next—bluffing one moment, raising the stakes the next. He knew that this game was not about beating the house; it was about outsmarting his opponents through discipline and expert strategy.

Jay's eyes burned with intensity as he placed his chips onto the felt-covered table. The other players around the Texas Hold'em table shifted uneasily in their chairs, some muttering under their breath as they weighed their odds while others had already folded. Jay's poker face remained stoic, with a hint of a smile, despite the two cards he'd been dealt in the pre-flop stage. His calculated betting style made him look eager to win, but when his hand improved, his expression turned sour. He called it a reverse bluff. Later, he would reverse the reverse bluff at will.

The flop revealed three community cards for all the players to use in their hands, and another round of betting ensued. Jay put up a larger bet than usual, and one more player folded out of the game. In the next round known as the "turn," the dealer showed an additional fourth card, and another round of betting began. Amateur players were losing their nerve at this stage but Jay kept steady and only raised minimally with a disappointed grimace on his face as part of his bluff.

By the "river" –the fifth and final card open on the table—only three players remained: Jay, an eager newbie, and one hardened opponent. Unbeknownst to anyone else at the table, that fifth card gave Jay a lucky pair that would win him the pot. He knew he should never grow dependent on luck, but it sure came in handy now and then.

Jay sat at the table; eyes fixed on his cards as he calculated his odds of winning the pot. The glare from the overhead lights bounced off the shiny plastic surface of each card, making them difficult to read in the dimly lit room. To win, a player must have the best five-card poker hand using their two "hole" cards and three of the five community cards on the table. Players can use any combination of their hole cards and the community cards to make the best hand of the traditional five cards. Jay's fingers twitched with anticipation as he weighed his options and considered how much to bet. The room was tense with excitement as everyone waited to see who would come out on top.

The other two players took turns, the sound of their chips clacking together filling the small room. The dealer's gaze was sharp as each player revealed their hold cards, his eyes flicking between them in a way that made Jay feel like the dealer sized them up by the quality of their hands.

Then came Jay's turn. He swallowed hard as he laid down his two pairs of aces over nines, and the dealer declared him the winner. The pile of chips glinted under the harsh overhead lights, enticing and heavy in his hand —not a bad haul for one hour of work.

Jay folded very quickly on the next four hands when he calculated the odds were against him based on a certain personal betting style. He could feel his heart hammering in his chest as he swiftly assessed each card that appeared on the table, silently cursing when it did not work out in his favor. That got him out of bad hands instead of depending on luck to get him out of the hand with cash. Luck is not a good strategy to depend upon, he reminded himself firmly.

As he rose from the table, Jay felt both relieved and exhilarated by his winnings. Two hours of work had paid off handsomely, but he knew better than to push his luck any further tonight before his shift at the Top of the Tunnel. Instead, he carefully stacked his chips and headed for the cashier.

CHAPTER 6

Through banks and Chinatown, her steps resound,
Echoing in the tunnel's dark surround.

Jiewen strolled through the Stockton Street tunnel, making her way from work at the bank to her family's food market. Her shoes clacked against the sidewalk, stylish yet practical for her long journey to visit her parents. As she walked, she noticed a sign for the Top of the Tunnel bar above her on the left. It felt as though electricity filled the air, as she left behind the high-tech world of the Financial District and entered the old-world charm of Chinatown. Each time she felt as if she entered a time warp that transported her through a portal. Inside the tunnel, fluorescent lights flickered in sync with each step, creating an otherworldly atmosphere.

Today's task with the family was the weekly chore of cleaning up the family's books at the market. She thought deeply about the narrowing margins that consumed the family's efforts by making them work harder and harder each day. On the bright side, they owned the three-story building where Li's Food Market had remained open for nearly sixty years. They even had renters on the top floor to help defray the costs of ownership.

Jiewen walked into the market and glided past the rows of colorful food. The aromas of ginger, soy sauce, and star anise wafted from Li's Food Market and out into the bustling streets of Chinatown. The market stood three stories tall, with the ground floor brimming with fresh produce, exotic spices, and delicacies like dumplings and noodles handmade by Grandma Yu Chen Li herself.

Wei Guo Chu, Yu Chen Li's son-in-law, whom she prodded constantly and intentionally mispronounced his name, as "Way to Go" each time he messed up, stood at the entrance of the shop. He smiled as he watched tourists snap photos of his perfectly ordered fruit stands while locals rushed in for their weekly shopping routine. In the back-of-house area, the Li family worked tirelessly to keep up with demand, grinding spices, roasting meats, and preparing sauces according to traditional recipes passed down through three generations.

The matriarch, Yu Chen Li, stood at the heart of it all, silver hair pulled tight into a bun and eyes aglow with pride for her family's legacy. She offered guidance to her children and grandchildren while managing finances, but when it came time to taste-test new dishes? That was her domain alone. The family's story weaved tightly into the fabric of San Francisco's history, serving as a testament to both the hard work and love that went into building a business from scratch. Here in Chinatown, they flourished—a symbol of community spirit that showed no signs of slowing down anytime soon.

Wei Guo Chu, the unaccepted son-in-law, embraced his wife Meiyu Li as they walked through the aisles of their family market. Though their origins were from different regions of China, they both wore vibrant traditional clothing that represented their individual heritages. When their daughter Jiewen joined them, they welcomed her affectionately with kisses on each cheek. Curious, they asked if her brother Yuze would be joining them as well.

"He has a shift at the Top of the Tunnel tonight," Jiewen replied and then continued walking, only after stopping to adjust one out-of-place fruit.

Meiyu Li smiled gracefully, and went back to greeting customers with her melodic voice filled with enthusiasm for the Chinese cuisine they offered. Behind her, Wei Guo hummed an old song from his childhood as he inspected the kitchen and made sure that only the freshest ingredients found their way into each dish.

"Our customers do not like your constant whistling," Yu Chen Li shouted as she stormed down the stairs from her lair on the second floor and stared at her son-in-law. Wei Guo instantly stopped whistling and went back to work.

The next generation of children at the shop, Yuze and Jiewen, had different plans than to be heirs to the family market. To them it seemed stoic and steady like a slow river that flowed on endlessly. Finance whiz Jiewen worked at a bank and loved planning events for the market in the evening while keeping the business's books in good order on the weekends. In the day, she crunched numbers at the bank in the Financial District, and during the evening helping out at the market and created new ways to engage their community. Younger brother Yuze was a passionate bartender at the Top of the Tunnel bar—he'd grown up surrounded by their Grandma Li's food but decided to pursue something entirely different than the family business, much to Wei Guo's chagrin.

Wei Guo took his turn at the entrance, greeting and welcoming customers as they entered. His wife, Meiyu Li, went to the back office, meticulously managing the stock on the shelves while her mother, Yu Chen Li kept an unspoken watch over the business. Partially retired but far from absent.

As Wei Guo strolled through the brightly-lit aisles, he was surrounded by vibrant scents of Bok choy, ginger, garlic, and mushrooms. The ambiance of the store was enhanced by traditional Chinese music playing softly in the background, adding to the sensory experience. Every shelf held a variety of exotic ingredients sourced from both local and international suppliers, including tofu, noodles, and teas. A section dedicated to Asian snacks and ready-made meals offered customers a taste of something new and exciting while also providing tourists with a quick exotic treat.

Customer service was at the forefront for the Li family. Their staff members were fluent in English, Mandarin, and Cantonese to cater to their diverse customer base. One even spoke Italian for those living close by in the North beach area. They went above and beyond by offering personalized recipe suggestions, insights into the culinary world, and even giving cooking tutorials or demonstrations upon request. The store was also adorned with decorations and artwork celebrating Chinese culture, creating an authentic ambiance that mimicked a bustling warehouse. The soft sounds of traditional Chinese music could always be heard playing in the background, adding to the warm and inviting atmosphere.

To spread the word about their market, Wei Guo often used newspapers to advertise and booked occasional radio spots on local channels. But they didn't stop there –the Li family also made it a priority to strengthen ties within their community by actively participating in events such as cultural festivals, charity drives, and school clubs. This not only helped promote their business but also allowed them to give back to the community that supported them.

Despite its warm aroma of fresh produce and the friendly tone of the conversations around him, Wei Guo was aware of the complex web of politics beneath the surface. The close-knit nature of the city meant that any misstep could easily become public and tarnish his family's reputation in an instant. He had to be careful not to step on anyone's toes, especially those of powerful tongs within the community. Then, there was the competition from rival businesses, some of whom were willing to use underhanded tactics such as spreading rumors to gain an edge over their competitors. With gentrification came shifting customer preferences and demographics that the

Li family had to navigate through carefully if they were going to keep up with new trends and remain profitable.

Yuze and Jiewen grew up watching their parents from the sidelines as the family juggled customers, orders, and paperwork at this locally famous market in San Francisco. As first-generation immigrants, their parents had worked hard to build a successful business and now were trying to transfer its legacy onto Yuze and Jiewen. Yet, the two siblings were uninterested in taking over the market —much to their parent's dismay. Despite this setback, the older generation still ensured that Yuze and Jiewen had all the knowledge and skills necessary to carry on the family business should they ever choose to do so.

The family was striving to keep up with other markets in a constantly changing city, where regulations and customer tastes shifted rapidly. To stay relevant in such an environment, they had to balance modern convenience with traditional practices while also catering to a different customer base that was largely younger than before. It was an arduous task that the family balanced out carefully.

Navigating the complex bureaucracy of Chinatown politics was daunting, as obtaining licenses and permits requires extensive paperwork and often entails unexpected delays. To maintain good standing in the community, businesses must also commit to various events and causes, such as charity drives or cultural celebrations, in order to avoid criticism or exclusion from certain circles.

The Li family was no exception. With language barriers and cultural misunderstandings causing friction, and with Wei Guo marrying into the family, he knew he must find a way to bridge their traditional roots with the ever-evolving modern needs of the neighborhood.

Later that same day, Wei Guo crept out of the second-floor apartment as soon as his mother-in-law dozed off. He made his way out the back door and through cramped alleys and cobblestone streets until he wove his way around the side streets to reach the Stockton Street tunnel. The shadows across the opening of the tunnel made it look like an ancient cave dug into the city itself. The carved pillars on each side indicated the architectural style from nearly two hundred years ago.

With a weary feeling, he walked through the tunnel and then slogged up the winding stairs before stopping to catch his breath at the top of the tunnel walkway. He looked out at the Financial District at the end of Stockton Street in the distance, its tall buildings standing sentinel-like at the end of the long street, then he turned to his right, where he spotted his son Yuze through a window of the Top of the Tunnel bar at the end of the walkway.

Wei Guo slowly eased the front door of the bar open, peering inside with caution. His gaze fell upon Yuze, whose expression conveyed a mix of shock and confusion at the sight of his own father entering.

"Hello, father," Yuze said politely as Wei Guo nodded and took position at a bar stool in front of one of the televisions lining the back bar. Wei Guo asked for an Anchor Steam with little foam and watched as Yuze carefully poured it for him. He had changed out of his market clothing and into a standard pair of loose-fitting jeans, sneakers, and a sweater.

Charles Kang, who sat a few bar stools away from Wei Guo, interrupted their moment. "Your son is doing quite well here, you know," Charles said, while folding up his laptop. He walked over to sit next to Wei Guo and paused while waiting for an acknowledgment to sit beside him.

Wei Guo nodded at Charles and glanced at Yuze with newfound admiration and asked, "Is that so, Yuze?"

"Yes, father," Yuze replied. He carefully dried off glasses as he removed them from the dishwasher one by one. He looked at his father and said cautiously, "Jimmy converted me to full-time bartender now."

Charles took his seat next to Wei Guo and re-opened his laptop computer on top of the bar. The base of the device was three-inches thick and shaped like a wedge. A small six-inch screen folded up from the keyboard and Wei Guo leaned in closer to get a better view of the unfamiliar machine. Charles noticed the curiosity from Wei Guo and explained, "That's a Macintosh portable computer."

Charles deftly inserted a five-inch floppy disk into the side of the device, which opened like a hungry mouth and swallowed it whole. Wei Guo's eyes grew wide with astonishment.

Yuze stepped in to explain how Charles worked on this computer all the time, and then Yuze left and took an order from another patron down the bar further.

"I'm studying computer software at the University of San Francisco," Charles explained. "I'll graduate in the spring."

Wei Guo lit up with pride as he shared that his daughter had also gotten her degree from the same college.

To his surprise, Charles interjected, "I know her. She does the finances here for Jimmy and Frank, too."

Stunned by the unexpected turn of conversation, Wei Guo shook his head in amazement. "Who knew the children would leave the market?" he muttered before taking a long sip of beer.

Charles realized he must have unintentionally revealed new information. He looked over at Wei Guo and tried to comfort him. "Times are changing."

Wei Guo glanced at Charles and replied. "Who knew I would see a Black man using a computer at a bar?"

Yuze's cheeks reddened, and he whispered harshly to Charles, "Father! We do not use that term. We say African American now."

Charles' lips curled into a grin and he tried to hide his amusement as Wei Guo looked puzzled. "I prefer you simply call me by the name Charles," he said. "Why do we have to put a label on me at all? If anything, I am an American, the same as you all."

We Guo looked confused and said, "I meant no offense, sir."

"None taken. I am neither Black nor African American. My family is from Somalia and Korea. If anything, I'm more of a mocha color." Charles chuckled at his own joke.

"I, too, know what it is like to be labeled unfairly," Wei Guo replied and glanced at his son.

Charles lifted his glass of beer toward Wei Guo in a gesture of solidarity, and the two men clinked their glasses together in silent agreement. At that moment, a third glass of beer suddenly appeared between them as Frank Renado, the owner of the bar, joined the toast from behind them with a mischievous smile on his face. Frank declared jovially, "Can a 'dago' join the toast?"

The two men turned to Frank and remained frozen as Frank continued, "When my father came to America, people called his whole family a bunch of dagos. He told me stories of the mistreatment he had to overcome. Seems like every generation has a new group to pick on."

Another glass appeared from behind and a tall, thin, elderly Italian-looking man added, "Hell, they wouldn't even let me in this place fifty years ago. Except to do the dishes!"

Everyone laughed, and Frank introduced the older man as the longest-running customer at the Top of the Tunnel bar. Frank explained how the man sat most days having a single shot of whiskey and a "schnit," the term for a free half-glass of beer chaser in German bars. The man's order every day was a shot and a schnit, and the man prided himself on getting a free glass of beer. Some of the bartenders simply poured the glass full to be nice, but then the old man only drank half of it.

The four men then solemnly toasted once more and drank from their beers in unity. Frank concluded with a wink, "And if anybody treats my customers like the old days, I will throw 'the sons-of-a-bitches' outta the bar!"

CHAPTER 7

Noiseless entrance, clad in woolen thread,
Numbers assured for what lies on ahead.

Jimmy sat across from Frank Renado, his fingers tapping nervously on the polished wooden table. He couldn't believe he was about to become the new owner of the Top of the Tunnel bar, a local establishment that had been in Frank's family for two generations.

As they went over the details of the purchase, Jiewen quietly entered the room and took a seat at the table. Her long wool dress swished against her calves as she sat down, giving glimpses of her elegant boots. She pulled out a ledger sheet and unfolded it, revealing columns upon columns of numbers.

"Which pieces need replacing now?" Jiewen asked as she scanned through the columns from January 1989 to the future 1993. Jimmy felt grateful for her help, knowing that her sharp mind and keen eye for detail would be invaluable in running the bar over the next four years.

They started reviewing the list and looked over at the refrigerators, which rattled and hummed loudly in the corner of the kitchen. Then came the grills, caked with layers of grease and grime from years of use. Next were the dishwashing machines, their hoses leaking water onto the already wet tile floor. But as they reached the end of the list, Jimmy paused before mentioning the walk-in refrigerator. It was by far the most expensive item on the list, but also the most crucial for keeping the bar up to health code standards. He held his breath as he waited for Jiewen's reaction.

After much discussion and guidance from Jiewen, Jimmy made the difficult decision to take out a mortgage on his beloved Victorian house he inherited from his aunt to provide the down payment for all the new equipment. His brother Jay helped by turning over his minority ownership in their aunt's house to secure the loan. In exchange, Jay would have free drinks for life at the bar. Jimmy couldn't help but wonder who got the better end of that bargain.

Jimmy would need to take in more renters in the old home to afford the mortgage payments. Luckily, the long-ago builders of the house designed Victorian homes with many small rooms, so owners could easily convert the rooms into rented spaces. Victorians all over San Francisco now contained rental spaces with multiple tenants. The thought of shared bathrooms often caused a bit of trouble, but the low rent made up for the inconvenience.

Jiewen and Jimmy made their way through the dark, musty rooms of the Top of the Tunnel bar, clipboard in hand. Jimmy's eyes scanned every inch of the space while Jiewen jotted down notes about each piece of furniture, fixture, or equipment they saw.

Frank sat at the old kitchen table upstairs, overseeing the inventory process with trust. The room was small, with a single bed tucked into one corner and a small kitchen off to the side. A bartender came in for a break and Frank reminded him of his strict rule: only one person could use the room at a time, and no fraternization would be allowed on his watch. He added that one more infraction, and the bartender was out.

Jiewen and Jimmy made their way to the main area of the bar, with Jimmy carefully measuring each item with his eyes and verbally noting its value. Shelves lined the walls, filled with odd trinkets and curiosities. A narrow hallway led to more rooms including restrooms, a pool room, and storage space. In the back was a forgotten pinball machine from 1972 and a dusty classic arcade cabinet.

Jimmy and Jiewen followed their inspection path back to the bar area and took inventory of the attached fixtures on the first floor. The builders of the bar top constructed it with natural wood stained with a dark mahogany color. The bar top bore nicks around the edges where generations of people scarred it, along with other marks from the many years of use.

"How's the deal going?" Jay Baumers said as he entered the bar unexpectedly.

Jimmy looked surprised at first and rushed over to shake his brother's hand. "I couldn't have done it without you."

"Easy bro," Jay replied and said hello to Jiewen with a wink and a smile. He noticed Yuze wiping down the bar top and staring at him with more intensity than usual. Jay nodded at Yuze who looked away quickly. Jay turned back to his brother and said, "The house was always yours anyway."

Jay was taller and healthier looking than Jimmy, but there was no mistaking they were brothers. The angular nose and muscular physiques were traits handed down from their Dutch lineage. Jimmy added, "Mom would be proud of you."

After a while catching up with his brother about the state of the bar purchase, they agreed Jay must reduce his hours behind the bar now that his regular job was so demanding. Jay reluctantly agreed, and Jiewen nodded and smiled.

Later, while continuing the inventory after several hours, Jimmy's golf shirt stuck to his back with sweat as he walked back into the break area upstairs again. Frank sat at the main table by himself, looking over old inventory logs as Jimmy and Jiewen joined him.

"I think we got everything now," Jimmy said as he offered a chair to Jiewen. She set the bulky ledger on the table for everyone to see and slid gracefully into the chair. She moved the ledger for Frank to see the total at the bottom.

"Thirty-one years," Frank said and moved his old ledger in front of Jiewen. "I would never have guessed this place would triple in value."

"This was a great investment, Frank," Jiewen replied and smiled kindly while pointing at some numbers in his ledger. She looked over at Jimmy and said flatly, "If you handle it well, this will triple again by 2020."

"If I can just get through the first few years, I think I can make it work." Jimmy patted Frank on the shoulder and stood up to retrieve another coffee.

"I'll help you," Frank said in return. "I'm retiring—not dying."

Jiewen stood up and kissed Frank on the cheek. "I'll get all this entered into my spreadsheet at the bank and finish drawing up the papers tomorrow."

A book fell off a nearby shelf and hit the floor flat, making a loud noise that startled all three of them. Then, the floor started moving in a quick rolling action. Jiewen sat back down on the chair and said, "Earthquake."

Jimmy and Frank braced themselves as more books fell from the shelves, beginning to form a haphazard stack on the floor. Several glasses bounced off another shelf and hit the floor, shattering into a burst of broken glass and noise. All three of the people placed their hands palms down on the table to steady themselves.

Jimmy said, "That's about a 5.2."

"Another one," Frank added while shaking his head. "Holy shit, that's about the third big one this year."

Jiewen looked worried and got up to look out a window as the rolling subsided. The tops of the street lights and telephone poles wobbled back and forth several inches, causing the telephone wires to bounce up and down in response to the swaying poles. As the rolling stopped, Jiewen looked at Jimmy and said, "I want to check in on the market."

"Take Yuze with you," Jimmy said. "We can manage the bar this afternoon."

Frank grabbed a broom and dustpan and started sweeping up the broken glass in a practiced routine. Jimmy and Jiewen went downstairs to check on damage elsewhere. An earthquake that big can knock a lot of items down, and sometimes even open up cracks in unexpected places. It may have been Jimmy's imagination, but the space between the stairsteps and the wall seemed a little bit wider now.

CHAPTER 8

Their income mirrors dreams and goals aligned,
In turbulent times, love's anchor they find.

In the summer of 1989, Jay Baumers oversaw the bustling construction site with precision and finesse. He darted between the clangs of metal and hum of machinery, effortlessly navigating financial complexities with the ease of a well-practiced artist.

His partner in both love and ambition, Jiewen, carved her own path to success in the heart of the Financial District. She presided over a team of loan officers at Bank of America with grace and authority, their combined incomes symbolizing their dedication and shared goals.

Despite their hectic schedules, Jay and Jiewen found solace in each other's company. Their love served as an anchor in a constantly changing world, reminding them of what truly mattered. As the sun set on another productive day, they stood together, basking in the promise and possibility of their future. For Jay, there was no greater joy than being with Jiewen, with her smile a constant beacon of light guiding him through life's uncertainties.

They were part of a growing trend of DINKs (Double Income No Kids), and their friends often joked that they were "Jay When and Jay Now." Jay laughed as he remembered this while entering Jiewen's cozy third-floor apartment.

"Did you feel that one today?" Jay asked as he entered Jiewen's flat on the top floor of a house in the hills leading up to a prominent part of town. Her studio apartment was small but seemed large compared to Jay's room at the Victorian. He spent most of his time at Jiewen's place lately and contemplated finally getting his own apartment or condominium.

As Jiewen crossed the room, her steps were purposeful, her gaze locked on Jay with an intensity that spoke volumes. Without a word, she closed the distance between them, her lips meeting his in a fervent kiss that ignited a spark between them. It was a moment of shared passion, a silent affirmation of their love amidst the chaos of the world outside.

Breaking away reluctantly, Jiewen's eyes sparkled with a mixture of amusement and concern as she recounted their recent excursion to the market. "Yes, we lost some items at the market. Stuff flew off the shelves."

Jay nodded, a hint of perplexity playing at the corners of his lips. "That was a big one," he acknowledged, setting his belongings down on a chair near the small kitchen. "I read a report that it's a good thing that we are having these big earthquakes because it relieves pressure off of the San Andreas fault line."

Curiosity piqued, Jiewen reached for a newspaper article, her fingers tracing the lines of text as she sought to shed light on the article she had read only a few moments before. With a deft motion, she presented the article to Jay, her fingertip guiding his gaze to a map that accompanied the piece. "The fault goes from down by Santa Cruz all along the mountains," she explained, her voice tinged with a note of fascination.

Jay looked concerned as he studied the intricacies of the map, his mind racing to connect the dots between their conversation and the physical landscape that sprawled before him on the map that accompanied the article. "It kind of follows Highway 280 all the way to right here," he mused aloud, tracing a finger along the fault line as it snaked its way across the page.

Jiewen leaned in and looked closer at the spot where Jay pointed. She glanced at him and then looked away and out the window. "It ends up right here in San Francisco, doesn't it?"

Jay caught the worry in her eyes and replied, "More to the west part of the city, though."

Jiewen remained quiet as she glanced out of the window at the rolling neighborhoods that extended out to the Golden Gate Bridge. She told Jay that she loved the view and wanted to make sure that if they ended up living together, the place must have a view of the bridge.

Jay went and sat on the couch near the window, engrossed in the article about the San Andreas fault line. He continued on to another article talking about geography and geology. Jiewen crossed the room, her heels clicking against the hardwood floor as she disappeared into her bedroom. She quickly changed out of her crisp business suit and into a flowy blouse and jeans, catching Jay's gaze as he checked her out.

"Ready to go?" Jiewen asked after finishing her wardrobe change while grabbing a jacket from the coat rack near the front door.

Jay stood up, his posture tense. "More importantly, are your parents ready?"

Jiewen's family worked tirelessly at the bustling Li's Food Market in Chinatown. Every time Jay visited them, he felt uncomfortable under their disapproving stares. Despite openly dating each other, their relationship was still a point of contention among Jiewen's relatives.

When Jiewen introduced her Caucasian boyfriend to her parents, they only focused on two things: His skin color and the fact that he gambled at night. They never bothered to ask about his successful job at Apple.

After a brisk walk down from the hillside, they traversed the city to enter the Chinatown area from the west. Jiewen and Jay turned right on Stockton Street and entered the market while immediately sensing the stares from some of the employees. Wei Guo stood at his usual spot, and stopped his whistling once he saw Jay.

"Hello, father," Jiewen said as she approached him and kissed him on the cheek. Wei Guo smiled in response and greeted the two people politely.

"Hello, Mr. Chu," Jay said and received a nod in response. At least some progress was evident.

Wei Guo took his daughter's hand and guided her to the back of the store as he explained a new idea. He dismissed her questions about damage from the recent earthquake only a while ago. Although as they walked through the narrow aisles, evidence of broken glass and spilled fruits and vegetables were testament enough that the cleanup remained unfinished.

Wei Guo pulled his daughter to the back area where a wooden desk stood at barstool height with a small Apple computer sitting upright along with a small printer on a stool to the side. He tapped a button on the side of the eight-inch-wide screen that sat attached to a bulky keyboard. "I cannot change the price of this item."

Jiewen smiled at her father and said, "You should be asking Jay that question. He's the one that got you this computer."

Wei Guo looked stoically at Jiewen and then moved his eyes toward Jay while frowning slightly and letting out a sigh. "Pengyou, please tell me how to change the price on this fancy new computer."

Jay seemed puzzled at first at the strange name just used but moved to a spot in front of the computer as Jiewen stepped back to allow room in the cramped space. Wei Guo stayed close to watch the screen. Jay immediately saw the edit button on the upper right corner of the website —familiar with its every spot because he designed this new website by himself. He explained to Wei Guo how to find the edit button and how it indicated whether it was in edit mode or not. He pressed it to edit the displayed contents. "And make sure you turn the edit button backoff before publishing the finished page."

Wei Guo moved quickly to the screen and changed the price then turned off the edit button. He hovered over the publish button for a moment and then turned to his daughter with a smile. "This is my favorite part."

Jay stepped back and saw the new web page published with the updated price. He smiled at the other two and moved back another step.

Wei Guo looked at Jay and said, "My younger customers are looking at the website now. They say that we cannot be a real business if we do not have a website."

Jiewen replied, "A place in the Yellow Pages isn't even needed any longer now that the worldwide web is taking over."

The three discussed other plans for their fledgling website in an excited tone. Wei Guo seemed alive with energy over the potential of making sales over the internet someday. Suddenly, the loud voice of Wei Guo's mother-in-law echoed over the market calling for him to get back to his post by the front door. Wei Guo politely excused himself and rushed to the assigned spot.

Jiewen finished some entries in her ledger for the family business while Jay wandered through the rows of fruits and vegetables, selecting several items unavailable in his normal market. He paid for the items under the watchful stare of an employee and waited outside for Jiewen to join him.

The two walked out of Chinatown and up Stockton Street to go through the tunnel and then climbed to the Top of the Tunnel where Jiewen continued her accounting services for Jimmy. They snacked on an Asian pear that was so watery it was difficult to eat without dripping the juices on their shirts.

Jay paused for a moment and asked, "What was that word your father called me back there?"

Jiewen smiled. "That's progress, my father called you, Pengyou, which means friend."

Jay smiled and acknowledged the compliment. He walked quietly while thinking of the potential in this relationship now that the idea of race may not be as big of an issue.

Jiewen teased and said quietly. "Maybe someday he will call you Nuxo."
"What does that mean?"

Jiewen pushed Jay and walked quicker while giggling. "Son-in-law."

With each step, Jiewen and Jay's feet landed on the cracked pavement of

Stockton Avenue, a subtle reminder that they were walking on the San Andreas Fault. They couldn't help but think about the map they had studied earlier, tracing the fault line from San Francisco to Point Reyes. The Pacific Plate and the North American Plate, two massive tectonic plates, clashed deep below the earth's surface. Molten rock churned and bubbled in the mantle, fueling their never-ending dance.

As they walked, they could feel a sense of anticipation in the air, as if even the Earth itself was holding its breath for what was to come. Jagged rocks and ridges along the fault line served as silent witnesses to the immense forces at play, but here in downtown San Francisco, repair crews quickly patched the cracks from each earthquake with fresh pavement like adding a fresh band aid to a wound.

CHAPTER 9

Shops fade into a bustling market's call,
A corner stall stands tall, renowned for all.

As Liz Mawbry emerged from the tunnel onto Stockton Street, she was immediately transported, like a time warp, into a bustling Chinatown. Four-story buildings adorned with balconies overflowing with drying laundry, metal fire escape stairs, and window-mounted air conditioning units, lined both sides of the busy street. Every storefront displayed vibrant Chinese characters, with only a few displaying English translations. The first two blocks after the entry gates contained electronics stores, hair salons, nail shops, foot massage parlors, trading companies, and camera shops. But as she continued down the street, the scene transitioned to rows of food markets bursting with fresh produce and hanging chickens in the windows. One particularly well-known market stood on the corner of Stockton and Clay Street: Cheong Kwan Jang Market, run by another well-respected family in the neighborhood. Most people called it Jang's Market.

Liz strolled down past each of the first three food markets and said hello to several people working the food bins lining the sidewalks in front of each store. She received very polite but wary responses, as each person could not remember if it was their day for an inspection.

"Hello, Ms. Mawbry," a shopkeeper said to her as she walked by. "Would you care for a Chinese pear?"

Liz thanked him warmly, appreciating his kindness despite their professional relationship. To Liz, being a health inspector was not about shutting down businesses but instead about ensuring a safe environment for everyone involved —from customers to employees. She made sure to give ample warning and assistance to those who needed to make improvements, always striving for fairness and understanding in her inspections.

Liz finally reached today's destination at Li's Market, the first inspection for this place in nearly six months. She went past the food bins on the outside and waited for Wei Guo Chu to escort her around the kitchen and food storage areas. She spotted him and he looked at her. He quickly glanced around out of habit to see if the place was tidy then walked toward Liz.

"Hello, Ms. Mawbry," he said and offered his hand to shake. "We are ready for you today."

"Thank you, Mr. Chu," Liz said and began paging through her notes from the last inspection. She looked up, smiled at Wei Guo, and added, "You keep the place in fine order, so there is very little to review from last time."

Liz noticed Wei Guo smiled broadly at that comment and watched him as he quickly glanced around the store again only stopping when his eyes reached the stairs. Liz turned and noticed movement at the top of the stairs and saw Yu Chen Li, the matriarch of the store, quickly duck away from the opening. Up until a few years ago, Yu Chen Li was the one who escorted the inspector around the shop. It took nearly five years of inspections before earning her trust and cooperation. Wei Gu, on the other hand, cooperated right from the start.

"Let's check the bottom of the deep-fat fryers first," Liz said after studying the notes on her checklist. She followed Wei Guo through and around various food bins and containers before arriving at the rear of the market where it transitioned into a very busy kitchen. Three rows of stainless-steel benches stood in the very center where people stood and chopped, sliced, packed, folded, and stir-fried every type of food imaginable. On the far side stood a row of flat top griddles, gas-fired woks, stoves, stock pots, and deep-fat fryers. On the other side was a row of reach-in refrigerators and a door to a walk-in refrigerator. A large dishwashing operation sat in the far corner. A light mist hung in the air that smelled like flowers and antiseptic soap at the same time.

Wei Guo crouched down and pointed to the bottom legs of the fryers as if studying a science project. "See, all cleaned up."

Liz bent down and shined a flashlight at the sturdy little legs that held up the immense weight of the deep-fat fryers. Each one looked as if it had been cleaned only moments before. Liz bent way down and shined the flashlight underneath as far as she could see as she checked for rat droppings—the telltale sign of not cleaning in unseen locations. Keep the small things clean, and the big things stay clean by themselves. She nodded in approval.

"How about the rat traps out in the garbage area?" Liz asked next after scanning her checklist.

Wei Guo eagerly escorted Liz through the rear door where she instantly smelled the familiar odor of the rear of nearly any kitchen. Where there was food preparation, there would be garbage at the rear open to the elements and the rats. Wei Guo pointed out a half-dozen bait traps all in the proper locations as prescribed in the previous inspection.

"And now let's check that condensing unit," Liz suggested. The previous inspection detected a cooling problem with the walk-in cooler, perhaps the single most costly item in a food market.

"I had it serviced, and we changed the freon," Wei Guo explained while moving down the alleyway to see a large boxy-looking machine mounted on a shelf above their heads.

Liz shined the flashlight at some gages on the box to take readings to compare them to the last inspection. "That's better, but I think you are going to have to replace it at some point, though."

Wei Guo looked sad as he must have known what that could mean to his profits. Liz saw the look and added, "Try not to worry for now. I think if you keep the door closed and the filters clean, you should be able to squeeze another year or two out of it."

Wei Guo suddenly looked much happier and nodded in agreement. He agreed to the suggestions and then confided to her, "I better start setting some money aside, though, just in case it goes out suddenly."

"That is very smart," Liz acknowledged. "No wonder your market is one of the best on the street."

Wei Guo began talking animatedly about fresh ideas for the market. They walked back to the front and Liz stopped to pick out two Chinese pears, her favorite. The large apple-like pears were difficult to find in the regular grocery stores. Wei Guo offered to pay for them himself but Liz had a strict rule of paying for her own food.

*   *

After a long day of inspecting Chinatown businesses, Liz walked wearily up Columbus Avenue toward her apartment in North Beach. Her feet ached, and she couldn't wait to kick off her uncomfortable heels. She turned the corner onto Chestnut Street and saw the familiar three-story building that held her second-floor apartment. Parking garages lined the entire first floor for the tenants, each with an assigned space behind individual garage doors. Liz and her partner, Greet, shared a small stall just big enough for their

Subaru wagon.

Greet happened to arrive at the stairs from the opposite direction as Liz walked around the corner on her way home from her busy day of inspections. Greet wore her long, thick blonde hair in a ponytail today, and Liz noticed and complimented her after a tender kiss.

Liz had always known she preferred being with another woman, but Greet had previously been in relationships with men before realizing her true preference. They had been together for two years now, and their love continued to grow stronger every day. The only peculiarity that Liz noticed about Greet was her penchant for collecting life-size plastic animals that she decorated for each season on their front porch. A large buck-tail deer was her favorite but it took up enough space on the deck that sometimes Liz simply sat down on it like riding a small horse.

After reaching the apartment and settling in for the evening, Greet glanced nervously at Liz and voiced a concern she had been thinking about for a while. "Hey, Liz," she called out, "did you see that the garage door doesn't quite close all the way?"

Liz took a sip of wine before responding, "Yeah, unfortunately, the building shifted during the last earthquake. I've tried fixing it, but it just won't budge."

Greet's eyes widened as they both walked out to their porch and she surveyed the deck for any signs of damage. "Is this place safe? What if another earthquake hits?"

Liz reached over and lightly touched Greet's leg in a reassuring gesture as Liz sat down in a chair and Liz threw a leg over the large plastic deer. "Don't worry. This building has been standing for over seventy years. It can handle a few earthquakes."

Greet relaxed back into her chair, still looking hesitant but noticeably calmer. After a moment, she shook her head and said, "I don't think I'll ever get used to those things."

The two enjoyed their wine and cheese while speaking of more pleasant topics. The sun began to lower behind the Golden Gate Bridge, casting long shadows down the North Beach area of the city. A golden color washed over nearly every nook and cranny of the similar-style of buildings that filled each of the narrow streets. Greet leaned over the railing as a handsome young man walked by, and she waved back at him after he had glanced up and saw her on the balcony one story up.

Liz sat in silence, pondering the effects of the last big earthquake on the garage door and the shifting foundation of their seventy-year-old building.

She couldn't understand why the building was still settling after all these years. Standing up, she leaned over the railing to get a better look at the garage door directly below them. The door and top trim seemed almost inseparable now, explaining why the garage door would not open.

CHAPTER 10

Through heights they roam, with grace in each step's sway,
Towards North Beach's end, where their hearts will stay.

Brian and Joanne strolled through the quiet streets of Pacific Heights, admiring the elegant Victorian homes as they made their way west after a nice outing together. Turning onto a bustling northward street, they eventually reached North Beach, where Joanne's cozy apartment awaited on the third floor of Frank Renado's building. Funny how Frank's nurturing soul at the Top of the Tunnel bar seemed to draw people into moving into his family's apartment building.

As the two waited for the traffic light to change at a busy intersection, Joanne brought up an article she had read about a recent interview with Mikhail Gorbachev. Brian nodded in agreement, commenting on the significant changes happening in Russia in 1989 and the potential end of the Cold War. Joanne smiled and reached for Brian's hand, intertwining her fingers with his —always appreciative of his intelligence. Brian welcomed her touch and allowed her to guide his hand into a comfortable position that fit her height and stride perfectly.

Remembering their fervent efforts during Governor Michael Dukakis' campaign in the 1988 election for President of the United States, Brian and Joanne shared similar thoughts on the current political landscape. Despite being supporters of Ronald Reagan during his eight years as President, they were not fans of George H.W. Bush, who had served as Reagan's vice president and ultimately became president himself this year. With open minds toward both Republicans and Democrats, Brian and Joanne believed in voting to ensure that no single party controlled all three governing bodies at once. Joanne theorized that with last fall's election, it would be ideal for a

Democrat to take the presidency to offset the power held by the Republicans in Congress.

She also recalled a moment when Bush, then vice president, stumbled over a simple question about the cost of bread. She could not believe that someone isolated in luxurious offices for nearly two decades could possibly understand the struggles of everyday life. This only strengthened Joanne's resolve to see a change in leadership.

Her prediction was that the Republicans would take the Senate and the Democrats would maintain control of the House, leaving the presidency up for grabs. Joanne believed it should go to a Democrat to balance the power of the Senate. Plus, after spending eight years as vice president, Bush seemed completely out of touch with reality.

But all of Joanne's theories were shattered when Michael Dukakis tried to appear tough by driving a tank at an army base during his campaign. His handlers suggested he wear a navigator's helmet instead of a standard one, not realizing it was much larger in size and volume due to requiring space for headphones. As the tank jolted along rough terrain, Dukakis sat awkwardly with his oversized helmet bouncing on top of his head like a bobblehead doll. The media pounced on this comical image, and Bush ultimately won the election by a large margin. Joanne's plan failed on every level. The Republicans held onto the presidency, and the Democrats held the House and Senate, thereby ensuring another four years of getting nothing done on Capitol Hill.

Brian and Joanne weaved their way through the bustling streets, strolling along with their fingers still intertwined as they approached Joanne's apartment building. A row of slightly crooked garage doors lined the ground floor, a testament to the building's age. But above them, elegant porches adorned the second and third floors, exuding elements of Italianate architecture.

As they approached the stairs to the third floor, Brian felt a sense of excitement in his chest. This was a special place for Joanne, her own private sanctuary that she rarely shared with others. He wondered if she was going to invite him in this time.

Joanne unlocked the gate leading to the stairs and paused as she heard a familiar voice from above. Frank Renado, their friend and now only a coworker at the bar, leaned over the railing of his third-floor balcony. He waved excitedly to both Brian and Joanne and shouted jokingly, "Who's doing my bartending duties if both of you are here?"

Brian chuckled and shouted back, "Jimmy sent us home early. He said you were coming in to lend a hand tonight!"

Frank feigned shock and laughed before waving to them and disappearing inside his apartment.

Joanne's melodic laughter filled the air as Brian laughed along with her. She unlocked the main latch and motioned for Brian to follow her through the wrought iron gate and up the grand staircase. His heart raced with anticipation, wondering if tonight would be the night she finally let her walls down.

As they reached the top of the stairs, Joanne turned to him with a playful grin. She unlocked the door to her penthouse apartment and invited him inside. Brian entered and felt a sense of awe at the extravagant space, with its floor-to-ceiling windows and modern art pieces adorning the walls. No wonder she loved her place so much.

As they settled onto a plush couch, Joanne poured them each a glass of red wine. Brian tried to focus on their conversation, but he couldn't shake the thought of where their relationship was headed.

Finally, Joanne opened up about her career aspirations at the hospital. After years of hard work, she had finally obtained her nursing credentials and was now interning. Brian listened attentively, acknowledging her dedication and drive.

But when he mentioned something about their future together, Joanne's expression softened and she placed a comforting hand on his knee. "I know you want more," she said softly, "but can't we just enjoy what we have right now? No labels, no expectations. Just two people enjoying each other's company?"

Brian wanted to push for answers, for a label to define their relationship. But as he gazed into Joanne's warm saphyre eyes and felt her touch on his skin, he realized that maybe she was right. For now, all that mattered was this moment and being with her. Deep down though, he couldn't ignore the nagging doubts that things were far from simple between them. But he knew this was going to be worth the wait.

CHAPTER 11

His ardor firm, though burdens bend his frame,
Yet weary, his spirit remains aflame.

Jimmy Baumers had always been a man of dedication and hard work, so his first year as owner of the bar was difficult but rewarding. The bar, which had been his pride and joy since 1988, was more than just a business to him; it was a labor of love. With sweat glistening on his forehead and calloused hands gripping the worn wooden bar, Jimmy exuded a sense of determination and tireless dedication. For the last year, he had poured his heart and soul into the bar that he proudly owned.

But as the year passed, the physical toll of lifting kegs and stocking shelves all by himself began to wear on him. His broad shoulders sagged slightly, and gray strands sprinkled throughout his once jet-black hair spoke of the year that flew by. Though he cherished every moment spent behind that bar, it was becoming increasingly difficult to keep up with the constant hustle.

As September of 1989 rolled around, Jimmy knew it was time for a change. He started handing over responsibilities to the evening shift earlier each day, finding solace in moments of quiet reflection as he contemplated what would come next for him and his beloved bar.

On this particular day, two of his regular patrons, Daniel Kim and Charles Kang, sat at the bar, deep in conversation. Daniel, the well-dressed investment banker, and Charles, the former cable car driver turned software programmer, huddled over a laptop, their minds engrossed in a revolutionary idea they had conceived. Their plan was to transform the way the company scheduled the cable cars where Charles used to work. The new scheduling software would ensure smoother routes and provide exacting and guaranteed times at each stop.

Jimmy watched with interest as the two men spoke animatedly, their faces illuminated with passion and excitement. Their determination mirrored his own when he had taken over the bar, determined to make it a success. He knew that look all too well –the spark of innovation and ambition.

Jimmy noticed Jorge Freeman enter the bar. He interrupted the two men's conversation abruptly, a mischievous grin forming on his face. He swiftly grabbed three shot glasses from the back bar and placed them in front of the two men who looked slightly bewildered. "Hold that thought, boys," he exclaimed, his enthusiasm evident. "Jorge needs to hear it from the top."

Jorge Freeman, still a cable car repairman and Charles's best friend, had just arrived and took a seat next to the duo. "Sorry I'm late," he apologized.

Jimmy poured shots of their favorite whiskey into the glasses and raised another of his own, proposing a toast to their future endeavors. Jimmy looked Jorge in the eyes. "No worries, Jorge. You're just in time for the start of something big. I've heard a lot of crazy ideas in this place, but what you guys have here is solid gold."

The four friends clinked their glasses together, sealing their commitment to a new venture that would bring their dreams to life.

CHAPTER 12

Beyond nature's grasp, at the edge of their home,
Seeking the west coast pulse, why people come.

The sun began its descent as Brian and his visiting high school friend returned to San Francisco on October 17, 1989 around 5:00 p.m., to meet other friends for plans that night. They had just finished a challenging hike through Castle Rock State Park, where breathtaking views of the rugged terrain and lush greenery rewarded their efforts. As they drove back to the city, the pine-scented air mixed with wildflowers filled their car, a reminder of the natural beauty that previously surrounded them. Soon, the quiet outskirts gave way to towering skyscrapers and bustling streets as they entered the city center. Brian's friend talked about how much he loved California and even talked about potentially moving here himself. This was no surprise –with its vibrant culture and stunning landscapes, California had a magnetic pull that drew people from all walks of life. The concept of "chain migration" was evident in this state as well –one person's move could inspire others to follow suit, creating a domino effect of relocation. As they made their way into the city center, Brian felt grateful for his decision to make California his home five years ago. He had found his own slice of paradise amidst the diversity and captivating allure of this state.

As they chatted and laughed while driving along Sansome Avenue, the road near the pyramid-like TransAmerica Building, the car suddenly swerved awkwardly all by itself. Brian thought they must have a flat tire or even two of them with the way the car swayed so much. Looking into the rear-view mirror, he saw rocks tumble down from a steep hillside behind them. Bricks fell from a nearby three-story building, and people ran out of their apartments in a panic as traffic came to a halt.

The power lines overhead swayed dangerously and began bouncing like a jump rope. More bricks fell, and more people emerged onto the chaotic street. Brian pulled the car over and quickly got out, but the violently shaking and rolling ground below him almost knocked him off his feet. The ground continued to roll and sway, causing buildings to lose bricks and crumble before their eyes. A serious crack in the street formed and spread like icy fingers under Brian until reaching for the curb and splitting it like a bolt of thunder.

To Brian's left, a three-story building started to move sideways, its soft ground floor giving way as it collapsed in slow motion onto the cars parked below in the garage. After sinking down and kneeling over, the top two floors stopped short of toppling over into the street on top of the panicking people. The once bustling street filled with screams, chaos, crashing, and destruction as the earthquake wreaked havoc on everything in its path.

Brian and his friend, disoriented and dazed, staggered through the chaos, their eyes darting around desperately as cries for loved ones pierced the air like anguished wails. Panic and confusion reigned supreme as people scrambled for their bearings amid the wreckage as an aftershock hit only moments after the first big eathquake.

As Brian surveyed the grim display of destruction, his gaze drew him to the buildings on the opposite side of the street. There, over the tops of the structures, a column of dark smoke billowed ominously into the sky, originating from Embarcadero Drive at the waterfront only four blocks away. The plume, a sinister sentinel of disaster, marked a foreboding presence that was a short distance away but hidden behind rows of crumpled buildings. It was a stark reminder that danger lurked at every corner, and safety felt elusive, but Brian began walking toward the noise and smoke down an alleyway he knew would lead that way.

Suddenly, another ferocious tremor rocked the ground, and the grating noise of highways collapsing upon each other reverberated through the air. Brian watched in helpless horror as the very earth beneath him seemed to groan and convulse. It was as if the world itself was rebelling against its inhabitants.

Amidst the deafening chaos, Brian's eyes fixated on the horrifying spectacle unfolding before him. The top of the causeway, a massive concrete structure that once connected distant shores, descended like a ribbon unfurling in slow motion. It cascaded down toward ground level, its enormous slabs crashing mercilessly onto cars and people caught in its unforgiving grip. The air filled with the sound of screeching metal, shattering glass, and the agonized cries of those trapped beneath the merciless concrete.

On Sansome Street, chaos descended like an unexpected storm. The once bustling thoroughfare now resembled a battlefield strewn with debris —bricks, shattered glass, and disoriented individuals struggling to make sense of the sudden devastation. The cacophony of screeching brakes and blaring horns had given way to an eerie silence broken only by sporadic sobs and gasps of disbelief.

Among the sea of immobilized vehicles, trapped motorists wore expressions of sheer despair. Some remained trapped inside their cars, tears streaming down their faces, while others had stumbled onto the cold curb, their eyes glazed over as if frozen in time. The disarray around them was palpable, a testament to the abruptness of the catastrophe.

As the wild symphony of crumbling masonry and shattering glass gradually subsided, a sinister undertone emerged. The hissing of gas, water, and sewer lines venting their contents into the air became audible, accompanied by the ominous snapping of severed power lines. The scent of natural gas, acrid and menacing, hung heavily in the air.

A few natural leaders emerged from the midst of the disoriented crowd. With resolute determination, they began to assess the situation and began lending a helping hand to those in need. Compassion guided their actions as they escorted terrified individuals away from the precarious structures, shielding them from the looming threat of falling debris.

One person, their voice cutting through the confusion, shouted orders that rang out with authority. "Clear the area! Move away from that building!" Their urgency conveyed the imminent danger, and as if on cue, people started to scramble to a safer distance.

The race against time and the pungent smell of natural gas pervaded the surroundings, and the looming disaster had not yet concluded. Suddenly, a spark ignited the volatile fumes, and a building erupted into flames, a fiery manifestation of the peril that had unfolded on Sansome Street.

As Brian's heart pounded in his chest, his mind raced with the vivid image of Joanne in her modest apartment in Frank Renado's building up in the North Beach area. It was as if he could see through the buildings, envisioning her waiting for him, unaware of the cataclysm unfolding outside. The thought of her safety consumed him.

He scanned the chaotic scene before him, his eyes darting toward the building that had tumbled onto the garages, reminding him of Frank's place, which shared an identical structure —a soft ground floor with two stories above. Determination etched across his face, Brian tore his gaze away from his trapped car, surrounded by people and debris, and made a snap decision. He had to reach Joanne, and he had to do it now.

Without hesitation, Brian bolted down the street toward the Renado apartment, his feet pounding against the pavement. He could almost hear Joanne's voice calling out to him, a distant yet urgent plea. Each step was a desperate race against time, fueled by love and fear for the woman he cherished. The commitment to their dinner date was how he knew she would be at her apartment. Hopefully it had not toppled over like he saw other buildings in every direction.

Brian's friend, though bewildered by the sudden turn of events, instinctively followed Brian's lead. With each stride, they left the chaos and confusion behind them, their focus unwavering. As they sprinted past other individuals, desperately seeking aid or escape, the two men paused only for a moment to assist an older woman with an injured leg. Using a piece of clothing they found hanging from a collapsed railing of a nearby building, they quickly fashioned a makeshift bandage to cover her wounds, ensuring she had at least some solace amid the turmoil. She told them to get to their loved ones in a cry of thanks to them.

Their mission propelled them forward, surging over, under, and around streets ravaged by equal measures of chaos and destruction. The world around them blurred into a chaotic mosaic of debris, but their determination to reach Joanne remained firm, their journey giving evidence of the unbreakable strength of love in the face of catastrophe.

CHAPTER 13

Their tiny home, a legacy of kin,
Nestled in hearts of the people within.

As the clock struck 5:04 PM on October 17, 1989, the ground beneath Liz's cozy apartment began to roll ever so slightly. Liz and Greet were both out on their front porch, enjoying a glass of wine and surrounded by Greet's quirky collection of plastic animal figurines and watching a tiny television perched on a shelf built just for that purpose on the side wall of the deck. Liz sat atop the life-size deer, its saddle digging into her thighs. Greet sat in the only chair on the porch in her usual spot. Vibrant shades of orange and pink painted the sky as the sun began to set.

Their tiny apartment was part of a building owned by the Renado family, with Frank Renado as their landlord. A legacy intertwined with the community's history, the Renados had maintained this modest complex for nearly half a century. In fact, Frank's father had been part of the Scavenger Garbage Company, a beloved garbage collection company serving San Francisco for over a century.

The design of their apartment building was practical and affordable; the first floor had a soft-floor configuration that allowed residents to conveniently park their cars beneath the living spaces above. Liz and Greet often enjoyed sitting on their deck above the garage doors, watching various activities unfold in their neighborhood. All of these details added layers of history and familiarity to their home, making it more than just a place to live.

On the fateful evening of the Loma Prieta earthquake, they had decided to stay home at their second floor apartment, absorbed in the excitement of the World Series game that pitted cross-bay rivals, the San Francisco Giants against the Oakland Athletics. But within seconds, the peaceful scene was shattered by the devastating force of an earthquake, turning their evening upside down. With a sudden, violent jolt, their once-stable abode transformed into a chaotic maelstrom of destruction. Then the rolling started and would not stop as the ground below the building moved like waves in the ocean.

In what felt like an eternity compressed into mere moments, Liz and Greet found themselves sprawled on the unforgiving pavement in front of their apartment building. The second-floor living space they had occupied only seconds earlier had plummeted to the sidewalk, descending as if the earth itself had opened up to claim it.

The top two floors of the structure, now resting precariously upon the crushed garage below, had flattened the parked cars when the first-floor walls gave way, "raking" to the side in a brutal, unforgiving motion. The entire building had collapsed upon itself, obliterating its first floor in a relentless cascade of destruction, leaving Liz and Greet to confront a horrifying reality amidst the rubble.

Greet's prized and decorated plastic deer broke all four of its legs as Liz had ridden it down and through the railing of their porch. Greet flew over the railing and bounced onto the street after ricocheting off of a parked car. She sat stunned on the pavement. Her eyes scanned the devastation, her heart pounding in her chest, as she took in the surreal sight of their second-floor deck now inexplicably resting at the level of the first floor. Among the debris, she spotted her beloved smashed deer and Liz, slowly trying to rise from the shock of the fall. Without hesitation, Greet rushed to her partner's side, her concern overriding the chaos that surrounded them and the deep bruises in her hip and thigh.

Their hands reached for each other, a reassuring connection amidst the mayhem, as they then embraced tightly as if trying to separate themselves from the world. But as they clung to one another, the building emitted an ominous groan, sending shivers down their spines. With a shared instinct, they abandoned their position near the fallen porch and dashed to the middle of the street, seeking refuge from potential falling bricks and further destruction.

In a horrifying symphony of destruction, the buildings on both sides of the street followed suit, collapsing upon themselves in the same devastating manner. The street echoed with the anguished cries of those trapped within, their voices a desperate plea for help amidst the crackling of flames and crumbling debris. Among the cacophony, one voice stood out, a voice that Liz recognized with a mixture of hope and fear. Liz cried out, her voice quivering. "Joanne? Is that you? Where are you?"

From deep within the collapsing structure, Joanne's frantic response resonated as if from the depths of a cavern. "Liz! I can't find Frank! Is he outside yet?"

Liz's heart sank as she scanned the chaotic scene, her eyes meeting those of her neighbors, all shaking their heads in response to her questions. Panic surged within her as she urgently conveyed the gravity of the situation. "Joanne! You have to get out of there now! The whole thing is going to collapse!"

Amid the chaos, Greet took charge. She ushered her neighbors to safety, leading them to a spot in the middle of the street away from the danger. A van had come to a halt and sat with its engine still running, its driver mysteriously absent. Greet squinted and read the words on the side of the vehicle: "Chef's Laundry Service." Without hesitation, she flung open the back door and grabbed armfuls of freshly washed tablecloths and napkins. She handed them out to her distressed neighbors, providing a small sense of comfort and warmth amidst the chaos.

Looking back at the collapsing building, Liz's desperate cries for Joanne went unanswered, and she watched in helpless agony as the roof began to crumble between the interior walls. Smoke began to seep out from an unseen fire that had evidently ignited somewhere deep within. Fear gnawed at her heart as she called out again, her voice trembling, "Joanne! Are you okay? You have to get out! Frank, are you in there?"

Amidst the rubble and debris, figures began to emerge slowly, their movements sluggish and dazed. Sirens wailed in the distance as police cars screeched to a halt near some collapsed buildings down the street. The call for fire trucks echoed through the street, but the city's resources were already stretched thin with multiple emergencies. The race to save lives had only just begun, and Frank's building was just one of many in dire need of help.

Pausing to look around at the chaos and the confusion of the people, Liz suddenly caught sight of Brian and another man charging toward her like marathon runners, their clothes stained with sweat, dirt, and smoke. Panic etched on his face; Brian frantically scanned the wreckage for any sign of Joanne before coming to a stop in front of Liz. She urgently gestured toward the building, fear evident in her eyes as she tried to explain where she thought Joanne might be trapped. Without hesitation, Brian instantly moved to the ruined structure, strategizing his entry point as Liz's desperate pleas followed him.

"Joanne! Joanne Stoddard!" Brian's voice rang out very loudly, a desperate plea that he repeated over and over, each cry filled with mounting concern. There was no response to his calls and no sign of Joanne emerging from the wreckage.

Brian's eyes scanned the building, his mind racing as he assessed the situation. He spotted a railing within jumping reach and a broken patio door leaning against some patio furniture that had managed to survive on what remained of the deck. He leaped up to the railing, a move that prompted a policeman to shout for him to return to safety.

For a brief moment, Brian hesitated while hanging from the railing, his gaze locking with the officer's. The gravity of the situation hung in the air, but Brian's determination to find Joanne overrode any concerns for his own safety. With a resolute nod, he pulled himself onto the deck and ducked through the patio doorway and into the heart of the crumbling building. His shouts for Joanne grew faint to those outside as he ventured deeper into the collapsing structure. His perilous mission had begun, and time was of the essence.

With careful steps, Brian maneuvered through the maze of shattered furniture and debris that littered the abandoned apartment. He gritted his teeth as he pushed against the stubborn front door, but it wouldn't budge. Frustrated, he took a step back and charged forward, feeling his heart race as he broke through the splintered wood.

The hallway beyond was eerily quiet and dimly lit, a sharp contrast to the chaos outside. Despite the danger, Brian felt some relief at recognizing a few numbers on the doors lining the hall, but he was still on the second floor and must go up one more level.

He found the staircase and began to climb, cautiously making his way up as smoke seeped into the confined space from all directions. The air grew thick with the acrid smell of burning debris, burning his throat with each breath.

At the top floor, Brian saw a terrifying sight. As he pushed open the door to enter the narrow hallway, a wall of flames roared toward him, engulfing Joanne's nearby apartment and consuming the number on her front door. Panic surged through him as he desperately called out for Joanne, hoping she was still within reach amidst the raging inferno.

From a nearby apartment tucked in a short hallway to the side, cries for help pierced the air. Brian immediately called out Joanne's name once more, his voice a lifeline in the midst of the turmoil.

"Brian!" Joanne's voice, laden with sheer panic yet tempered with newfound relief, rang out through the door. "We can't get out. The door is blocked!"

Brian's chest ached with a mixture of dread and determination. He recognized Frank Renado's apartment door immediately and rushed to the entrance. With every ounce of strength he could muster, he forced the door open just a fraction, allowing Joanne's trembling fingers to protrude through the narrow gap. Brian touched her fingers, and they froze for a moment. Her desperation fueled her efforts as she tugged with all her might, while Brian threw his shoulder against the door in a desperate bid to free her from the fiery prison that had become their reality.

Yet, despite their relentless struggle, the door refused to yield another inch. The flames danced ever closer, their crackling fury echoing the urgency of the situation. Brian and Joanne's fate hung precariously in the balance as they battled the unyielding obstacle that separated them from safety.

As the flames closed in on them, Joanne's voice trembled with fear as she yelled out, "Brian, I'm scared. The fire is coming through the walls!" Her words were interrupted by a fit of coughing, and her fingers disappeared from the narrow opening. Desperation gripped her as she continued, "I can't get Frank up."

Brian's heart raced as he assessed the dire situation. Time was running out, and he could feel the heat and smoke intensifying with each passing second. With a determined resolve, he yelled back, "Stand back from the door! Stand way back! I'm coming through fast!"

Taking several steps away from the door, Brian knew he had only one chance to break through with all his strength unleashed in a single moment. He closed his eyes briefly, focusing on his goal with unwavering determination. He visualized bursting through the door, stopping ten feet past it, and getting both Joanne and Frank to safety.

With a deep breath, Brian began to run, building up speed as he approached the door. At the last possible moment, he turned his shoulder toward the doorframe, and his shoulder collided with the side of his face as he crashed through the opening. The doorframe came away with the door, exploding into splinters as Brian tumbled to the floor about five feet beyond the entrance. Disoriented but determined, he quickly regained his composure and looked up to find Joanne sitting on a kitchen chair cradling Frank's head on her lap as he sat on the floor.

Frank, somewhat dazed but remarkably composed, muttered, "Jesus, Brian, all you had to do was knock first."

Joanne, her relief palpable, let Frank lean against the chair and moved toward Brian to embrace him. A sense of urgency washed over them as she embraced Brian and kissed him on the lips, her voice filled with determination. "We have to get him out of here, now!"

Brian's eyes widened as he took in the sight of the bone protruding from Frank's leg. He knew they were running out of time. Ignoring his own dizziness, he moved away from his embrace with Joanne and lifted Frank's limp body in his arms. He noticed a piece of wood had been tied to his leg as a splint.

Joanne rushed to help, but Brian was determined and he used every ounce of strength to carry Frank out of the room and down the hallway. He paused briefly to make sure Joanne was following, and a sense of love and protectiveness washed over him as he gazed at her tender smile.

"The stairwell is still safe," Brian reassured Joanne, pointing her in the direction of escape. "Hurry!"

Joanne, her determination mirroring Brian's, retorted, "Not without my boys." She held the stairwell door open so Brian could carry Frank out.

The older man was on the verge of passing out, but Brian had Frank's arm wrapped securely over his own shoulder, holding him as if he were a lifeless rag doll. All three of them made their way down the stairwell as the noise of collapsing beams grew louder and more ominous. The entrance to the hallway where Brian had entered was now blocked by fallen debris. Panic set in as they assessed their limited options.

"This way!" Brian yelled over the escalating noise, feeling the heat from the encroaching fire. They had only seconds to spare. "Through the trash room!"

Joanne initially looked incredulous, but understanding dawned on her, and they rushed down a side corridor, bursting through a metal door that led to the trash chutes and dumpsters. However, the stairs that had led down one story were now reduced to a jumbled pile off to the side. They looked around desperately, and Brian spotted the garage doors, crushed like an accordion.

Brian set Frank down momentarily and began pulling at the aluminum garage doors with all his might, resembling someone trying to unroll a stubborn carpet. In a moment of desperate effort, an opening appeared, revealing a faint glimmer of light outside. Without hesitation, Brian lifted Frank once more and dragged him through the opening, pushing Joanne through first. Finally, Brian emerged from the makeshift escape route, relief washing over him as he wrapped his arms around Joanne, showering her face with kisses to express his gratitude and love for her safety.

Frank, lying prone on the ground, couldn't help but comment while groaning, "Get a room, guys."

Joanne bent down and carefully adjusted the splint she had applied to stabilize Frank's damaged shin bone, the tibia, preventing it from causing further harm to his skin. Frank winced but did not hide his admiration as he remarked, "You are one hell of a nurse."

Joanne smiled affectionately and continued to bandage the leg, her hands steady and experienced. "I do this all the time now, Frank." In the midst of disaster, her calm and competence provided a glimmer of hope and reassurance for them all.

With Frank held up and bouncing on one foot, they moved further away from the building, putting as much distance as possible between themselves and the engulfing flames that roared behind them. As they retreated, torrents of water from a firehose suddenly drenched the entire side of the building, dousing the relentless inferno. A vigilant firefighter had spotted the three survivors in the alley and yelled at them to move away.

Frank, his dry humor never deserting him, muttered quietly, "No shit, Sherlock."

On the other side of the building, they finally reunited with Liz and Greet, who had been tirelessly assisting others with bandages from the makeshift hospital at the laundry truck. Brian's friend, who had remained active in aiding those in need, saw Brian's return and looked visibly relieved. He could not help but inject a touch of humor into the situation, saying, "You sure know how to show a fellow a good time."

Brian chuckled in response; his spirits buoyed by their reunion. "Next time I'm in Wisconsin, I expect a good tornado then." Amid the chaos and destruction, their camaraderie remained unshaken, and a sense of resilience emerged in the face of adversity.

Liz devoted her time to aiding people in their escape from buildings all around them, guiding them through the shattered windows of the damaged buildings. As she worked tirelessly, shouts for loved ones pierced the air, the desperate voices of people trying to reconnect with those they held dear. Greet, by her side, shared in the efforts, and together they navigated the chaotic scene, offering support to those in need.

Meanwhile, Brian, his friend, and Joanne had managed to get Frank to an awaiting ambulance, ensuring that he received the medical attention he desperately required. With Frank safely in the care of the first responders, they began making their way toward the Top of the Tunnel bar, anxious to see if it had survived the devastation.

Attempts to contact their friends yielded only frustrating busy signals, as the overloaded cell phone system struggled to handle the surge in calls from everyone trying to reach their loved ones. Joanne paused and glanced back for a final view at her crumbled apartment building, a moment of reflection on the loss of all her possessions in the fire that now consumed the entire structure. Brian, attuned to her emotions, noticed the sorrow in her expression and asked if she was okay.

Her response was a testament to their enduring bond. "I'll always be okay with you, Brian Lomax," Joanne replied, her arms enveloping him in a long and passionate embrace.

Brian held her gaze, his eyes filled with love and gratitude. "I love you, Joanne. I don't know what I would have done if I lost you back there."

Joanne's response was simple yet profound, a testament to the strength of their connection. "Stick around. Me and Frank would be dead right now if it wasn't for you."

In the midst of chaos and loss, their love blossomed and remained a source of solace and resilience, a beacon of hope amid the turmoil that surrounded them.

At the time the Loma Prieta earthquake struck, the ground shook violently as the Pacific Plate and North American Plate slipped past each other along the San Andreas Fault. The intense movement released built-up stress within the plates, causing significant damage across a large region of California.

In the aftermath of the quake, smaller aftershocks continued to rock the region as the tectonic plates readjusted. These aftershocks would last for days, weeks, and even months after this major seismic event and caused even further destruction to already weakened structures.

The shifting of the tectonic plates also resulted in changes to stress distribution along fault lines and surrounding areas, potentially triggering future earthquakes in surrounding fault lines. The whole nation watched in disbelief.

CHAPTER 14

Walking the marina's brim with grace,
Hearing the city's secrets in shadows' space.

Jay Baumers had been walking quietly along Embarcadero Avenue near the waterfront when the Loma Prieta earthquake hit. He strolled along the wide avenue in the shadows of a two-story freeway that towered overhead, his steps synchronized with the rhythm of the city's pulse. The vibrant tapestry of humanity unfurled before him, each person a thread in the intricate fabric of daily life. As he moved forward, he drank in the kaleidoscope of sounds that filled the air: snippets of laughter, scraps of conversation, the constant hum of traffic above him. It was as if the very city itself was whispering its stories to him.

The warm October sun bathed the city in its golden embrace, casting long, graceful shadows from the towering monoliths of glass and steel lining the waterfront. The result was nothing short of a living postcard, a picturesque scene that Jay couldn't help but to embrace. Squinting up at a nearby glass wall, he marveled at the reflection of Coit Tower, a historic sentinel overlooking San Francisco. It stood like a guardian of the past, its history etched in stone, a silent observer of the ever-changing city.

Jay's path unfurled ahead, leading him to the steep staircase that wound its way through lush gardens and up the formidable Telegraph Hill. This was his sanctuary, the place where he sought solace and perspective in the midst of the urban chaos. Each step upward was a meditation, a journey into tranquility amidst the bustling city below. The stairs wound through beautiful gardens on a street so steep, they never actually built the street and it had become a series of terraced gardens for the neighbors instead.

Dressed in blue jeans that bore the faint traces of countless adventures and a crisp white shirt with sleeves casually rolled up, Jay was the embodiment of urban elegance. He moved with a grace that was both effortless and confident, his thoughts already drifting to the dinner plans he had made with Jiewen, his girlfriend who would be joining him later at a place on Montgomery Street.

As the clock ticked to 5:04 p.m., the city's symphony of life was punctuated by a deafening crash, shattering the serenity of Jay's stroll and rocking the earth beneath him. A massive rock, seemingly detaching from the very cliff above, gave in to gravity's pull. It fractured into a chaotic dance of shards, each fragment descending upon Jay like a tempest of nature's fury. The harsh reality of the moment snapped him out of his tranquil reverie, and instincts took over. He leapt back, his heart pounding, his breath quickening, his pulse racing in sync with the chaos that had erupted.

But the turmoil was far from over. Nature seemed determined to cast aside any semblance of order or tranquility. More rocks dislodged from their precarious perches, tumbling down the steep stairs with an unforgiving gravity. They seemed to possess a malevolent intent, striking at Jay with the force of a vengeful deity.

The ground beneath Jay's feet morphed into a treacherous storm, shaking violently, leaving him swaying unsteadily. The very earth quivered beneath him like a beast awakening from slumber. Nausea surged through him, his senses overwhelmed by the disorienting chaos, the world around him jolting and quaking.

For a never-ending moment that stretched into eternity, Jay fought a fierce battle against the relentless tremors. His arms outstretched like a tightrope walker, feet rooted to the earth like an ancient oak; he grappled with the raw force of the earthquake. His muscles strained and his resolve held firm as he desperately clung to the semblance of control on this moving staircase on the edge of the cliff.

And then, as if mocking the resilience of humanity, the calamity escalated further. Jay turned toward the waterfront about six blocks away and watched in horror as the top roadway of the Embarcadero Freeway, some fifty feet in the air but at his own eye level as he stood on the stairs, began collapsing one section at a time onto the roadway below it. The metallic symphony of twisted vehicles and the shrieks of terrified souls filled the air. Cars and trucks trapped between the crumbling roads were transformed into grotesque pancakes as if the world had suddenly turned into a giant, unforgiving car crusher like those found in a junkyard.

Jay stood frozen in place, the weight of the unfolding tragedy pressing down upon him. He envisioned the swift and brutal fate that befell so many people in that heart-wrenching moment. The dust and debris from the collapsing highway soared into the sky, obscuring the fading light of the evening sun, casting the world into a chilling grayness that matched his despair.

A three-story building to his left shook violently and a large pain of glass shattered and dropped large glass pieces onto the sidewalk below. Several people scrambled to get out of the way of the falling glass, with one of them suffering a large gash on his shoulder as he sprinted away. Then bricks rained down from above as Jay stumbled down his staircase and out into the center of the street, looking up to see what could fall on him. A mother and daughter joined him in the street, and he instinctively tried to shield them both. He yelled for others to meet them in the middle of the street as others poured out through the shaking buildings.

The ground continued rolling violently, sending bricks and glass crashing to the street. People stumbled out of bars in shock, clutching their drinks as they looked around in disbelief. A four-story building bent precariously, crushing parked cars beneath its weight, while a fire escape lay crumpled on the ground with a person clinging to it six feet off the ground.

Jay sprang into action, running toward the crumbling building to help the person on the fire escape. He shouted instructions over the cacophony of screams and sirens, and guided the person to safety.

Amidst the chaos, Jay heard cries for help coming from inside a damaged building. He scanned the area for a way inside and spotted a patio door, partially open and radiating screams. With adrenaline pumping through his veins, he jumped onto a nearby railing and climbed up to the second-floor deck. Ignoring the sharp edges of broken glass, he entered the apartment and felt his way through the dust-filled room.

"Hello?" he called out.

A woman's voice answered him in relief. "Oh, thank God! I can't get out! There's a fire. Please help me!"

He rushed toward a faint flicker of light in the corner of the room, his heart pounding in his chest as he realized it was a small flame growing larger by the second. Squinting through the smoke, he spotted a large appliance on its side blocking a door. He pushed with all his might, sweat pouring down his face as he struggled to move it.

With a loud groan, the refrigerator finally shifted enough for the woman to crawl out from behind it. He rushed over to her and carefully helped her up, checking her for any injuries.

The acrid smell of smoke filled their lungs as they stumbled toward the patio, Jay's arm wrapped firmly around her trembling body.

Jay helped the woman climb down the deck as debris fell around them. The street below was a chaotic mess, with people rushing in different directions and buildings leaning precariously. Jay spotted a familiar face in the crowd —Yuze from the bar —and called out to him for help. Yuze recognized Jay's voice and rushed over to a spot below them.

As they tried to get the woman safely onto the ground, smoke billowed out of the top floor windows of her apartment building. Yuze yelled at her to keep climbing down while he and Jay steadied her.

Finally, she reached the street and turned back to look at her collapsed apartment building. Panic set in as she asked if anyone else was still inside. She grabbed onto Yuze's collar for support.

Meanwhile, sirens wailed in the distance as rescue vehicles made their way through the debris-littered streets. Jay saw an ambulance approaching and people swarmed around it. Paramedics jumped out and were bombarded with pleas from frantic onlookers.

Together, Jay and Yuze discussed the situation as they surveyed the streets and absorbed the extent of the damage. The shock of what had happened spread through the crowd, bringing a sense of urgency and fear to the already chaotic scene.

Jay and Yuze frantically dialed their flip phones, but they couldn't get a signal. Frustrated, they looked over at the young woman next to them who had just pulled out her phone to answer a call.

As she spoke into the phone, Jay and Yuze watched in disbelief. "How did you get a signal?" Yuze asked.

"I don't know," replied the woman, her brow wrinkled in confusion. She listened intently to her mother's voice on the other end of the line before it abruptly cut off. Turning to look at Jay, she gasped, "My mom said the Bay Bridge collapsed."

Both Jay and Yuze shook their heads in disbelief as they turned to look toward the waterfront. They started walking with the woman alongside, then broke into a run toward the bridge, determined to see if the report was true. As they ran down a two-block street, their pace slowed as they came upon the wreckage that lay before them.

Where there once stood a sturdy two-story freeway now lay a haphazard maze of crushed concrete and steel debris scattered across Embarcadero Road. Cars were crushed beyond recognition, their twisted metal frames sticking out from beneath the decimated upper deck. Jay pointed out one car with a headlight still visible among the destruction, blood dripping from its smashed front end.

The three of them stood in stunned silence before slowly backing away from the scene, trying to make sense of what had just happened. It was like something out of a nightmare.

Jay's eyes widened as he pointed up at the Bay Bridge, now visible from this vantage point due to a collapsed section of the freeway. Cars and trucks were at a standstill on the Bay Bridge in both directions, with people spilling out onto the roadway and staring in shock at the gaping hole in the bridge.

His phone rang in his hand and he answered it without thinking, still transfixed by the scene before him. Daniel Kim's voice came through the receiver, asking for an explanation. Jay shook himself out of his daze and quickly explained their location near the freeway.

Within minutes, Daniel arrived on the scene after abandoning his train sitting motionless on the middle of Mission Street —only fifty feet short of his normal stop. Together, they made their way toward one section of the collapsed road where desperate cries for help could be heard amidst the rubble. With Yuze's sharp vision, they spotted a hand waving frantically from a space next to a crumpled truck.

Without hesitation, they used all their strength to move chunks of concrete and twisted rebar in order to reach the trapped person. And then, finally, after what felt like hours but was only minutes, they saw more of a little girl emerge from the debris, her voice meek as she pleaded for help.

With renewed determination, they continued digging, until eventually, they were able to pull out the little girl —battered and bruised but alive thanks to their efforts. The group stood together in awe at their accomplishment as more hands reached into the rubble and voices joined in the search for survivors. A few other onlookers joined the digging, sweat and dirt cascading from everybody's faces as they reached for some bastion of hope in the middle of this death and destruction. Words of hope filled the air as they dug.

After the chaos and destruction subsided, screams pierced through the air in the growing quiet. The group scrambled to find the sources, their hands reaching through broken concrete and twisted metal. After moving a large slab, they uncovered another young girl, her body pinned by another slab of concrete. Jay quickly organized the rescue effort, calling for pry bars and utilizing a fallen light pole to create a makeshift lever. They positioned it carefully next to the girl's body, making sure it wouldn't slip during their risky attempt to save her.

"Ready?" Jay shouted, his voice steady and commanding.

On the count of three, they all pulled with all their strength while Yuze used every ounce of his being to pull the girl out of harm's way. Miraculously, they managed to free her just as the concrete collapsed in on itself. The exhausted group collapsed onto the ground, with Yuze and the rescued girl embracing each other tightly amidst tears and gasps for air. They were quickly helped up and brought to safety by their grateful companions.

The young girl kept thanking everyone and then started asking for her mother. She looked at the space where she had been trapped and explained they were walking hand in hand right before the roadway fell on them. She began sobbing uncontrollably as she yelled out her mother's name at the pile of rubble.

CHAPTER 15

He sifts through rubble, thoughts of loved ones in mind.
His heart beats fast, to those loved he will find.

As Jay tirelessly dug through the rubble with Daniel and Yuze, his mind kept wandering to one thought: Where was Jiewen? He glanced over at Daniel and noticed a determined look on his face. Then he looked at Yuze, who caught his gaze and gave him a sympathetic nod. Jay could see the pain in Yuze's eyes, knowing that he was also struggling with thoughts of leaving to find his own family in Chinatown. But then Yuze shook off the emotions and went back to digging, waving goodbye to Jay as he did so.

After running around cars and debris in the roadway, Jay spotted an old bicycle abandoned on the sidewalk. Without hesitation, he grabbed the bike and pedaled through streets choking with dust, twisted metal, and broken glass. His heart beat rapidly as he weaved between stopped cars and struggling pedestrians, barely aware of his surroundings as he thought about Jiewen, hopefully waiting at home for him at their planned rendezvous place now interrupted by this event.

After thirty minutes of strenuous effort, Jay finally made it to Jiewen's apartment, after stopping occasionally to try using his cell phone only to discover that all lines were busy when he tried. When he arrived at her front door, he found a note saying she had gone to their family's market to help.

He hopped back on the bicycle and headed straight for Chinatown down a busy street filled with gridlocked cars, broken traffic lights, and people walking. The people's faces told their stories outright, some with tears streaking down their dusty faces, others with panic in their eyes as they rushed to find their loved ones, and some walking slowly and looking dumbfounded. An occasional policeman or firefighter assisted people. Some people helped direct traffic, and others sat in stunned silence as aftershocks stacked up like tormentors. Meanwhile, the ominous smoke began choking the sky as the sun set on a darkened city —all but for the lights of the growing fires.

Jay reached Chinatown and saw its intricate green gateway had crashed to the ground, and now lay pushed off to the side to make way for cars. He bicycled right up to the front of Li's Food Market and tossed the bicycle to the side. A frantic-looking man instantly grabbed the bike and took off down the street. Jiewen, standing in front of their food market, saw Jay and quickly jumped into his arms and sobbed uncontrollably. Wei Guo and Meiyu Li came over and placed their hands on Jay's shoulders in comfort.

"Wai Po won't come out," Jiewen said between tears, using the maternal grandmother term affectionately. Jiewen's beautiful blue wool suit carried food stains and dirt, looking like she found them in a garbage pile. "She won't leave her home."

Wei Guo and Meiyu Li rattled off their efforts to coax her out of the building, which was badly damaged but still standing. Jay glance up and down the street and saw that most of the buildings stood tall and erect, but glass, clothing, and bricks dotted the street, along with overturned food stands and toppled market trinket stands. Their owners had already begun righting the stands and began picking up the pieces. Shopkeepers lit paper globes to help their way through the darkening sky. But Jay smelled smoke. The scent of natural gas burned his nostrils and alighted his awareness.

"We have to get the gas turned off in all of these buildings," Jay said to Wei Guo after releasing Jiewen.

"But what about Yu Chen Li?" Wei Guo asked. He moved his arm around his wife of thirty years, Meiyu Li, trying to comfort her and knowing fear must be consuming her thoughts.

Jay looked up and down the street, began developing a plan with his razor-sharp mind, and replied, "Where is the gas meter? We have to get that turned off, or the whole place could go up."

"Jay, I smell smoke," Jiewen said and looked at the others.

Wei Guo released his wife and stood for a moment one step away, and then he motioned for Jay to follow him through the store. They both rushed into the front door, hopping over overturned racks, equipment, and spilled food. Jiewen and her mother stood stunned outside, not knowing what to do. But then Jiewen took off running down the street, leaving her mother to watch alone. But only a moment later, Meiyu Li began picking up spilled food and overturned racks as a way to keep busy and helping in any way to take her mind off of her mother stubbornly sitting inside. Other people started helping. Meiyu Li looked like the anchor person in an army of volunteers.

Wei Guo and Jay made their way through the market and out the back door into the alleyway. Wei Guo motioned for Jay to follow him to the far corner of the building where a row of gas meters sat side-by-side to feed the neighboring buildings. Wei Guo reached behind one of the meters and pulled on a red-colored rope that revealed a gas meter wrench on the other end. He immediately began turning off the gas at each meter one by one. He turned to Jay when he recognized his questioning look and said, "Liz made us add this gas wrench in her last inspection."

Jay and Wei Guo finished the task of turning the gas off and went back into the building. The odor of burning plastic stung their nostrils, so Jay suggested Wei Guo continue upstairs while Jay searched for the source of the fire. Jay ducked into the kitchen area while Wei Guo headed for the stairs, taking them two at a time to reach the third-floor living quarters.

Wei Guo made his way down the hallway to their family's apartment. The door was locked but Wei Guo always carried his key with him. He unlocked the door but found it bolted with the chain. He felt the chain and then yelled out his mother-in-law's name. She would not or could not answer.

Wei Guo thought for a moment, stood back, and then rammed his shoulder into the door several times until the chain broke away from the door frame. He rushed inside only to see Yu Chen Li sitting on a kitchen chair holding a large wooden spoon.

"What kind of man breaks down his own door?" Yu Chen Li chided while waving the spoon in Wei Guo's direction.

Wei Guo was in no mood to be lectured once more. "I will not let my children lose their grandmother, and I will not let my wife lose her mother. Think what you will of me, but that is a fact."

Yu Chen Li began reciting a litany of Wei Guo's failures as Wei Guo only paused momentarily before asking once more for her to come with him. She refused again, and Wei Guo stood glaring at his passive aggressive mother-in-law, finally having enough of the years of torment. Both stayed gridlocked while staring at each other when the odor of chemical-filled smoke filled their nostrils. A wisp of smoke came through the open door behind Wei Guo.

Wei Guo grabbed the spoon away from his mother-in-law and threw it across the room, shattering the window above the kitchen sink. The spoon flew through the window and sailed out to land on the street below, only a few feet from where Meiyu Li was busy picking up food.

Wei Guo grabbed Yu Chen Li as if he were picking up a bag of potatoes, lifted her aggressively from the chair, and threw her over his shoulder. She lashed out kicking and screaming while Wei Guo remained stoically strong and quiet as he moved her through the front door.

Suddenly another aftershock hit as they reached the stairway, at which point Yu Chen Li chose to stop struggling from Wei Guo's tight grip on her as he balanced in the very strong rolling of the building. He and his human cargo arrived at the rear stairwell door, and he tried hard to open the door but it would not budge. He stood back and kicked his foot as hard as possible against the door knob. The sound of the doorknob breaking and the sound of his ankle shattering came at the same time. The door swung open and Wei Guo limped down each step, wincing in pain but continuing on at the same time.

Finally, they reached the lower floor and came face to face with Jay, covered in soot and grease and carrying a fire extinguisher. Jay looked at Wei Guo carrying his mother-in-law so disrespectfully, and Wei Guo looked at the fire extinguisher in Jay's hand.

Jay held up the fire extinguisher and asked, "Liz?"

Wei Guo burst out laughing and began limping to the front door. He said casually to Yu Chen Li, "I am tired of being afraid of what you think of me."

Yu Chen Li remained quiet and motionless. Right before they emerged through the front door, the old woman replied, "You do not seem to be afraid of anything… my son."

Wei Guo carried his mother-in-law to the street as Meiyu Li burst into tears at the sight of them and rushed to them. She gently combed back her mother's hair and helped Wei Guo lower the old woman to the ground. Meiyu Li quickly found some chair cushions lying in the street and helped prop her mother up against a wooden rack tipped on its side.

Yu Chen Li looked up and down the street at the people frantically trying to save each other and their village. She looked up at Wei Guo and Meiyu Li and then began crying. "I had no idea it was this bad."

Meiyu Li expressed her love and hugged Yu Chen Li, who looked up at Wei Guo standing strong in front of them. Yu Chen Li looked straight into her son-in-law's eyes and said, "Make sure you get something to eat before you help other people."

Wei Guo never heard words of love from his mother-in-law. Love is through the stomach with Chinese families so people rarely use the words of love in any other way. "Yes, Zhang Mu Niang," Wei Guo said, using the reverent term for his wife's mother for the first time.

Jiewen suddenly appeared with a bag full of plastic fittings in one hand and a heavy metal monkey wrench in the other. Over her shoulders hung two coiled garden hoses that made her look like a military combat person carrying a string of bullets. Jay and Wei Guo looked perplexed and Jiewen stated, "We are on our own here. The fire department is busy, and Chinatown is probably last on the list."

Jiewen opened the bag and pulled out a large 3" plastic pipe adapter as well as several transitions to the garden hose size. She handed it to Jay and ordered him to get this on the fire hydrant. Jay instantly recognized the plan and said, "We are going to need more hoses."

Wei Guo kissed Meiyu Li's cheek and smiled at Yu Chen Li still sitting on some cushions leaned against a food cart, then took off running into the market once more. Yu Chen Li grinned a satisfying grin and leaned back to close her eyes.

Within an hour, fire hydrant after fire hydrant sat connected to long strings of garden hoses reaching deep inside the buildings that had shown evidence of smoke or fires. Families of the entire Chinatown society worked together to save their village. Shouts of more water or more people to combat the flames, as well as roaming groups shutting down gas meters at every building, and other groups turning off electricity at the main panels to each building ensured that more fires could not start.

Families began setting up tables and chairs in the street, while others used paper lanterns with candles to light the way. People cleaned the street and set up their stores outside, feeling the danger of more aftershocks that might continue for days. Several restaurants carried their cooking gear into the street and used broken pieces of wood from the damaged buildings to light fires under the woks.

Somebody yelled out, "I have more chickens to cook tonight!" Then a group of chefs ran to gather the perishable food to cook and eat before any of it spoiled. Rows of coolers sprang to life as restaurants emptied their ice into the coolers before it melted.

The toughness, camaraderie, and shared experiences allowed the entire Chinatown to come together in spite of their politics, religion, social statuses, and ages to band together until some sense of normalcy returned.

DAVID LEE LUEDTKE

CHAPTER 16

After the quake, they toil in makeshift inns,
Trading meals for goods, the healing begins.

As the aftermath of the earthquake settled down in the following days, Jimmy and Yuze worked tirelessly to tidy up the bar. With banks still closed, the bar remained a hub for the community, offering meals at discounted prices or in exchange for goods. This system of trading and cash would have to continue for a few more weeks until the utility companies could restore essential services like electricity and water to the devastated city of San Francisco.

Yuze stood on a wobbly chair, his hands carefully positioning broken pieces of the shattered sports memorabilia that used to hang on the walls. Jimmy leaned against the wall, a pen and a roll of duct tape dangling from his fingers as he watched with a mixture of frustration and amusement. "Go ahead and take that one down. I don't think I can fix it anyway."

"But it's got Joe Montana's signature on it," Yuze protested.

"Well save that part," Jimmy replied. "We can put all the broken ones together at some point."

Jay emerged from the hallway, balancing a large black trash bag overflowing with debris. He dumped it onto the growing pile outside the bar's entrance, joining the other businesses who were also cleaning up after the recent natural disaster. A quick glance up and down the street revealed that every building had its own pile of rubble and destruction waiting for the garbage trucks to wind their way through the debris. A nearby six-story building was missing a section of its parapet wall at the very top, looking like jagged teeth and adding to the grim scene.

Jay walked to the sidewalk overlooking the tunnel and peered down at the Financial District below in the distance. It was still eerily quiet, but signs of life were slowly returning as people trickled back to work after spending time rebuilding their personal lives in the aftermath of the disaster.

Despite the devastation caused by the earthquake, the local bar remained open. It quickly became the center for this community, serving as a makeshift living room and kitchen for those who had lost their homes. Jimmy, Jay, and Frank worked diligently to keep the bar stocked with food and supplies, navigating through damaged streets to get whatever they could from their suppliers.

Although Jimmy's supply chain was sporadic at best, the three friends found ways to make it work. Jay even constructed a makeshift rickshaw to transport supplies up the steep hills, maneuvering around debris and rubble in the streets.

Jay decided to move back into his old room at the Victorian for a few days. The grand old dame was relatively untouched after surviving both the 1906 earthquake and now the recent Loma Prieta quake. He saw Jiewen every day as they worked together to help get Li's Food Market back up and running. While their official jobs at the bank and Apple wouldn't start until next week, for now they were focused on supporting their families.

Unfortunately, Frank's apartment building had collapsed in the quake, so Jimmy offered him a temporary place to stay in one of the rooms above the bar until insurance could help rebuild his building in North Beach. Everyone who lived there had to find alternative shelter, as it would take two years to rebuild.

News later confirmed that the earthquake had registered at a magnitude of 6.9 on the Richter scale after consulting with monitoring stations around the world. The effects of the Loma Prieta quake were felt as far as San Diego and western Nevada. A magnitude 5.2 aftershock occurred just three minutes after the initial quake, and in the following week there were a total of 20 aftershocks with magnitudes of 4.0 or greater, along with over 300 smaller ones recorded by monitors in the region.

A few months later, details of the destruction revealed that 63 people had died, 3,757 were injured, and 12,053 were displaced. Damage estimates reached upwards of $10 billion, with over 18,000 houses damaged and nearly 1,000 destroyed. Additionally, 2,575 businesses sustained damage and 147 were completely destroyed. Major structural damage included the collapse of a section of roadbed on the Bay Bridge, the collapse of the Embarcadero freeway in San Francisco, and the failure of an elevated Cypress Structure on Interstate 880 in Oakland that killed dozens. Downtown Santa Cruz and San Francisco's Marina and North Beach Districts also experienced extensive damage. The Bay Bridge was rendered unusable for almost a month, and even the highly anticipated World Series between the Giants and A's was delayed for over seven days.

Geologists had forecast a major earthquake in this area based on historical data, especially the lack of a major seismic event along the San Andreas fault since 1906 –the 8.3 San Francisco earthquake. In the 83 years since the 1906 quake, seven damaging earthquakes of magnitude 6.5 or greater occurred. Several 5.0-plus seismic events in the two years preceding Loma Prieta also served as warnings. Geologists warned the frightened people of San Francisco that there was a 50 percent chance for a magnitude 7.0 earthquake in the next 30 years.

The San Andreas Fault is the boundary between the North American plate and the Pacific plate. Land west of the fault has been moving to the northwest relative to land on the east at an average rate of 2 inches per year for millions of years. This motion typically occurred in sudden jumps during large earthquakes. The Pacific plate moved 6.2 feet to the northwest and 4.3 feet upward over the North American plate during the Loma Prieta earthquake.

Like a ticking time bomb, the earthquake-prone area had the ability to alter the lives of millions of people, but only temporarily interrupt the race toward artificial intelligence.

CHAPTER 17

In Chinatown's streets, smoke and spice abound,
Proud fighters they are, amidst the ruined ground.

Jiewen and Jay, or Jay When and Jay Now as friends called them, arrived at Li's Food Market, their family's quaint establishment nestled within the bustling heart of Chinatown. The aroma of sizzling dumplings and simmering soups wafted through the air, mingling with the familiar scent of incense and with the remnants of smoke and fire. Greeting them with a warm smile was Wei Guo, Jiewen's father, whose eyes shone with pride and gratitude as they crossed the threshold of the disheveled store. Jay had become more than just Jiewen's boyfriend; he was now a fellow warrior in the battle they had faced together.

The aftermath of the 6.9 magnitude earthquake that had rocked the city just days earlier left its unmistakable mark. A fine, ghostly coat of dust had settled on many of the surfaces of the market, casting an eerie shadow over the once-vibrant shelves and bustling aisles. Wei Guo's wife, Meiyu Li, and his mother-in-law, Yu Chen Li, were still taking refuge in another family's home, awaiting the elusive permission from the building inspectors that would allow them to reoccupy their beloved store and home. However, Jiewen had chosen to stay behind, driven by an unshakable determination to help her family in the arduous task of cleanup. After a few days and nights working clandestinely to avoid the health department, they began piecing the place back together in spite of the warnings to stay out.

Jay's entry into the market was not through the usual welcoming embrace of the front door but instead by lifting the yellow tape and sign that warned against entry prior to inspection. The once well-stocked shelves now lay bare, their contents scattered haphazardly across the floor in a chaotic mosaic of spilled rice, noodles, and sauces. Several stacks of bins, once neatly organized, now lay spread out and thinning as their supply chain dwindled. Most of their precious cargo miraculously survived the destruction that had occurred outside. Bricks from crumbling walls were strewn across the street, some still clinging to chunks of plaster, like remnants of a battle long fought.

As Jay and Wei Guo engaged in conversation, Jay's sharp eyes noticed scorch marks that marred the stairwell walls. He couldn't help but recognize that those marks were a testament to the valiant efforts it took to contain the fire and get the natural gas turned off. His and his future father-in-law's quick thinking in turning off the gas main valve had prevented further chaos from engulfing the building, sparing the market from an even more devastating fate. He observed as Wei Guo struggled to walk on his injured foot, a result of kicking down the door yesterday. The cast on his foot was now covered in well wishes from those who had signed it earlier today.

The metal fire escape, which had seen better days, hung precariously outside, appearing as though it had suffered some serious damage during the earthquake's upheaval. Pots of once-green plants and various debris were scattered around its base, a poignant reminder of the chaos that had ensued. It was a stark contrast to the warm, bustling market that had thrived just days earlier.

Wei Guo and Jay crouched in between the cramped space among food bins. Their clothes were dusty from the debris that surrounded them, but their faces were set with determination as they recounted their harrowing rescue of Yu Chen Li. The wailing sirens and distant sounds of helicopters provided a constant soundtrack to their conversation, which was filled with stories of bravery and love amidst the chaos and destruction. As they spoke, Jiewen felt overwhelmed by the unbreakable bonds of family that had been strengthened in the face of this disaster.

After spending hours inspecting other buildings, Liz Mawbry arrived at the Li's property. She, along with Wei Guo and Jay, began their inspection by checking for any potential damages to the ceilings on the top floors. They then made their way up to the roof, where Jay noticed bricks scattered nearby the three-foot-tall parapet. As he approached the edge, he saw that the bricks had fallen onto the fire escape below and bounced off onto the street.

Curious, Jay picked up one of the fallen bricks and examined it closely and said, "Seems like the mortar was pretty thin."

Liz took the brick from him and inspected it herself. "Yeah, that's the way they used to build it in the old days. But this building was built in 1945, so it had enough structural steel to withstand this kind of earthquake," she explained, then looked up across the neighboring buildings and began scanning the North Beach area as if searching for something.

Wei Guo placed a comforting hand on her shoulder and gazed out toward North Beach with her. "We heard about your apartment. We're sorry you lost your home."

Jay also reached out and placed his hand on her other shoulder. "We're just grateful that you and Greet made it out safely. Brian told us everything."

Liz felt comforted by their touch as she carefully placed the brick back into its rightful place. A tear rolled down her cheek as she remembered her friend Frank's apartment that had caught fire right away.

"I'm glad Frank made it out," she said, sniffling.

"And Joanne, too," Jay said solemnly. "That was a close one for both of them."

Liz completed her inspection of Li's Food Market, and the group gathered outside the front entrance. She carefully reviewed the inspection card once more before showing it to Wei Guo. The approval would only allow them to reopen the first floor of the market; the broken fire escape made the top two floors unsafe. Liz inquired, "When do you anticipate being able to make the necessary repairs on the upper levels?"

"We will have to open the store without them. I do not think we can afford them anyway. We will make do with what we have."

"I can get some bricks to fix the parapet wall. And some steel to reinforce the fire escape," Jay offered, thinking about the construction site at Apple which had more than enough to share.

Jay offered to assist with the cleanup of Li's market and get contractors to donate materials leftover from a project at Apple. He also suggested some financing might be in order. Taking out a loan to repair the damage would have been a common step in the recovery process, with the hope of eventually returning to normal business operations.

"This I cannot do," Wei Guo explained. "That is not the way we do business here."

"But how will you be able to repair the place?" Liz asked incredulously and with emotion. "We cannot let you move back in until you pass the fire inspection."

"We will find a way," Wei Guo replied. He bent over and picked up a piece of pottery that must have fallen from the metal fire escape above him. Several other planting pots sat precariously near the edge of a broken railing two stories up. He tossed the shard onto a pile of rubble near the front door of his closed store. The food bins survived the hail of bricks from above, so they sat stacked to the side awaiting a fresh load of food deliveries.

Liz looked at her checklist and debated whether to check the box for the red tag and officially close the market, or whether she should check the box for the repairs required for reopening. She watched as Wei Guo pleaded for her to do the right thing and open the market that people depended upon. She checked the repair ticket.

"Thank you, Ms. Mawbry," Wei Guo said and held her hand after she handed him the paper. His eyes began to water, and Liz could not help but hug him.

Liz looked inside the market one more time and then turned back to Wei Guo. "I'm coming back after work to help cleanup."

"That is not necessary, Ms. Mawbry."

Liz reached out and grabbed Wei Guo by the shoulders, surprising him with her strength. She stated factually, "Yes, it is necessary. We are all in this together."

Liz Mawbry, a building inspector in San Francisco for 15 years, had faced many challenges in her career. But nothing could have prepared her for the aftermath of the Loma Prieta earthquake.

The Loma Prieta earthquake, which occurred on October 17, 1989, at 5:04 p.m., was a significant seismic event in the San Francisco Bay Area, including Chinatown.

"We must find a way to serve the people," Wei Guo explained. He picked up more debris from the floor and tossed it into a waste basket that overflowed its top. "Our customers have to eat. It's not only about keeping the business alive."

Liz knew that she had to act quickly to assess the safety of the buildings in the rest of the city. She must assemble a team of inspectors and begin to survey the damage. They must work determinedly, inspecting hundreds of buildings each day.

Liz's job was not easy. She had to make difficult decisions about which buildings were safe to reoccupy and which buildings needed to be demolished. She also had to work with building owners and engineers to develop plans to repair damaged buildings.

Liz's heart grew heavy as she surveyed the destruction of her beloved city. She had to push back tears when walking past homes that had been reduced to rubble. Everywhere, people were picking up the pieces and doing whatever they could to rebuild.

With a determined resolve, Liz and her team put on their hard hats and set out to start the assessments. They first evaluated buildings to determine which were at immediate risk of collapse –those were red-tagged and evacuated. The more detailed inspections followed, examining each structure from its foundation up through its walls, roof, windows, doors and ceilings. With engineers, Liz also discussed plans for rebuilding and developing strategies for making buildings more earthquake-resistant.

Liz looked out over the city in awe. She had never seen so much destruction. The skyline was unrecognizable, and rubble and debris covered the streets. As Liz carefully made her way through the wreckage, she encountered San Franciscans filled with grief and determination. They wanted nothing more than to start rebuilding their beloved city.

DAVID LEE LUEDTKE

CHAPTER 18

More than a ride, with a test in each stride,
And chips that power this unusual glide.

With a determined grip on the steering wheel of his 1988 Chevy Sprint, Brian weaved through the hilly streets of Pacific Heights. The car's unique electric motor hummed softly as it effortlessly tackled the challenging inclines, drawing the curious gazes of passersby. The bold letters, "Electric," emblazoned across its door panels could have been a bit more subtle.

This unconventional vehicle was a testament to Brian's unrelenting curiosity and dedication to the exploration of computers and electric cars. Despite its innovative design, the Chevy Sprint had its limitations –its modest battery capacity restricted Brian to short trips within city limits. But for him, this car was more than just a mode of transportation; it was an ongoing experiment with the early adoption of computer chips operating the energy that drove the car's motor.

However, this passion for experimentation also came with setbacks. The collaboration between Chevrolet and Suzuki, though ambitious, ultimately failed to generate enough sales and the Chevy Sprint had already been discontinued after only one year. But for Brian, this journey was like a winding road full of unexpected obstacles and dead ends –challenges that he saw as opportunities for growth and discovery.

As they made their way through Pacific Heights, passing by homes seemingly untouched by the huge Loma Prieta earthquake only a few months ago, Joanne sat beside Brian in the passenger seat and stared out the window at barricades and rubbish piles from the endless cleanup. Her face showed a mix of tension and acceptance as she took in their surroundings.

Thanks to Brian's success at National Semiconductor, he was now able to afford a third-floor Victorian condo for them to live together —a move that Joanne had finally agreed to after her own apartment in Frank Renado's building was gone. With their final boxes in hand, Joanne and Brian ascended three flights of stairs to their new home.

As they reached the top, Joanne looked around the hallway with a smile, but there was a melancholic edge behind her confident expression. She turned to Brian and asked softly, "Are you sure about this?"

Brian didn't hesitate as he replied, "Absolutely. I want you to have the spare room all to yourself."

Relief flooded over Joanne's face as she wrapped her arms around him and teased, "But we are still going to sleep together, right?"

Brian chuckled and hugged her back tightly. "Of course. But I also want you to have your own space."

With that settled, the couple continued unpacking and settled into their new home, a symbol of their commitment to each other and their sense of adventure. Joanne squeezed Brian's hand and they moved to the window, taking in the view of the city below. The earthquake had left its mark on the landscape, with smoke from fires still lingering in the air and buildings standing tall amidst the destruction.

The once bustling Bay Bridge remained closed and stood unusually silent now, its collapsed span tragically taking lives when a large piece of the bridge fell onto the deck below. And looking down to the waterfront below them, a two-story roadway remained crumpled and flattened, a stark reminder of the devastation caused by nature's fury. The surface of the tectonic plates experienced a shift, almost as if the earth itself had hiccupped and now was recovering from the jolt.

Despite it all, Joanne felt grateful for this new beginning with Brian by her side. Together, they would brave whatever challenges came their way and create a beautiful life together in this resilient city by the bay.

CHAPTER 19

Years pass by, with new inventions in time,
Unlocking doors, discoveries sublime.

Brian Lomax guided his light blue 1998 Toyota Prius into the narrow driveway below his flat. The car's unique appearance, resembling a friendly boulder with rounded edges and bulging fenders, stood out in the sea of conventional vehicles. With its meager 74 horsepower, it was hardly a beast on the road.

As he stepped out of the car, Brian noticed the lock on the garage door ahead and debated whether someone had been tampering with it. It was an old padlock, worn from years of use and rusted over. He fumbled with the key, causing it to clatter against the metal as he tried to unlock it. The sound reverberated through the quiet neighborhood street before finally yielding to his efforts. Brian pushed open the creaky wooden door, revealing a garage filled with tools and gadgets all perfectly aligned with their outlines drawn on the walls, although his recent inventions from his various tinkering projects sat in organized piles as if swept together with a broom.

His eyes immediately landed on an electrical cord hanging from its designated spot on the hook overhead. With practiced hands, he connected it to another cord dangling from under the hood of his Prius, like a lifeline connecting to a patient. As soon as the two cords met, a low humming noise filled the air.

Brian watched intently as the battery level on his Prius' dashboard began to rise from absolute zero to a mere one percent charge in just a few minutes. A sense of satisfaction spread across his face, a rare occurrence when dealing with this finicky machine. Retrofitting a hybrid car with an external charger was always a risk, one that likely voided any remaining warranty. But Brian didn't care; he had affectionately named his creation the PIP —Plugged-in Prius —and it was worth all the effort and uncertainty.

With the success of his experiment momentarily secured, Brian turned his attention to his sleek black briefcase resting in the passenger seat. Its surface bore the initials "BL," embossed in silver on one corner, a touch of personalization on an otherwise nondescript accessory. Opening the side pocket with a practiced motion, he retrieved an Apple PowerBook, a sleek machine that contrasted sharply with the aging tools in his garage.

He placed the laptop on the hood of his Prius which was still warm from the day's drive. As he lifted the laptop cover, the bright white screen illuminated his face, making him look almost otherworldly in the dimly lit garage. His fingers danced across the keyboard, inputting data and meticulously tracking every aspect of his unconventional invention. Brian couldn't help but marvel at the speed and efficiency of the computer, a far cry from the clunky old PCs he used to work with at National Semiconductor. What once took minutes now only took seconds, a testament to the never-ending advancements in technology. It was hard to believe that it was already the year 2000.

"What the hell is that thing?" said a voice from a neighbor walking by as he pointed to a spot inside the engine compartment. He stepped close after seeing Brian's smile.

Brian looked up at his neighbor, who seemed to stop by with increasing frequency whenever he worked on this contraption. "Remember, I told you about the charging system I added. I can plug this thing in at night and by morning I have fifty miles of range on the battery."

The neighbor's jaw dropped in awe as they both leaned in under the hood while inspecting the loose wires spread out throughout the surrounding areas of the engine. "Does it work?"

Brian excitedly explained his process and the neighbor asked many more questions, each one drawing out more fascinating details. Brian offered a beer to the man while they talked but then remembered that Joanne was expecting him upstairs for a quick dinner before she hurried off to work.

As their conversation continued, the neighbor suddenly paused and stepped back to study the outside of the vehicle while gesturing toward the unconventional design of the car. "Why does it have to be so damn ugly though?"

Brian laughed and shrugged. "It's beautiful on the inside," he replied with a grin.

The main entrance to Brian and Joanne's top-story flat lay behind a security gate to the left of the garage door. Brian closed up the car after assuring himself the charger was working, said goodbye to the neighbor and pressed the four digits into a security lock and the whirring noise of the latch signaled the release. The gate squeaked as the heavy springs tried to close the door before he walked through. Climbing to the top floor, only a little out of breath, he paused to look out at the view from their front entryway, never ceasing to be amazed at the view of the bay only a dozen blocks away.

As Brian entered the house, he set his black leather briefcase on a mahogany desk in the foyer. The polished surface reflected a large mirror on the wall behind it. He shouted out a greeting and was met with heavy footsteps and a high-pitched scream of excitement from his little boy, Dexter. The nine-year-old ran toward him, clad in green soccer cleats, shin guards, and a white jersey with the name of a local dry cleaner printed on the front.

"Daddy! Can you take me to my game now?" Dexter pleaded, jumping into his father's arms.

Brian's heart sank as he remembered his business trip scheduled for that evening. "I'm sorry, buddy. I have to fly out tonight."

His wife, Joanne, emerged from a nearby room and leaned in to kiss Brian before kneeling down to finish tying Dexter's shoes. The laces were frayed and torn from being constantly untied.

"Don't worry, Dexter," she reassured him. "I'll take you to your game. We have to leave in five minutes, though." She glanced at her watch and hurried off down the hall.

"But Mom, I thought you had work tonight?" Dexter asked with a pout.

Joanne smiled and said, "I do, but Jiewen offered to pick you up after the game. I can take you to your match, and then you can stay over at their house tonight."

Dexter's frown turned even more dejected as he exclaimed, "Bradley is such a pain in the butt," he muttered under his breath. "He's only a first grader."

Dexter, all four-feet tall of him, slim and lanky, stood with outstretched arms pleading to not have to stay with a much younger boy again. He saw the looks on his parents faces, then turned and thumped down the hallway, surely bothering their renters on the floor below them.

Brian cringed as he asked Dexter to slow down. Brian and Joanne embraced. She wore her nurse's uniform, the traditional light blue at Saint Francis Hospital.

"Do you have the long shift tonight?" Brian asked and kissed her on the forehead.

"Yes. Dexter can spend the night with the Baumers again." She noticed the airplane tickets sticking out from a side pocket of Brian's briefcase. "What time is the flight?"

"At nine," he replied and kissed her again. She smiled but there was a sadness in her eyes. He added, "I'll be in Taiwan until Saturday."

Joanne's smile faded as she remembered all the times she had been left alone while Brian traveled for work. "How much longer will you be doing this?" she asked.

"Not much longer," Brian promised, rubbing her back. "We're launching the 300mm wafers next month and after that I can stay at Apple headquarters from now on."

Joanne traced her finger along the kitchen countertop and looked up at Brian. Many previous conversations laid the groundwork for her next comment. "You'll be commuting again though, right?"

Brian sighed and pulled her into a hug. "I know. Maybe we should consider moving to the east bay. That way the commute wouldn't be so bad."

A small smile tugged at Joanne's lips as she thought about living closer to her family and even working at Eden Medical where she was born. They excitedly discussed potential plans and which city near the hospital would be the best location. Suddenly, little Dexter burst into the room, begging to go to his soccer game.

"Say goodbye to Daddy then," Joanne said with a smile.

Dexter ran over to Brian, who lifted him up with ease. Joanne noticed how big Dexter had gotten —taller and more muscular than most boys his age. He was only nine, but he already seemed bored with school and always eager for something new.

As Brian finished his preparations for his flight, he reviewed his travel itinerary and the list of meetings scheduled for his three-day trip to Taipei. The first meeting stood out, as it was the third time that Dr. Phillip Burnet had requested a meeting with him. Brian looked upon this meeting as if the weather was about to change —more than likely this would result in some big changes in Brian's life whether he liked it or not.

CHAPTER 20

A gamble in mind, he sees cards in view,
Eyes searching for foes, his options are few.

The murkily lit card club was bustling with activity, but Jay Baumers sat at his designated table, his focus solely on the cards in his hand. He took a sip from his scotch on the rocks and glanced around the room, keeping an eye on his opponents. They did not know that his scotch was only water with a splash of cola to give it some color.

But as he studied his hand, a nagging feeling made him question if this type of gambling was right for him anymore. After all, he had just landed a dream job at Enron, one of Silicon Valley's largest and fastest-growing energy companies in the year 1999. The salary was generous, the benefits package unprecedented, and they even offered him thousands of stock options appraised at $23 per share. It seemed like a once-in-a-lifetime opportunity that he couldn't resist, especially because it was simply another type of gambling.

Jay thought about Enron's transformation from a traditional energy supplier to a dot-com high roller under the leadership of ambitious CEO Kenneth Lay and young executive Jeffrey Skilling. With Lay's determination and Skilling's untamed style, the company was taking advantage of market deregulation and expanding on a global scale.

As for Andrew Fastow, Enron's notorious CFO known for his complex schemes and sub-entities, Jay saw an opportunity to learn from the inside how such a mastermind operated. He liked the thought of getting rich from it.

Despite the long commute to Silicon Valley with his friend Brian, Jay found contentment in his life. He and his wife, Jiewen, were happily married and living in a beautiful home in the affluent neighborhood of Pacific Heights. Jiewen still worked at Bank of America, using her skills to assist families affected by the Loma Prieta earthquake a decade ago. She took great pride in her job and the positive impact it had on the community.

As Jay walked in through the front door of their spacious flat late in the evening, he announced his arrival to his family. Jiewen greeted him with a warm embrace, accompanied by their first-grader Bradley Baumers. With bright blue eyes and dark blonde hair, Bradley was the spitting image of his father, though with just a touch of darker hair. In the hallway just outside Bradley's bedroom stood Dexter Lomax, a friend of the family. A smile spread across Dexter's face as Jay waved to him, then the little boy quickly disappeared back into the bedroom. Jay walked in and patted Dexter on the head as he brushed by him to look at his son playing with a toy on the floor.

Jiewen sighed from the doorway as she explained, "Bradley just won't go to sleep tonight."

Jay scooped up his son and met his gaze sternly. "Listen here, kid. You need to go to bed right now and stay there."

"Yes, Daddy," Bradley replied obediently, though he wore a small frown on his face. But as soon as Jay kissed him on the cheek and directed him toward his bed, Bradley's expression transformed into a smile.

"He's just so excited that Dexter is here," Jiewen explained as she kissed her husband, who escorted Dexter to the makeshift bed alongside Bradley's.

The couple walked hand in hand into the living room and gazed out at the city lights below. The soft glow of the Golden Gate Bridge in the distance provided a peaceful background for their conversation.

Jay and Jiewen settled in after the kids were now safely in bed. They sank into the plush cushions of the couch near the large window that led out onto their balcony. Stars dotted the night sky, their twinkling lights casting a serene glow over the city.

"I'm going to quit playing cards," Jay said, breaking the peaceful silence between them.

"I've heard that before," Jiewen replied with a laugh as she rose from her spot and made her way to the kitchen. She returned with a chilled bottle of Chardonnay and two glasses. Her white silk blouse hung slightly open, revealing a glimpse of her smooth skin and curves. Jay couldn't help but steal a glance at her as she sat down on his lap. She grinned and kissed him on the forehead.

"No, I mean it this time. My heart just isn't in it anymore," he explained, his thoughts consumed by Enron's financial shenanigans instead of the game in front of him. "Working at Enron is like gambling, but with much higher stakes and with other people's money."

Jiewen nodded in agreement, pouring them both a glass of wine. As they toasted and sipped their drinks, she leaned in for a passionate kiss.

"And all while the stock price continues to skyrocket," Jay added, gazing out at the city lights through the window before locking eyes with Jiewen. "Like that Kenny Rogers song, you got to know when to hold 'em, and know when to fold 'em."

"But this time it's our life on the line," Jiewen reminded him softly.

"We'll make enough off of this one deal to set us up for life," Jay assured her confidently. They clinked glasses again, both lost in their own thoughts about the risks they were taking for their future together.

DAVID LEE LUEDTKE

CHAPTER 21

In dot-com rush, he treads a cautious path,
But temptations of quick gains spark his wrath.

Daniel Kim sat in his designated office space within the expansive Sequoia Capital building, enveloped by the lights from other offices in the Partner's section. Two large video screens accompanied his PowerBook laptop, shielding anyone passing by from seeing anything besides the top of Daniel's head. His strong forearms, a product of his recent fitness regime, extended out from under his rolled-up shirt sleeves and rested on either side of the screens.

Despite the other Partners' high-risk investments and wild successes, Daniel studied his investments cautiously and slowly, often questioning if his long-term approach was still relevant in this age of dot-com companies, who raked in huge investments without ever turning a profit. Daniel's rise to this level was by steering investments and people into the long haul by following Xerox Park's investments as well as the projects DARPA funded.

Let the other Partners hit and miss, scoring amazing returns sometimes and complete failures most times. But Daniel began questioning whether he should take a chance on one of these fledgling companies himself.

Suzan Bolstock sauntered into the room, her hands confidently stuffed in the pockets of her dark grey suit and a proud, determined look on her face. She was tall, too slender since her recent divorce, and wore her dark grey suit much like a coat hanger. "Did you hear the news?" she asked as she peered through Daniel's office door. "That Petco company is really taking off!"

"I don't understand it—who would buy dog food on the internet?" Daniel replied and stood up to face her. "And now the infusion of that new venture capital rates them at a billion dollars —with only twenty million in revenue. I just don't get it."

"It's all speculation," Suzan said and stepped into his office. "But I steered some investors into it, and their value doubled in one month."

Daniel stood from his leather chair and circled his desk, pausing to take in Suzan's presence in his office. His eyes lingered on her for a moment as she fidgeted with her jacket pockets before taking a seat in the armchair facing him. Daniel moved to the other chair and spun it around, joining her in close quarters. A small smile formed as he spoke about their company motto, "But what have you done for me lately?" Their laughter soon faded and he watched Suzan study him intently; something he hadn't seen her do before.

They talked about the NASDAQ's meteoric rise of 500% over the past three years and how it correlated with advances in technology. Suzan marveled at how the internet expanded people's access to information and revolutionized whole industries.

Daniel leaned back in his chair, gesturing extravagantly while describing the "digital divide" and how computer ownership had shifted from a luxury to a necessity in American households. He spoke passionately about the shift into the Information Age and how new companies were founded because of it.

The conversation turned to interest rates and capital gains taxes, and Suzan found herself drawn to Daniel's eloquence as he explained economic theories she'd never heard of. She listened to how Alan Greenspan, the Chair of the Federal Reserve, influenced investments in the stock market with his glowing positivity and wondered if she could ever be that optimistic.

As they talked late into the night, Suzan felt something stir within her—a sense of excitement for what Daniel was building, and maybe something more.

"Maybe I should look into one of those startups?" he asked suddenly, turning toward her. "I feel like I'm always working on long-term projects."

Suzan smiled and then got up to leave the office. She paused at the door, though, turning back to him again. "As the top performer for two years running now, you can do pretty much anything you want."

Daniel got up, quickly put on his suit jacket, and followed her to the door. He stopped as she opened the door to leave. "Listen, I have a friend doing some interesting software right now. Maybe we should look at funding a startup?"

Suzan's eyes lit up at the suggestion of the "we" in Daniel's question, and she leaned forward eagerly. She lightly touched his arm and prompted him to continue.

Daniel began to explain how his friend Charles Kang had created a train scheduling software as a side project while working at a small software company. Daniel had helped him get the new job after Charles graduated from the University of San Francisco with a degree in software development.

Enthused by the idea, Suzan walked over to the whiteboard that hung on Daniel's office wall and began jotting down words they used during the ensuing brainstorming session. She circled some words and underlined others, occasionally erasing those that seemed unsuitable for their goal. Both of their jackets soon lay over the backs of the chairs in front of Daniel's desk, revealing rolled-up white shirt sleeves and markers, one red and one blue, in each of their hands.

Bringing her attention back to her query, Suzan wrote a dollar sign followed by a blank space and an explanation below it. "What is the revenue for all of the trains in the area right now?" she asked.

Daniel went to his computer and paged through a painfully slow website for the Department of Transportation that said all of California for 1999 would be $7.2 billion dollars. He did some quick calculations and replied, "If the annual ticket sales are calculated at $420 million for the cable cars in San Francisco, we could add a one percent fee and take in $4.2 million dollars. For just one train company. There must be hundreds or thousands across the globe."

Suzan frantically jotted all the recited numbers down on the board and began extrapolating numbers for several other train lines. She worked feverishly, and soon her white blouse began to show signs of sweat. Daniel paused for a moment and admired her beauty, feeling a little closer to her in their shared exuberance. Daniel continued reciting numbers from his laptop that represented train lines from all of the major cities.

"What are you trying to show here?" Daniel said and approached her at the white board. "That's not possible. Is it?"

Suzan looked at the board, then at Daniel, then at the board, and she appeared to make some sort of decision. Daniel's eyes widened as Suzan presented the number of $1 Billion in revenue for the year 2004. He studied her face intently, as though trying to read her mind, and then stepped forward and opened his mouth to speak. But Suzan was quicker, grabbing hold of him before he could utter a word and pulling him close. Their lips met hungrily as they swirled around each other, oblivious to the open door that offered a view into the hallway.

Daniel came up for air first, quickly closing the door and shutting the blinds to ensure their privacy. With newfound urgency, he moved over to Suzan, who had perched herself atop his desk, her eyes devouring him. His hands were soon everywhere, taking off any clothing in their way while their passion rose higher and higher until they fell back onto the desk.

At two o'clock in the morning and nearing exhaustion, the two continued on like first-time lovers, risking their careers and reputations for a built-up heat that went beyond money and into their shared passions. Neither of them felt awkward later on while getting dressed and they talked about working together on several other projects as if they were old friends already.

CHAPTER 22

Tracking records from a paper to the screen,
A decade gone with a sadness yet unseen.

Jimmy sighed as he looked from the back bar to his laptop, where he was tallying up the inventory of liquor bottles. It had been ten years since he took over the small bar, Top of the Tunnel, and although he had been successful in rebuilding it after the big earthquake and paying off Frank Renado, Jimmy felt a tinge of sadness at the thought of his brother Jay, who had moved away from the bar and had a successful career and a new family. But Jimmy missed the camaraderie of bartending with him.

The sound of keys clinking on Yuze's key chain brought Jimmy's attention back to the bar. Yuze managed the bar and also oversaw the renters at Jimmy's Victorian house up the hill. He handed two keys to a new bartender who had just moved in.

Yuze said to the new man, "This one is for the front door. And this one is for your room."

The man left the room and Jimmy looked a little forlorn, but then went back to his work on his laptop. Assigning Jay's room to another renter had a finality to it that his brother was out of the house for good.

"We can move him if Jay ever comes back," Yuze said quietly after seeing the look on Jimmy's face before returning to the kitchen with an order ticket.

Just then, a small boy of about seven years popped through the saloon doors that led to the back kitchen. He took in all he could see of the full bar —at least all that he could see from his vantage point with his eye level matching the top of the bar. To him all of the patrons must have looked like floating heads. He wore pajamas, had slightly blonde hair like his mother, and the eyes identical to Yuze's own. "Daddy, I want something to eat."

Yuze walked quickly over to the saloon doors and ushered little Lawrence back into the kitchen area. He quieted the boy and led him to a small bowl of rice with deep-fried chicken pieces spread evenly over the top. Lawrence smiled and said it was his favorite.

Jimmy admired how Yuze treated his son and ran a hand through his thinning hair. He glanced around, taking in the view of his loyal customers from Chinatown's affluent business owners, several customers from the Financial District –and, of course, all the locals coming in nearly every day.

As he watched Yuze disappear into the kitchen, Jimmy reflected on how much he missed his younger brother and how different life would be if they were still working together at Top of the Tunnel. But then he thought how nice it was to have Yuze and his son working and living at the bar. Yuze felt like a brother from another mother. And little Lawrence added yet another generation to the bar family. Too bad his mother, Donna, who was one of the waitresses at the bar, had left town for good. Yuze was a good father, but he worked weird hours for raising a child. The new bartender should help take over some of the late-night shifts after a while.

Jimmy was focused on the task at hand, typing away on his laptop while simultaneously counting the various liquor bottles that filled the back bar. Dim yellow lights illuminated the intricate carvings of the bar's tall wooden columns, giving a nostalgic feel to the entire room. At the other end of the bar sat Frank Renado, nestled in a traditional spot –a place adorned with a small brass plaque thanking another longtime customer for his years of patronage up until the old man's death three years ago. Frank looked content as he accepted offers for drinks from many of the regulars, who believed it fitting that Frank should occupy such an honored spot.

Daniel came in after work later than usual and settled down into his usual seat next to Charles Kang. Charles' navy blue suit jacket and tie contrasted against his blue jeans and no-socked loafers. Jorge Freeman, Charles' best friend from former days working on the cable cars, took the seat beside him. Jorge also wore a suit jacket now, a strange sight for those accustomed to seeing him in his repairman's outfit for so many years.

"We only want the train scheduling software," Jorge said while studying the display on the laptop Charles moved in his direction. Jorge took a sip of his beer and glanced down at the bar to avoid eye contact.

"But the ticket purchasing software can increase your revenue ten-fold." Charles implored. He looked to Daniel for help.

"We can start with the scheduling software and get into contract so you can lock in pricing," Daniel added and motioned for Yuze to fetch him a beer. Daniel shifted in his chair, facing Jorge, his eyes intense. "TrainSeek is moving quickly, and our prices are going up, so you should act fast."

Jorge studied his friends' faces, his expression uncertain. Was their speech coming from a place of friendship or from salesmanship? Daniel turned his laptop back toward him and resumed typing as if he'd made a decision. He spun the screen around to Jorge again and said confidently, "I'll send it over for the scheduling program then."

Daniel smiled at Charles before lifting his glass in toast among all three men. Then, retrieving his flip phone, Daniel tapped away at the buttons before quickly slotting it back into his pocket.

The trio discussed ideas on how to implement the software. Jorge asked endless questions about the new office Charles had leased for TrainSeek. Daniel and Suzan Bolstock had arranged for $3 million of capital funding to kickstart the internet ticketing program, causing Charles to leave behind his software job and become the first employee at TrainSeek. Interviewing prospective candidates now filled his days to hire enough people to help develop the program that would eventually take them public. Charles felt uneasy as he hired people to work at a company that just made its first sale and was already millions in debt.

DAVID LEE LUEDTKE

CHAPTER 23

With confident strides through neon-lit streets,
She turns, skyscrapers shift to old-world meets.

Liz Mawbry strode with confidence along a short street in the Financial District, her sturdy heels echoing against the pavement. The city of San Francisco was buzzing with the excitement of the booming tech industry. Countless startups had sprung up from Silicon Valley, and the promise of the digital age was palpable in the air. As she made a turn onto a smaller side street, Liz noticed how the landscape changed from towering buildings to a more industrial look.

Approaching a brick building with exposed steel beams protruding from its facade, Liz marveled at the blend of old-world charm and modern innovation that seemed to define the era. This area, now known throughout the world as "Dot-Com Alley," was home to new startup companies that embraced this industrial yet contemporary aesthetic. It symbolized the merging of traditional business values with the bold ambitions of tech entrepreneurs.

Upon entering the building's lobby, a young receptionist with impeccable makeup and hair greeted Liz with a warm smile. Her friendly demeanor and flawless appearance stood out in contrast to the casual dress often associated with the tech industry. She offered Liz a bottle of water and a freshly baked cookie from a nearby cafe.

Liz graciously declined the refreshments, and instead focused on her purpose for being here. This was an important step in approving the permit necessary for this fledgling company's final signoff on their Certificate of Occupancy.

Liz had inspected three of these types of startups today alone. The lobbies often took a former manufacturing space and added glossy finishes while polishing the bricks and structural steel to a glow. The architects often accepted some blemishes on purpose to show the new age thinking.

A very young man came out wearing a golf shirt and blue jean shorts with flip-flops and again offered her a bottled water and a cookie. Liz declined again and followed the young man through a large double door as he opened it in a grand gesture to display the bullpen of the workers inside. Liz glanced left and noticed a ping pong table with some young people playing energetically. Just then, a young woman drove by on a push scooter, nearly knocking into her as she excused herself by saying, "On your left."

The escort motioned for Liz to keep following as they passed by various groups of people huddled at desks that looked randomly placed around the columns of the old building. One very large window stretched from floor to ceiling, some thirty feet above. At the end of the bullpen area, a lone glass-lined office sat elevated ten feet above the floor. A thirty-year-old slender woman sat alone in the office, which had an extremely wide staircase without railings leading like a pyramid to the boxy office's front door. Liz glanced left and right and stopped to make a note about the railings.

The escort saw Liz pause and said, "We took them off because they didn't fit with our aesthetics."

Liz stared for a moment and replied, "That's between you and the Building Department. I'm here for the health inspection."

The young escort shrugged and motioned for Liz to follow him up to the top of the stairs, where he held the door open for Liz to enter.

"Good afternoon, Ms. Mawbry," The woman in the box said while marching over and extending her hand. "I'm Elly Taylor, President of Silcoo.com."

Liz shook her hand and went right to business. "Hi Ms. Taylor. I'm here to inspect the kitchen for the Health Department."

"Please call me Elly," the woman responded and went back to her desk. "I'm sure you will find everything in tip-top shape. Our chef is one of the best and most successful chefs in all of San Francisco."

Liz asked question after question about the operations of the kitchen and received vague answers to each. Liz entered as many notes as she could into her paper ledger as Elly tapped into her laptop to display menus and working hours on a very large video screen behind her. The dichotomy between the electronic answer and the quaint pencil-to-paper was palpable. Soon Elly escorted Liz down the stairs and toured her around the wide-open floor, stopping to explain various activities with pride.

As they ventured further into the building, Liz could feel the energy and optimism radiating throughout. The possibilities were endless in this digital frontier, with every corner holding potential for innovation and success. It was an exciting time filled with transformation.

Finally, Liz asked to see the kitchen area and serving area. Elly brought her down a hallway and to the side of a large bullpen where they entered another large glass box where the serving area, with about a dozen people eating, led to several trays of ethnic foods for self-service. The amount of food and selection was incredible. Liz had seen large spreads of food at other dot-coms, but this one was way over the top.

Liz began by examining the refrigerated and heated serving compartments lined up next to each other. She then inspected their splatter shields, took note of the cleanliness beneath the equipment, and observed how the staff handled the new and used utensils. "I need to see the kitchen next," Liz stated and checked another box.

Elly replied, "Chef doesn't like anyone in his kitchen."

Liz often heard retorts like this at Michelin Star-rated restaurants, but never in a corporate setting. "Well, tell Chef that this is the Health Department." Liz paused for only a moment and started walking through the kitchen door. "Never mind, I will tell him myself."

Elly followed Liz in through the door with only minor protests. Liz stopped in amazement when she stepped inside, noting the size and complexity of the kitchen, which was equivalent in quality and magnitude to any restaurant she had ever seen before. She went right to work to inspect the first piece of equipment and began jotting notes down. She looked to the left and saw the next piece of equipment, and at that point, she decided this would be a very easy inspection because everything was in immaculate condition. Not only because it was new, but because the chef's staff really knew what they were doing.

"Hello, Liz. I trust everything is on order?" a handsome man of about forty-years-old with a pure white chef's uniform and hat said to her as he walked up.

Liz recognized the voice immediately. "Of course, it is." She turned, and the two exchanged kisses to each other's cheeks. "Jean Claude, it has been way too long."

"I agree. I've been away since I closed Le Claude."

"That must have been two years ago?" Liz said as they continued holding both hands between them.

The two exchanged small talk as Elly looked bewildered. Jean Claude suggested Elly leave them alone to finish the inspection. Elly paused and quickly left.

Jean Claude leaned in to whisper to Liz, "They offered me so much money I could not refuse."

Liz laughed heartily and the two continued to speak of the past and how Liz was the inspector at several restaurants where Jean Claude perfected his culinary skills. Liz checked a few boxes to finish off her inspection and handed Jean Claude the passing paperwork. They spoke for a short while more and Jean Claude escorted her out the door with a fond farewell.

Liz had one more inspection at a new address she did not recall seeing before. She walked down a long busy road and turned left at a street only one block long lined with four-story brick manufacturing buildings. She paused at an address number that led into a freight elevator where a man in a tuxedo waited inside.

The man in the elevator noticed Liz, and he recited, "You seek TrainSeek." He lifted the screen part of the freight elevator door, and the solid part slowly sunk into the floor like a giant clam shell opening. He motioned for her to enter. She had a bewildered look on her face as she stepped into the highly polished interior of the freight elevator.

"Is this the lobby?" Liz asked the operator.

"That is on Level Four," the man replied, closed the clamshell doors, and pushed buttons on the panel. The elevator shook as it roared to life; repurposed for passengers but still acting like a freight elevator. The two stood facing the doors as floor after floor appeared and disappeared as they rose to the top. The elevator came to a stop, and the man opened the doors again.

Liz entered a large open space, sparsely populated with furniture and individuals. In one corner of the vast area, there were a few desks clustered together. Every surface, from the structural beams to the bricks in the walls, had been meticulously polished to perfection. The floor appeared to be bare concrete, but upon closer inspection it was also expertly polished, any imperfections from years of use as a factory now smoothed over and filled in. The windows along the side of the large space stood floor to ceiling and gave a view of the neighboring identical brick façade. The roof of the neighboring building looked like it had a restaurant on top of it, palm trees and all on an exposed patio.

Liz walked down the long open bullpen, her steps echoing off the concrete and reverberating off the brick walls. She walked toward the small group of people who noticed her suddenly. One person in a finely tailored suit broke out and walked toward her.

"Liz! What are you doing here?" Charles Kang said happily. He walked straight to her and shook hands with her.

Liz looked puzzled at first and then put it all together at once. "This is your place? Oh my God!"

Charles waved his arm around, encircling the entire 360 degrees of the open office, and replied, "We moved in two weeks ago. I'm trying to hire people right now."

The office was a whirlwind of activity, with young professionals huddled in groups, brainstorming ideas, and typing away on sleek new computers. The dot-com era had brought with it a sense of urgency and limitless possibilities, and this office space was a reflection of that spirit.

As Charles and Liz caught up on the status of the business in the confines of their friendship, a thin woman in an expensive business suit approached them. Her walk was reminiscent of a runway model, with one foot placed perfectly in front of the other. Her presence demanded attention, and her confident stride seemed to echo the ambition of the times.

Without a hint of warmth, the woman extended her hand in a formal handshake motion and said coldly, "You must be the health inspector." Charles and Liz exchanged uncomfortable glances. It was clear that the woman assumed Liz's role based on her attire and demeanor and desired to get this bothersome step out of the way.

Charles quickly interjected, trying to defuse a tense situation. He introduced Liz to Suzan, then said to Liz, "Let me introduce my finance partner, Suzan Bolstock, of Sequoia Capital."

Liz nodded politely, and extended her hand to Suzan, and said with a warm smile, "A pleasure, Ms. Bolstock."

Suzan wasted no time, immediately switching gears to her business demeanor. "Let me show you around and then I can point out the exits for you to leave," she said briskly. Her tone suggested that she had little time for distractions, and she was all business.

Liz, although mildly irritated by Suzan's curt attitude, accepted it as par for the course when dealing with business owners in the fast-paced world of startups. Suzan, on the other hand, seemed pleased with herself, putting the lowly health inspector in her place and asserting her dominance in this new era of entrepreneurship. The office tour commenced, and Liz and Charles followed Suzan, fully aware that they were in the presence of someone who meant business in every sense of the word. They worked their way through the kitchen area where Liz encountered another scene of an exorbitant chef's kitchen and culinary delights.

After the inspection, Liz exchanged a parting nod with Charles, and a hint of a playful wink escaped her. Her day had been eventful, to say the least. As she headed toward the bus stop to make her way home across town, she felt a sense of satisfaction in knowing that the startup Charles was building was in good hands. She thought it was amazing how he transformed himself into an entrepreneur in the past ten years.

The bus ride took her through the heart of the city, passing by iconic landmarks that had become symbols of San Francisco's tech revolution. Eventually, the bus arrived at its destination, and Liz stepped off, making her way toward their three-story apartment in the tranquil Sunset District of the western part of San Francisco. The neighborhood was serene, far removed from the bustling tech scene of downtown.

Looking up at their apartment building, Liz recalled the reason they had chosen this spot a decade ago. It had been a decision born out of experience, specifically the Loma Prieta earthquake that had shaken the region and flattened their home. They had vowed never to settle in a liquefaction zone again; the memory of buildings swaying like pudding was not one they wished to relive.

Approaching the front porch one story up, Liz spotted Greet, who was sitting there, soaking in the afternoon sun. The warm rays of sunlight painted a picturesque scene as they bathed the porch in a golden glow. Liz smiled at the sight.

Greet looked down onto the street, her eyes crinkling with warmth as she saw Liz. Standing next to her on the balcony was Deery, her life-sized plastic deer with a hat gracefully resting on top of its antlers. The growing herd of animals on their porch was a source of both amusement and a forewarning of Greet's zany side. Lamby and Goaty, two other members of the plastic menagerie, also sported matching hats, creating a whimsical display that never failed to bring a grin to Liz's face.

Liz opened the front door and Greet hugged her just as she did every day. There was genuine affection in Greet's voice as she asked, "How was work today, honey?" The simple question conveyed a sense of care and interest that made Liz's heart warm. It was a reminder that amidst the fast-paced world of startups and tech, there was a peaceful oasis waiting for her at home, where love and simplicity reigned supreme.

Liz set her briefcase down on the side table in the cozy kitchen and again embraced Greet affectionately. Liz's expression was a mixture of frustration and bewilderment as she had been wanting to tell Greet about what she was seeing all day long. "I don't understand what's going on in the world," she sighed, her voice tinged with concern.

Greet, always the optimist, grinned and teasingly guessed, "Let me guess another dot-com company?" She knew that Liz had been spending her days inspecting various startup offices, and the dot-com frenzy had become a topic of frequent discussion between them.

Liz nodded and began to explain her day, her animated gestures emphasizing the opulence she had witnessed at one particular company that boasted an executive chef, among other extravagant perks. "I mean, how can they afford it all?" she wondered aloud, genuinely puzzled by the lavish spending she had seen.

Greet chuckled, offering her perspective on the matter. "Monopoly money is what I call it," she quipped, her tone carrying with it a hint of sarcasm. "And when they run out, they just grab some more money out of the box." It was a playful analogy that hinted at the ephemeral and speculative nature of the dot-com bubble.

Liz decided it was time to unwind, and she reached for a stemmed glass from the shelf, pouring herself a glass of wine from a bottle that Greet had thoughtfully opened. They both made their way out to the front porch, where the herd of whimsical plastic animals awaited them. Liz patted the tops of the heads of her favorites, Deery, Lamby, and Goaty, a traditional pattern for bringing good luck.

As they settled into their chairs, Liz and Greet continued their discussion about the dot-com situation that seemed to be taking over San Francisco. The city had become the central hub for new startups seeking venture capital from the prestigious Sand Hill Road investors. The allure of the gold rush atmosphere was undeniable, but Liz felt a sense of skepticism about the sustainability of it all.

Greet took a sip of her wine, her eyes sparkling with mischief. "Maybe we should go work at a dot-com," she suggested with a playful grin. "I feel like we're missing out on a gold rush."

This tempting thought had crossed their minds before, but both women knew that there was something special about their tranquil life in the Sunset District, away from the frenzied pace of the tech world.

Liz replied, "You should do it."

Greet looked up in disbelief, then grinned. "I know it's risky, but I really want to try it."

Liz smiled widely. "You go, girl. I'll keep my boring old job at the Health Department to pay the bills."

DAVID LEE LUEDTKE

CHAPTER 24

Tech's light beckoned, a manager embraced,
A gateway built, meeting long-craved haste.

With the dawn of the new Millennium, Wei Guo found himself standing at the forefront of technology. As a humble manager of Li's Food Market, he had little experience with the internet, but he boldly took on the challenge of expanding his business through online sales and deliveries. His children worked alongside him to create a state-of-the-art website for their family store, essentially forming an in-house tech team. Together, they navigated the ever-evolving world of ecommerce and catered to customers who had relocated but still craved the specialty foods from Li's Food Market.

In the bustling heart of San Francisco's Chinatown, Li's Food Market was a vibrant hub of activity. The matriarch of the family, Yu Chen Li, watched with pride as her daughter Meiyu Li expertly handled transactions and answered questions in both English and Mandarin at the wooden counter. Meanwhile, Wei Guo managed inventory and ordered supplies in the back room. As the dot-com boom raged just blocks away in the Financial District, this corner of Chinatown remained a peaceful oasis of culture and community. Yu Chen Li marveled at her daughter's ability to balance tradition and modernity in their family business. She also took note of her son-in-law's newfound computer skills, which greatly contributed to the market's success. As profits continued to rise, Yu Chen Li's curiosity about Wei Guo deepened, eventually leading to a genuine affection for him akin to that of a mother for her own son.

However, as Yu Chen Li's health declined, her visits downstairs to the food market became increasingly infrequent, marking a bittersweet shift in the family's dynamic.

As the year 2000 approached, the internet grew more sophisticated and Wei Guo realized that the website he had created was no longer enough to keep up with the demands of the online world. He hired Yuze as a consultant to help him overhaul the website yet again, creating a sleek new design that was both user-friendly and aesthetically pleasing.

Meiyu Li, always supportive of her husband's endeavors, watched in awe as Wei Guo transformed their small family business into a very successful e-commerce sales force. She had always known that he was capable of great things, but seeing it in action was truly remarkable.

Yu Chen Li sat perched on a cushioned seat in front of her window, gazing down at the bustling streets of Chinatown. She took a sip of her favorite green tea and looked on with pride as customers crowded into her market below. It was thanks to Wei Guo's hard work that their business continued to thrive both online and in-store.

Wei Guo strode confidently down the hallway toward Yu Chen Li's room, humming a tune he had heard on the radio. He passed by her open door and called out cheerfully, "Good morning, Yu Chen Li. How are you feeling today?"

For a moment, there was only silence. Then, from inside the room, Yu Chen Li's voice rang out playfully, "That depends on how well you've been selling."

Wei Guo couldn't help but feel a sense of pride as he responded, "Sales are up today. We even got an order from someone in New York City who used to live here."

Yu Chen Li stood up from her chair, her lips curved into a small smile. She walked toward the door, and Wei Guo quickly opened it wider, letting in more natural light. As she stood in the doorway, Yu Chen Li met his gaze with a playful twinkle in her eye and said, "If you're heading downstairs, I could go for one of our famous pears."

Wei Guo nodded respectfully, his posture conveying deep admiration as he replied, "Of course, mother. It would be my honor to bring that to you." With a slight bow, he gracefully exited the room and headed downstairs on his errand. In no time, he returned with a large, golden Chinese pear – handpicked from the freshest bins outside.

Later downstairs, Wei Guo and Meiyu Li worked together seamlessly, carefully packing a dried food order for a former customer in Minneapolis. The back of the market had undergone a transformation, now resembling a well-oiled packing company. Cardboard boxes lay neatly stacked, clear tape dispensers and bubble-wrap rolls were within easy reach, and postmarking materials for UPS and FedEx deliveries sat organized by color and size to maximize their packing speed. What used to be a neglected garbage space at the back of the store was now buzzing with productivity, slowly encroaching upon the traditional food market area as online orders became a significant portion of their sales.

As Wei Guo finished taping up one of the boxes with expert precision, he mused aloud while studying one particular box, "Perhaps we should limit the size of these orders. This box size seems to be the most profitable for us."

And with that thought in mind, he recalculated their profit based on an optimized shipping container size that would increase their margins.

DAVID LEE LUEDTKE

CHAPTER 25

As eve drew near, the tech world in suspense,
With a hustling staff and fears immense.

The clock ticked ever closer to 5 o'clock on December 31, 1999, and Jay's heart raced as he navigated through a sea of desks and computers at the Enron office. A mix of nervous excitement and apprehension charged the atmosphere.

As part of the Finance department, everyone knew the high stakes of the impending Y2K night, short for the "Year 2000" problem. They had been working tirelessly for months to update their systems and avoid potential disasters caused by the Year 2000 bug. The concern was that the software and computers only recognized the last two digits of the year from 1901 to 1999. With the turn of the century approaching, there were fears that the date would reset to 1900 instead of 2000, causing chaos in worldwide programs. Airplanes would fall from the sky. Trains would grind to a halt. And banks would shut down.

Everywhere, employees were checking and rechecking code, running simulations, and holding their breath as they waited for the clock to strike midnight. This wasn't just about technicalities; their jobs and even the stability of society hung in the balance.

The hustle and bustle in the office seemed to intensify as the world held its breath for the impending date change. Despite spending millions to ensure Y2K compliance, there was still an underlying fear of potential glitches. As an employee in the finance department, Jay had spent countless hours double-checking processes and monitoring systems.

The Enron office was a frenzy of activity as midnight approached. Jay kept stealing glances at the clock, counting down the hours with nervous anticipation. He and his co-workers were all on edge, exchanging anxious looks and trying to focus on their tasks. They were part of the world's preparations for Y2K, hoping for a smooth transition into the new millennium.

Jay's mind sat divided, torn between his work and his family. He wondered if his team could handle everything without him as he said goodbye for the evening and rushed out of the office for his commute home to San Francisco. But back at home, Jiewen, still employed by the Bank of America, faced her own challenges. She had decided to stay at home with their six-year-old son Bradley on this historic night, while her subordinates remained at the bank in case of any system shutdowns.

As the night wore on, Jay finally finished up at the Enron office, made sure all of his people had everything covered, and hurried home to join Jiewen and Bradley for the midnight event. The three of them sat huddled around the television, watching as the countdown to the Y2K moment continued. Their hearts raced as they watched footage from New Year's celebrations around the world —Europe, New York, Chicago, Denver —all transitioning from 1999 to 2000 without any major issues.

And then it was California's turn. As the clock struck midnight, a collective sigh of relief seemed to echo across the globe. Jay and Jiewen watched with bated breath as their own systems managed the date change seamlessly. There were no reports of airplanes falling from the sky or any other major disruptions. In that moment, they felt not just relieved but also proud to have been a part of such a monumental event in history.

Outside on their San Francisco porch, Jay and Jiewen stood together, holding hands, and looked up at the clear night sky. The fears of Y2K had largely been unfounded, and it was a moment of both celebration and reflection. They realized that the preparations, the late nights at the office, and the anxiety had all been worth it.

As they gazed at the stars, they couldn't help but feel a sense of hope and optimism for the new millennium. The Y2K bug had been averted, and they, like the rest of the world, could now look forward to a new era filled with possibilities and opportunities.

CHAPTER 26

A world paused, breaths held tight and lights aglow,
The millennium went like a vanquished foe.

Across town as the last moments of December 31, 1999 drew near, Brian and Joanne found themselves standing on the expansive deck of their Pacific Heights home with their 10-year-old son Dexter by their side. The evening air was crisp, and the city lights of San Francisco sprawled out before them. It was a night when the world held its breath, and Brian and Joanne were no exception.

The sky above was clear, a canvas of stars twinkling in the darkness. It was a stark contrast to the volatile spending on technology that had dominated the year. Companies had scrambled to prepare for the Year 2000 problem, fearing that computer systems across the globe might have trouble changing their clocks. The uncertainty had gripped the tech industry, and it was no different for Brian, who worked at Apple.

Brian leaned against the wooden railing of the deck, deep in contemplation. He thought about his job and the decisions ahead. His mind drifted to his recent meeting with Dr. Burnett, a brilliant mind he had crossed paths with in Taiwan. Dr. Burnett had been instrumental in directing Brian's efforts in advancing semiconductor wafer technology to a groundbreaking 300mm scale. The memory of their conversation lingered, and Brian was torn between his loyalty to Apple and the advice that had been imparted to him. The weight of his professional choices hung in the air, much like the uncertainty of the Y2K problem itself.

Beside him, Joanne stood, her eyes fixed on the horizon. She had chosen to be present at home on this crucial night, unlike her coworkers who were taking the evening shift at the hospital. Her thoughts were with them and the patients entrusted to their care. As a nurse, she understood the importance of her colleagues' dedication and the impact their work had on the lives of others. Her heart swelled with hope and concern for all those who depended on the hospital's staff, especially on a night filled with uncertainty.

Dexter, their young son, stood between them, his innocent eyes gazing up at the starry sky. He didn't fully grasp the complexities of the Y2K problem or the weight of his parent's thoughts. Instead, he simply marveled at the beauty of the moment, unaware of the world-changing events unfolding around him. Then he wanted to go and watch a National Geographic documentary interrupted by this weird moment with his parents.

On that deck in Pacific Heights, the three of them stood together, each lost in their own thoughts, watching the clock tick toward midnight. The stars continued to shine, and the world held its breath, hoping that the transition to the new millennium would be as smooth as the starlit sky above, and that the efforts of people like Brian and Joanne would contribute to a future filled with promise and progress.

CHAPTER 27

Friends gather beneath the New Year's bright view
Thinking of fortunes and wishing they knew.

Back at the lively atmosphere of the Top of the Tunnel bar, Jimmy, Yuze, Daniel, Suzan, Jorge, and Charles gathered to welcome the arrival of the new year. The bar's panoramic windows offered a breathtaking view of the city lights, a fitting backdrop to their reflections on the ever-changing financial landscape.

Charles, in particular, found his mind wandering through the complexities of his company's worth. On paper, it had become a staggering fifty-million-dollar entity, an astronomical figure that seemed to defy logic, especially considering their meager income, barely enough to cover the gas bill. The latest round of investments had fueled discussions of taking the company public, a move that could potentially solidify its financial standing.

In the late 1990s, the Nasdaq Composite stock market index had surged by a staggering 400%, a testament to the unprecedented growth in the tech sector. Companies like Charles' were seizing the opportunity to go public through Initial Public Offerings (IPOs), raising substantial capital despite not having turned a profit or in some cases, realizing any meaningful revenue at all. This financial landscape offered Charles the tantalizing prospect of his employee stock options, turning him into an instant paper millionaire once the IPO was executed.

Around them, they witnessed the frenzy of personal investing that had swept the nation during the dot-com boom. Stories abounded of individuals quitting their conventional jobs to pursue day trading and stock market investments. Jorge, who still worked as a repairman on the city's iconic cable car system, contemplated the allure of quitting his job to invest in Charles' burgeoning tech venture.

Yuze, the ever-attentive host, made sure their plastic champagne glasses were filled to the brim, and he adjusted the television to ensure they had the best view of the impending fireworks on the waterfront. The anticipation in the bar was palpable, mirroring the collective excitement of the city itself. He looked down at the other end of the bar, where he saw through the saloon doors to the back room where his eight-year-old son sat watching the countdown on a small television perched atop a stool next to his chair. Without a babysitter on a New Year's Eve, once again, little Lawrence wanted to be with his father in the bar instead of sitting alone in his room. Yuze and Lawrence now lived in two of the rooms on the top floor, so at least they didn't have to go far to get home.

Suzan, Daniel, and Charles found themselves in a quiet corner of the Top of the Tunnel bar, their glasses of champagne catching the soft glow of the city lights streaming through the windows. They exchanged meaningful glances, their thoughts interweaving in a silent conversation that delved deep into the heart of their venture.

In that moment, surrounded by the festive atmosphere of celebration, the weight of their responsibility bore down on them. Suzan's eyes, tinged with a hint of concern, reflected the gravity of their situation. She knew that the success of their software depended on the intricate web of computer systems that underpinned it. The code, the algorithms, the servers—all of it was the lifeblood of their company. Their dreams and aspirations hinged on these digital foundations.

Recently, Suzan had stumbled upon an intriguing piece of information that had lingered in her mind. She had read about two dot-com companies that had shelled out an astonishing one million dollars for a mere 30-second advertisement spot during Super Bowl XXXIII next month. The extravagance of it all struck her. It was a testament to the era's economic exuberance, where investors seemed willing to pour their resources into any dot-com company, regardless of its valuation. The allure of the Internet-related prefixes or the ".com" suffix in a company's name had the power to attract investors like moths to a flame.

Venture capital flowed freely, like a river swollen after heavy rains. Investment banks, keenly aware of the lucrative nature of initial public offerings (IPOs), fanned the flames of speculation and encouraged investments in technology firms. The soaring stock prices in this new sector of the economy, coupled with unwavering confidence that these companies would reap future profits, created an environment where investors were willing to disregard traditional financial metrics, such as the price-earnings ratio. People wondered how could a new dot.com company with very little revenue be valued more than a hugely-profitable company like Pepsi? Or even more than Walmart?

Charles, sitting across from Suzan and Daniel, absorbed their concerns and shared an understanding of the times. They all knew that the dot-com bubble was inflating rapidly, a bubble that would soon reach its zenith before the inevitable burst. But for now, they were caught in the excitement of the moment, sipping champagne and watching the city come alive with the promise of the new year. The allure of technology's advancements and the hope for their own success overshadowed the looming uncertainties of the market. In that dimly lit corner of the bar, they were acutely aware of their roles as pioneers in a rapidly changing world, where dreams were woven into lines of code and innovation held the power to shape their future.

As Jimmy sat by the window watching his customers, he couldn't help but reflect on his own journey. He had come a long way since taking ownership of the bar. He leaned closer to the window, hoping to catch a glimpse of the fireworks bursting between the buildings, a visual testament to the explosive growth and opportunities that had come to define this remarkable era.

In the Top of the Tunnel bar, beneath the sparkling city lights, they rang in the new year, each lost in their thoughts, their dreams, and the myriad possibilities that the booming tech industry had brought to their lives.

Shortly after midnight, Liz and Greet wandered into the bar. Liz exchanged hugs with her friends while Greet awkwardly shook hands with most and only hugged a few of them. Liz explained they had become bored at home and wished to be with friends.

"I didn't see any airplanes fall from the sky," Greet explained as she described the view from their deck. She held up a bulky flip phone. "And the date on my phone changed too? So, what's the big deal?"

CHAPTER 28

Amid the finance flurry, screens aglow,
A sage plots trades, timing the house cash flow.

A few months later, Jay Baumers sat at his desk in Enron's bustling finance department, surrounded by screens displaying stock prices and market trends. He was a financial whiz, constantly crunching numbers and analyzing data to make smart trades for the company.

In 2000, Enron was the talk of Wall Street. Jay had been promoted to a special team responsible for creatively moving money between different divisions while timing gains and losses to coincide with industry events. It was an exciting and lucrative time to be involved in the stock market. Everyone seemed to be investing, and stories of average people becoming millionaires overnight were common.

On January 10, 2000, America Online, led by Jay Case and Ted Leonsis, announced a merger with Time Warner, led by Gerald M. Levin. The merger was the largest to date and was questioned by many analysts. Jay directed his team at Enron to invest in the merger.

Then, on January 30, 2000, twelve of the sixty-one ads for Super Bowl XXXIV were purchased by dot-coms (sources state ranges from 12 up to 19 companies depending on the definition of a dot-com company). At that time, the cost for a 30-second commercial was between $1.9 million and $2.2 million. Jay directed his team to invest in a company called, Pets.com, which delivered dog food to people's homes –an industry ripe for innovation.

But deep down, Jay couldn't shake the nagging feeling that this bubble would eventually burst, much like a run on the table during a session of gambling. He had seen the frenzy of the dot-com era and knew it couldn't last forever, much like when he spent more time at the casinos. And as share prices continued to soar, he saw more and more executives cashing out their stock options as soon as they were able.

While most investors became caught up in the excitement, not so much the legendary investor Sir John Templeton, who saw through the temporary insanity and began shorting dot-com stocks, referring to the time as a "temporary insanity" and a "once-in-a-lifetime opportunity." Templeton anticipated the expiration of lock-up periods, typically six months after the initial public offerings, correctly predicting that many dot-com company executives would sell their shares as soon as they could. This large-scale selling would inevitably force down share prices, and Templeton was ready to profit from the ensuing crash. Jay admired Templeton's foresight and knew he needed to tread carefully as well if he wanted to protect his own investments –small as they were.

During the peak of the boom, even companies that had never turned a profit or generated any substantial revenue could go public through Initial Public Offerings (IPOs) and raise massive amounts of capital. Employee stock options turned ordinary workers into instant paper millionaires when their companies executed IPOs. However, most of them were barred from selling their shares immediately due to lock-up periods designed to prevent massive sell-offs. Enron started looking more and more like a Ponzi scheme where only the first investors made a killing.

As the year 2000 progressed, Jay Baumers found himself in a precarious position. He had seen the euphoria of the dot-com bubble and the relentless rise of Enron's stock price. But deep down, he couldn't shake the feeling that it couldn't last forever. The financial world was changing rapidly, and Jay knew that he needed to tread carefully as he navigated the treacherous waters of the stock market in those uncertain times.

Jay continued to invest Enron's money into high-technology and emerging markets as directed by his bosses. He tried to get them to invest in stalwart types of companies, but his bosses insisted it was like burying money in a tin can in the backyard. The Nasdaq Composite stock market index rose 400% and reached a price–earnings ratio of 200 by the end of the year, dwarfing the peak price–earnings ratio of 80 for the Japanese Nikkei 225 during the Japanese asset price bubble of 1991.

In 1999, shares of Qualcomm rose in value by 2,619%, 12 other large-cap stocks each rose over 1,000% in value, and seven additional large-cap stocks each rose over 900% in value. Even though the Nasdaq Composite rose 85.6% and the S&P 500 rose 19.5% in 1999, more stocks fell in value than rose in value as investors sold stocks in slower-growing companies to invest in Internet stocks.

As the Chair of the Federal Reserve, Alan Greenspan raised interest rates multiple times in an attempt to slow down the rapid growth and speculative behavior of investors. However, his actions were met with resistance as the NASDAQ Composite peaked at a record high of 5,048.62 on March 10, 2000.

But just three days later, news of Japan's recession caused a global sell-off that had a disproportionate effect on technology stocks. This led Yahoo! and eBay to end their merger talks and resulted in a 2.6% drop for the Nasdaq, while the S&P 500 saw a rise of 2.4% as investors shifted their focus to more established companies.

The following week, Barron's published an article titled "Burning Up," warning readers about the financial struggles and potential bankruptcies facing many internet companies. This sparked doubts and reconsideration among investors. On the same day, MicroStrategy announced a restatement of its revenue due to questionable accounting practices. As a result, their stock price plummeted from $333 to $140 in just one day.

Adding fuel to the fire, the Federal Reserve also raised interest rates on March 21st, leading to an inverted yield curve. This caused temporary relief for stocks, but tensions continued to rise as Judge Thomas Penfield Jackson declared Microsoft guilty of monopolization and tying in violation of the Sherman Antitrust Act. This ruling resulted in a 15% drop in Microsoft's shares and an 8% decline in the Nasdaq.

Fast forward to the last few months of 2001, the cracks in Enron's facade were beginning to show. What had once been a seemingly invincible energy giant was now unraveling at an alarming pace. Jay Baumers, like many Enron employees, was growing increasingly concerned about the future.

Enron's financial woes were no longer a well-kept secret. Reports of questionable accounting practices and off-balance-sheet partnerships had begun to surface. The stock price, which had once soared to dizzying heights, was plummeting rapidly. Employees who had invested heavily in Enron's stock were watching their paper fortunes evaporate before their eyes.

In the midst of the chaos, Enron's top executives, including CEO Jeffrey Skilling and Chairman Kenneth Lay, were attempting to reassure both employees and investors that everything was under control. But the truth was far from it. The company's debt was mounting, and its financial stability was crumbling.

Jay Baumers, who had been part of the finance department's intricate financial maneuvers, couldn't ignore the warning signs any longer. He had seen how the company had manipulated its financial statements to create the illusion of profitability. The realization that he had been a pawn in Enron's elaborate financial games weighed heavily on him.

In December of 2001, the world awoke to the shocking news that Enron, the once-mighty energy giant, had filed for bankruptcy. This event reverberated through the business world like a seismic shock, sending tremors throughout the financial industry and beyond. Enron's collapse was not merely a financial disaster; it stood as an enduring symbol of corporate avarice and corruption on an unparalleled scale.

Jay Baumers, who had once seen his financial future seemingly secured within Enron's walls, found himself facing a stark and disheartening reality. As Enron's stock plummeted into virtual worthlessness, Jay, like countless others, watched his once-promising wealth disintegrate. The dream of paper millions had evaporated, replaced by the cold reality of financial ruin.

The aftermath of Enron's catastrophic fall was a landscape of legal battles, investigations, and regulatory reforms. The shockwaves from the scandal rippled through the corridors of power, prompting a national reckoning with corporate ethics and accountability. The public demanded answers, justice, and safeguards to prevent such a devastating event from repeating itself.

In those tumultuous days, Jay made a somber decision. He walked away from Enron, much like many of his colleagues. In their wake, employees carried their laptops, not as prized possessions but as a desperate attempt to salvage something from the wreckage. The certainty of a final paycheck had evaporated, replaced by the grim realization that the company's demise was all but inevitable.

Enron's once-proud headquarters, the three tall blue towers that had stood like watchful guardians over Highway 101 near the entrance to Silicon Valley, now appeared as somber monuments to irrational exuberance. They were no longer symbols of corporate success but stark reminders of the consequences of unchecked ambition and unethical practices. Enron's downfall would forever serve as a cautionary tale, a stark lesson etched into the annals of corporate history.

CHAPTER 29

Sunset on the city, post-dot-com strife,
They find refuge in friends, safety in life

The evening sun cast a warm glow over Castro Valley in the East Bay of the San Francisco region. Brian and Joanne had weathered the storm of the dot-com bust, finding themselves in a more stable place than many of their peers. Brian had stayed at Apple, a company that had managed to avoid the chaos of the dot-com mess. He now concentrated on the intricate world of 300mm wafer technology, working for a company whose stock had only dropped 30% during the collapse of the technology sector and the dot-com burst. In those uncertain times, few companies in the entire world had been spared the turmoil of the bubble bursting. Joanne had moved to Eden Valley Hospital, only a short distance from their new home in the quieter suburbs. She finally made it to the Trauma Center, fulfilling the dreams she had when starting nursing school.

Leaving their son, Dexter, in the care of trusted friends for the evening, Brian and Joanne decided to head to the Top of the Tunnel bar. It was a place where they could unwind and be with friends who had also navigated the turbulent waters of the investment world. Although loving the suburbs, most of their friends still lived in San Francisco.

As they walked into the bar, they were greeted by the familiar faces of Jimmy, the owner, and Yuze, his number one bartender. The Top of the Tunnel bar had always been a refuge, a place where people sought solace and camaraderie during uncertain times. Tonight was no exception.

The bar was buzzing with activity, a surge in customers driven by panic and uncertainty in the wake of the fall of the investment world. Friends and acquaintances gathered at the bar, their conversations filled with a mix of frustration and resignation.

Brian and Joanne found a spot at the bar, their glasses soon filled with drinks that offered a temporary escape from the harsh realities outside. They exchanged knowing glances with their friends, understanding that they were all in this together.

Liz and Greet had been sitting nestled in the cozy corner, the dim lighting creating an intimate atmosphere. But they soon went over to join their friends at the bar. The group of friends surrounded them and exchanged stories, their voices filled with nostalgia and camaraderie, much like veterans reminiscing about their time in the military. They shared tales of companies that had succumbed to the dot-com bust and those that had managed to weather the storm.

"That Pets.Com is the one that I can't believe ever went public. I mean, who would buy their pet food online?" Liz asked incredulously, her disbelief echoing the sentiments of many. "And from a sock puppet?"

Joanne couldn't help but laugh at Liz's comment, her bright blue jeans and a beautiful blouse tonight serving as a welcome departure from the usual hospital garb.

Brian added, "Not all of them were phony, you know," he chimed in, offering her unique perspective as someone with inside knowledge of the industry. Brian, feeling comfortable among friends, sported a stylish leather jacket over his golf shirt and dress slacks. "That eBay company is going to last, I think," he confidently stated, the conviction in his voice evident.

"Online auctions in order to buy stuff?" Jimmy questioned as he momentarily paused between filling customers' drinks. Jimmy and Yuze moved with remarkable efficiency, gracefully handling the influx of customers who sought refuge in the Top of the Tunnel. The bar had indeed become a sanctuary for those in search of solace in the company of kindred spirits who had navigated the same turbulent waters.

Liz seized upon the opportunity to defend her conviction. "You're right about that. I just bought a used bicycle and saved hundreds of dollars."

However, amidst the lively conversation, Greet had been unusually quiet. She spoke up softly, her voice tinged with vulnerability. "We should be saving our money, Liz," she said, casting her gaze downward.

Liz looked over at her partner, puzzled by the comment. Concern etched across her face, she placed a comforting hand on Greet's shoulder and gently probed for an explanation.

"I lost my job today," Greet admitted quietly, her tear-filled eyes finally meeting Liz's. "They closed the office today. I didn't want to tell you."

Liz immediately enveloped Greet in a warm embrace as her lover began to cry. The group of friends rallied to comfort her, offering kind words and reassurance. But the weight of the situation proved too much to bear in the midst of their lively gathering. Eventually, with tearful farewells, Liz and Greet made their exit from the bar, seeking solace in each other's company.

As the evening wore on, the conversations at the Top of the Tunnel bar shifted from despair to determination. People shared stories of resilience and hope, finding strength in their collective resolve to rebuild and move forward. In the midst of uncertainty, the bar remained a steadfast beacon of community and support, a place where friendships deepened and forged anew in the crucible of adversity.

DAVID LEE LUEDTKE

CHAPTER 30

Together they face their startup's plight,
Born to revolutionize, yet reckless in flight.

The mixed lighting of LED and incandescent bulbs washed over a meeting room at Sequoia Capital, with the hushed conversations of financial movers and shakers permeating the air. Daniel, now a seasoned investment banker at Sequoia Capital, sat at the head of the conference table, the expression on his face echoing his concern. Charles, the brilliant software engineer and the founder of TrainSeek.com, was visibly tense, his fingers nervously tapping the polished surface of the table. Suzan, another investment banker at Sequoia who had taken a significant financial stake in the startup, sat beside Daniel, her expression a mixture of determination and anxiety.

The trio had gathered to confront the harsh reality of their startup's financial situation. TrainSeek.com had burst onto the scene with ambitious plans to revolutionize the travel industry by making train travel more accessible and convenient. They had attracted substantial funding, but their spending had been nothing short of reckless during the heady days of 2001.

Daniel, known for his financial acumen, began the meeting by projecting a spreadsheet onto the screen, displaying a series of dwindling numbers that painted a grim picture. "We need to face the facts," he said somberly, his eyes fixed on the screen. "Our cash reserves are depleting at an alarming rate. We cannot sustain this burn rate any longer."

Charles sighed heavily, his dreams of transforming the travel industry fading in the harsh light of reality. "We believed we could change the world," he said, his voice tinged with regret. "We invested heavily in technology, marketing, and expansion but the whole dot-com bust hit us too."

Suzan nodded in agreement, her determination unwavering despite the dire circumstances. "We took calculated risks, and we knew the road would be challenging," she said, her gaze resolute. "But now, we have to make some tough decisions."

As they continued to examine the financial figures, it became painfully evident that TrainSeek.com had spent far more cash than it had earned. The dot-com bubble had burst, leaving a trail of failed startups and dashed dreams in its wake. TrainSeek.com was not immune to the economic turmoil that had gripped the technology sector.

Daniel leaned back in his chair, his fingers steepled in thought. "We have two options," he said, addressing the group. "We can continue to burn through our remaining cash, hoping for a turnaround in the market, or we can make the difficult choice to close the business before we exhaust all our resources."

Charles sighed again, his shoulders slumping with the weight of the decision ahead. "I never thought it would come to this," he admitted, his voice heavy with regret. "But we have a responsibility to our investors and ourselves."

Suzan placed a supportive hand on Charles's shoulder, her determination steadfast. "Closing the business is not a failure," she said firmly. "It's a strategic decision to protect our investors' interests and preserve our own financial stability."

In the days that followed, Daniel, Charles, and Suzan made the difficult decision to shutter TrainSeek.com. It was a painful choice, but one they knew was necessary to salvage what remained of their financial resources. The dot-com bust had claimed another casualty, but the experience had taught them valuable lessons about resilience, adaptability, and the unpredictable nature of the tech industry.

As the end of the year 2001 pressed on, the economic challenges facing the nation deepened, and the events of September 11, 2001, proved to be the final, devastating blow to an already fragile economy. The tragic terrorist attacks on the World Trade Center and the Pentagon sent shockwaves through the United States, leaving an indelible mark on the nation's psyche and its economic landscape.

In the immediate aftermath of the 9/11 attacks, financial markets closed, and uncertainty gripped the nation. Airlines grounded their fleets, and businesses across various sectors were paralyzed by the unprecedented crisis. The tragic loss of life and the widespread destruction of property were compounded by the economic fallout that followed.

The stock market, already reeling from the burst of the dot-com bubble, suffered a significant decline in the wake of the attacks. Investors watched in dismay as stock prices plummeted, and many businesses faced mounting financial pressures. The tourism and travel industry, which had already been struggling due to the dot-com collapse, was dealt a devastating blow as people canceled travel plans and opted to stay home amidst heightened security concerns.

The aftermath of 9/11 brought about a series of economic challenges, including increased security costs, reduced consumer spending, and a climate of uncertainty that affected investment decisions. The Federal Reserve responded by cutting interest rates to stimulate economic activity, but it would take years for the economy to fully recover.

As they moved forward in their respective careers, they would carry with them the knowledge that success in the world of startups required more than just a brilliant idea; it demanded prudent financial management and a willingness to adapt in the face of adversity. The story of TrainSeek.com became a cautionary tale, a reminder that even the most promising ventures could fall victim to the unforgiving winds of economic change.

DAVID LEE LUEDTKE

CHAPTER 31

In the wild tech world, a manager steers,
His family's ventures online amidst fears.

In the early months of 2002, amidst the tech turmoil of San Francisco's Chinatown, Li's Food Market stood as a beacon of resilience. Wei Guo, a humble manager with only a couple of years of exposure to the digital world, had embarked on a daring journey to propel his family's business into the online realm. With dogged determination, he had decided to expand their reach through online sales and deliveries, a leap into uncharted territory. He had been worried that the Y2K problem would take his online business and turn it into a complete waste of time. Now the downturn in the economy and the world in shock after the terrorist attacks on the World Trade Center in New York threatened his family's business.

In a cozy corner of their home above the food market, Meiyu Li stood by his side, her eyes reflecting a mixture of hope and trepidation. Their children, Yuze and Jiewen, joined their parents as much as their free time would allow in this ambitious endeavor. Together, they toiled tirelessly, fueled by the vision of crafting a state-of-the-art website that would encapsulate the essence of Li's Food Market. They aimed to cater not only to the locals but also to those who had relocated, yearning for the authentic flavors and specialty foods that were synonymous with their family's legacy.

Meanwhile, the matriarch of the family, Yu Chen Li, observed the unfolding saga with a sense of pride but with a deeper caution. Her daughter and son-in-law seamlessly juggled the responsibilities of managing inventory and procuring supplies in the bustling back room of the store. She sat by her bedroom window on the second floor, brandishing her shotgun just in case the world came in on them.

As the calendar pages turned in 2002, the once-thriving landscape of San Francisco's Chinatown seemed to crumble like old parchment. The city bore the scars of both the dot-com crash and the haunting memory of the September 11th attacks. This dual catastrophe cast an omnipresent shadow, and the streets of Chinatown bore the weight of the collective uncertainty.

Within the walls of Li's Food Market, the digital tides that had once carried a steady stream of online orders had receded to a mere trickle. The world had grown cautious, and the luxury of savoring the cherished delicacies of the market in person had become a rare indulgence. Their business, which had been a steadfast presence for years, now bore the brunt of economic turmoil, witnessing a decline of nearly thirty percent. Hope seemed to wane, and the path to recovery appeared elusive.

Amidst this turbulence, Jiewen maintained her position at Bank of America. She exemplified her commitment to her family by extending a helping hand during these trying times. Her husband, Jay Baumers, found himself adrift in the uncertain seas of a lost career. The wounds were still fresh from the abrupt closure of Enron, a company to which he had dedicated himself completely. In the face of uncertainty, he sought solace in assisting at Li's Food Market, relishing the physical labor that provided a temporary escape from the disillusionment that had settled over him like a heavy fog. He recently accepted a consulting arrangement with federal prosecutors to help unravel the financial shenanigans at Enron. Not full-time, but enough to pay the bills for another year.

One day, as they toiled together in the store's bustling back room, Jay turned to Wei Guo with a perplexed expression. He held a curious, large, bumpy, dark brown fruit in his hand, its surface resembling a formidable football. As he inspected it closely, a peculiar aroma wafted from the depths of the enigmatic fruit, reminiscent of a laundry hamper in a high-school locker room.

"My god, that smells like gym socks," Jay exclaimed, his face contorted with a mixture of amusement and astonishment.

Wei Guo chuckled heartily, his eyes twinkling with mirth, and pointed to a bin on the far side of the room. "Be careful with those," he advised with a knowing smile. "It's called a durian fruit, and it's not your average fruit. But despite the smell, it's highly prized for its nutrients and unique flavor."

Jay's curiosity piqued, and he appreciated the momentary diversion from the weight of his uncertain career. In the midst of adversity, the exotic durian fruit served as a symbol of unexpected discoveries and the resilience of family bonds that endured, even in the face of the darkest of storms.

Jiewen appeared from her diligent work on the family's financial accounting. She approached her father slowly and whispered something about reducing their orders to match the sales. Wei Guo nodded appreciatively and went back to stacking fruit. She turned to Jay and smiled. "I'll go pick up Bradley from school."

"I can get him," Jay replied and wiped his hands on his colorful apron, then began removing the apron to shift into father-mode.

"No, that's okay. You boys keep stocking the food bins," she replied and weaved her way through the bins and shelves toward the front door. She turned and added, "And play nicely now."

Jay and Wei Guo exchanged glances and grinned with a shared love and understanding of the brilliant woman leaving the store.

DAVID LEE LUEDTKE

CHAPTER 32

In a safe place, for hearts that are weary,
the host serves solace, binds friends in theory.

At the Top of the Tunnel bar in San Francisco, the dimly lit ambiance enveloped the patrons in a comforting haze. Jimmy, always the congenial bartender, glided through the bar, his practiced hands gracefully serving up drinks and taking orders from the patrons seated at tables. His best bartender, Yuze, held court behind the well-worn bar counter, where an eclectic mix of locals and visitors sought solace in the establishment's comforting embrace.

This bar, nestled between the Financial District and Chinatown, served as more than just a place to quench one's thirst. It was a living, breathing nexus where stories flowed as freely as the drinks, where people gathered to find respite and connection amidst the turmoil of recent times—the economic meltdown and the haunting aftermath of the September 11th attacks in New York City.

Among the eclectic crowd were Jiewen Li and Jay, affectionately referred to by their friends as "Jay-When and Jay-Now." Nestled at the bar, they shared tales of their daily struggles. Jiewen wore her business attire but with her suit jacket hanging over a bar stool. Jay still had a blue suit and jacket on from a fresh day at a lawyer's office in the Financial District.

They spoke of their life at Li's Food Market in the heart of Chinatown, where their family's store stood strong in these tough times. Jiewen, still dedicated to her job at Bank of America, navigated the financial world's challenges with unwavering determination. Meanwhile, Jay continued his role in the ongoing Enron cleanup, working closely with federal agents to untangle the complex web of financial deceit that had ensnared the once-mighty corporation.

As Jay recounted the labyrinthine of financial entanglements he had encountered, his friends leaned in, their eyes reflecting a mix of curiosity and empathy. His words painted a vivid picture of the chaos within Enron, mirroring the financial turmoil that had gripped the nation. His gaze shifted to Greet, a striking figure in tall black boots and snug-fitting blue jeans, perched at the bar beside him and listening intently to his stories.

"It was probably just like that where you worked?" Jay inquired, inviting Greet into the conversation.

Greet, her long legs crossed elegantly, leaned forward to take a thoughtful sip from her half-finished beer. Her expression conveyed a hint of nostalgia as she reminisced about her own workplace. "No, not at all really," she replied with a wistful smile. "We were just a typical dot-com that spent more than we made. And then we ran out of money."

Liz, Greet's partner of nearly two decades now, offered a tender gesture of affection, placing her hand on Greet's knee and offering a reassuring rub. Her eyes scanned the gathered friends, and she decided to share a significant piece of news. "Greet is thinking about staying in Belgium for a while," she announced, her voice carrying a sense of solemnity.

Jiewen, taken aback by the unexpected revelation, voiced her concern with genuine surprise. "Oh my God, why are you doing that?" she inquired, her concern for her friend evident in her voice.

Greet's eyes met Liz's with an unspoken understanding that transcended words, their shared history and deep love for one another speaking volumes. As Greet began to explain the reason for her upcoming journey, her voice carried the weight of filial duty and an urgency fueled by a daughter's love. Her words carried a profound sense of responsibility.

"My mother is sick," Greet revealed, her voice trembling slightly with emotion, "and I want to help her while I still can."

Jay, the silent observer who had experienced the complexities of caregiving for aging parents, leaned in to hug Greet, his embrace conveying a quiet understanding of the challenges that lay ahead. He recognized the unspoken reality that had woven itself into their group of friends –the inevitability of parents entering a stage of life that demanded care and attention.

His gaze shifted to Liz, who was caught in a web of emotions as she grappled with the potential strain Greet's departure might place on their relationship. Jay could see the conflict etched on her face, the worry that had crept into the corners of her eyes.

As if sensing Liz's inner turmoil, Greet leaned tenderly toward her partner and pressed a loving kiss upon her lips. The smile that followed was filled with warmth and reassurance, a silent promise of enduring love and commitment. "You make sure and decorate my pets now, you hear?" Greet teased, her voice lighthearted despite the bittersweet moment.

Liz's laughter echoed through the bar as she addressed the group, revealing the quirky details of their lives together. "She's leaving Deery, Lamby, and Goaty with me while she's away."

Greet gently wiped away a tear from Liz's cheek, her gaze staunch as she addressed their friends with a sense of resolve. "I'm not sure how long this will be. But I will be back," she declared, her words carrying a comforting reassurance to those who cherished her presence.

Before long, Daniel made his entrance, accompanied by Suzan Bolstock, a new regular at the bar and whose arrival piqued the curiosity of the group. Daniel guided Suzan toward their friends seated at the bar, his hand resting on Jay's shoulder as he introduced her to everyone as if they had never crossed paths before.

The group exchanged curious glances as they observed Daniel and Suzan standing closely together, their body language revealing a deeper connection than mere friendship. It was a subtle but unmistakable display of newfound knowledge, an unspoken confirmation of the bond that had formed between them. When Suzan leaned sideways and planted a gentle kiss on Daniel's cheek, the pieces of the puzzle fell into place, and the group shared in the unspoken understanding of their evolving relationship.

Jay, ever the astute observer, couldn't resist breaking the silence with a mischievous grin. "Something tells me you two are no longer just business partners," he remarked, raising an eyebrow playfully.

Jiewen, quick to react, smacked Jay's arm in playful recourse and admonished him for his insensitive remark, though her eyes twinkled with amusement. The group burst into laughter, their camaraderie and shared history evident in their easy banter.

After the laughter subsided, Daniel decided to clarify their changing circumstances. "Well, Jay's instincts are right," he began, his voice carrying a note of excitement. "We're no longer business partners. Suzan here decided to leave the firm." He glanced at Suzan, his eyes filled with affection.

"Let's not sugarcoat it," Suzan chimed in, playfully pushing Daniel's arm while locking eyes with him. "I was fired, plain and simple. They canned me."

Most of the others around the bar were familiar with the TrainSeek company's rise and fall, even though it had made only a minor blip in the local news. Nestled on the fourth page of the business section of the San Jose Mercury News, it might have seemed inconsequential compared to the larger dot-com busts, but to those in the know, it carried an intimate significance that traced back to the very heart of the bar where they now stood.

Liz looked awkwardly at Suzan –their relationship to this point was of a stand-offish business executive looking downward at a lowly health inspector. Liz was a strong and resilient person, but even a person with that type of inner strength can be hurt when another person treats them badly.

As if sensing Liz's glance and the unspoken words, Suzan stepped around Daniel and approached Liz directly. "And I owe you an apology for my behavior at TrainSeek."

Liz looked puzzled but accepted the apology gracefully. They shook hands, and Suzan added, "I was such an asshole. You know, the money… and the heady times. It all just took over me."

"You can say that again," rang out a booming voice. Charles Kang walked into the bar and caught the last part of Suzan's explanation. A terrible silence engulfed the bar as Charles walked up to the uncomfortable group of people –all of them painfully aware of what happened with the crash of their company. Charles walked around Daniel and stopped straight in front of Suzan while looking her coldly in the eyes. The others didn't know if they should step in or retreat in terror.

Suzan stepped even closer to Charles without saying a word, then suddenly wrapped her arms around Charles who returned the hug with equal affection. The others stood in amazement.

Charles released Suzan and turned to the others. "If it wasn't for Suzan, I would be flat-out broke." He explained how she arranged for the settlement of all of the bills and the closing of the place, while still making sure Charles was able to keep the rights to the software he developed. It cost Sequoia Capital plenty of money, but Charles came out without having to file bankruptcy.

The whole group asked question after question about the wrap-up and a newer and deeper friendship began to form with the group –all seasoned veterans of the capital world now.

Suzan explained how she stood up to her bosses at Sequoia and protected the investors and founders with so much effort and without seeking authority, then inked the deals, closed the company, and took the fall for it by losing her job. The look on her face told the story of how she must have felt wonderful about her own actions for the first time in many years.

Jay turned to Suzan and added, "I sure wish we had you at Enron instead of the con artists we had running that place. Maybe we would still be open now instead of becoming the definition of greed."

CHAPTER 33

Years on, sailing hills in electric glides,
A nurse signals new changes in the tides.

Brian cruised through the winding hills of Castro Valley, his sleek new 2019 Tesla Model S gliding effortlessly along the scenic route. The near-silent operation of the vehicle never failed to draw the attention of pedestrians and fellow motorists. The soft whirring noise was an added feature to help pedestrians along the way and to keep them from becoming startled when a silent three-thousand-pound vehicle snuck up behind them. As he navigated the twists and turns of the road, that faint whirring of the electric motor turned a few heads along the way as a stark contrast to the roaring engines of traditional cars revving their engines as they climbed each hill.

Brian drove slowly through the suburban streets, taking in the familiar sights of his neighborhood. The neatly trimmed lawns, the flower-filled gardens, and the houses with their gabled roofs and decorative fences all appeared unchanged for several years. Perhaps it was the way the sun cast long shadows on the pavement or the way the leaves had started to sprout, a reminder that spring was just around the corner, but Brian became contemplative for a moment and breathed deeply. This was the place where he and Joanne had raised their son, Dexter, and built a life together. It was a place of memories.

Parking the car in the driveway, Brian took a moment to just sit and watch the world go by. Across the street, a neighbor lady was tending to her rose bushes, while a group of children played tag down the street on the sidewalk. Brian reached for the garage door remote and with a press of a button, the door smoothly ascended, revealing the clean and organized interior of the garage. He eased the Tesla into its designated spot on the left, the vehicle's futuristic design a stark contrast to Joanne's traditional BMW parked in the right stall.

Once parked, Brian stepped out of the car, feeling the cool breeze of the suburban evening on his face. He retrieved the EV charger from the cradle of the high-powered charger that he had recently installed, a sign of his commitment to sustainable living. As he plugged the charger into his Tesla, the car began to silently recharge, a reminder of the technology's seamless integration into his daily life. He looked at the connector and remembered first drawing that up ten years ago when he joined Tesla on its journey to revolutionize the auto industry. His past life in the semiconductor industry seemed to be directed by a guiding force to where his talents yielded the strongest results. Once again, the long arm of DARPA, and directed by Dr. Phillip Burnett, moved Brian from Apple to Tesla to take the autonomous driving level up to the next notch. This was the third time Dr. Burnett dabbled with Brian's career. And this elegant Tesla was a gift to Brian for his ongoing efforts and the recognition of his impending retirement in a few months.

With his car charging and the tranquil surroundings embracing him, Brian took a moment to appreciate the serenity of his suburban oasis. The peacefulness of his home in Castro Valley was a stark contrast to the bustling cityscape of San Francisco, just a short drive away, and it was moments like these that made the winding journey through the hills all the more worthwhile. He loosened his handsome wool jacket and tucked a loose end of his shirt into his pants. He tapped his waist line and thought he might want to take a pound or two off.

The sound of Joanne's footsteps echoed through the stairway, signaling her approach. Brian stood alone in the garage, lost in his thoughts and the quiet stillness of the evening. But when she appeared in the doorway, dressed in her crisp nurse's uniform, he felt a sense of relief wash over him. The soft light streaming in from the stairway outlined her silhouette perfectly, emphasizing her curves and gracefulness. She moved with a sense of urgency, a testament to her staunch dedication as a medical professional. Her radiant smile lit up the room and Brian's heart swelled with affection as she closed the distance between them. He eagerly reciprocated her warm embrace, their bodies fitting together like two puzzle pieces, only slightly worn down by time. In that moment, everything else faded away as they held each other tightly, both content in each other's company.

"Hello, husband," Joanne greeted him with a tone that conveyed both love and the weight of her responsibilities. Brian, always one for metaphorical expressions, remarked, "like two ships passing in the night." Their passionate kiss was a momentary escape from the world's uncertainties, a reminder of the strength of their bond.

As they held each other, the seconds slipped away, but the demands of Joanne's profession soon beckoned her back to reality. She reluctantly pulled away from Brian, her eyes flicking toward her watch. Time was a precious commodity.

"I'll be home about 4:00 a.m.," Joanne informed him as she moved toward her car, the nurse's uniform still a stark reminder of the frontline battle she faced daily. Her smile was warm and her eyes glistened as she looked at Brian as if she were deeply in love. She opened her car door and fastened her seatbelt, her dedication to her work evident in every gesture as she began looking concerned about her own thoughts. Before driving away, she rolled down her window and leaned toward Brian. "You know, we got another one of those cases at the hospital again," she confided, her voice tinged with frustration and concern. "We can't figure out what is wrong, but another one died last night with the same symptoms."

They briefly discussed her rising concerns, and then Brian watched as Joanne drove away, her taillights disappearing into the distance. The early months of 2020 had brought with them an unsettling sense of foreboding, as healthcare workers like Joanne grappled with an unknown adversary appearing in all of the hospitals.

As Brian gazed out at the rolling hills, he caught a glimpse of headlights coming up the hill as the sky began to darken. Moments later, Joanne's taillights disappeared over the crest of the hill after what seemed like a brief exchange with the driver of an oncoming vehicle. A surge of excitement washed over him as he realized it must be his son, Dexter, arriving as planned. He watched intently as the vehicle grew closer, curious about the height of its headlights and what kind of vehicle his son drove now.

The deep rumble of the engine reverberated through the quiet evening, causing Brian to wince at the thought of how much gasoline this monster must consume on a daily basis. But despite his concerns about fuel efficiency, he also felt a sense of pride at his son's impressive ride.

Dexter skillfully maneuvered the truck up the steep driveway to park, then used the built-in step ladder that unfolded when the door opened to gracefully climb out. As Dexter approached, Brian saw him wave and then go back to retrieve something behind the driver's seat.

Brian noticed his son put on more muscle each time he saw him. Brian also studied Dexter's truck. This was no ordinary vehicle –it was a true adventure-seeking machine, perfectly embodying Dexter's bold and adventurous spirit.

"You really went all out with this one, didn't you?" Brian teased as he walked down toward Dexter.

Dexter grinned mischievously and climbed back into his truck to retrieve one more thing. "But just wait until I tell you my plans for this baby," Dexter said with an excited gleam in his eye. He jumped down and walk toward his father. "I found a crashed Tesla and I'm going to swap the engine in this truck for a Tesla motor."

Brian smiled broadly at the thought of another car project. It had been years since they had worked on one together. "Let me know if you need any help."

Dexter turned to his father and burst into laughter. "Help? Are you kidding me? We're doing this in your garage!"

Brian let out a hearty laugh, mirroring the infectious joy of his son, Dexter. He felt proud as he remembered how quickly Dexter had breezed through his master's degree in electrical engineering, with a special focus on semiconductor AI designs –just like his father.

As they reached the bottom of the stairway leading to the house, Dexter handed a few items to his father and bounded back down the steps to his truck once again.

With effortless grace, Dexter pulled out a sleek laptop from a hidden compartment on the dashboard. It was the latest model from Apple, thinner than a notepad and shining with modernity. The rapid advancements in technology over the past two decades were astounding. Gone were the bulky machines with their clunky interfaces; now, everything could fit comfortably in the palm of one's hand.

Looking at the sleek laptop Dexter showed him, Brian marveled at how far laptops had come since their inception. No longer were they cumbersome devices that required large interfaces for human hands to operate; now, they were compact enough to fit on a wristwatch and still provide powerful capabilities.

Dexter walked with his father; his laptop tucked under his arm. As they ascended the stairs together, Dexter eagerly opened his laptop and turned it to show his father a complex display of circuitry and notes. The only two people who could truly understand the intricacies were looking at each other's reflections on the polished screen.

"See, I've been making improvements to my chip design," Dexter said with excitement evident in his voice.

His father's eyes sparkled with curiosity as they climbed the limestone stairs, their footsteps echoing throughout the house. Dexter enthusiastically shared every detail of his master's thesis improvements with his father, their conversation barely pausing as they made their way to the front door. They entered the familiar living room where Dexter had grown up, and he set his laptop down on the foyer table before kicking off his shoes.

Still talking animatedly about his breakthrough in artificial intelligence, Dexter retrieved sodas and sandwiches from the kitchen. They settled around a unique coffee table that doubled as a taller kitchen table thanks to Brian's genius addition of a small hydraulic cylinder. Over an hour of chatting and eating, Brian asked questions and Dexter eagerly responded, barely pausing to take bites of his sandwich or sips of his soda. Despite all the movement, Dexter remained focused on his exciting discovery. Finally, he paused, and Brian summarized, "That is truly impressive work," taking a bite of the sandwich prepared by Dexter himself.

"Thanks, Dad," replied Dexter, also taking a bite and causing a pickle slice to fall on the floor. Without missing a beat, he quickly cleaned it up and added, "I'm taking it to MAST Technologies."

Brian looked up with surprise and fixed Dexter with an intense gaze that caused an alarm in Dexter's body language. "Make sure you get the patent first."

"That's going to take too long," Dexter answered quickly. "Let's go to your lab. I want to show you something on the big screen."

Brian finished eating his sandwich and wiped the crumbs from the table while pressing the button to lower the table back down. The sound of the table's tiny pump resonated off the high ceiling of the living room. The table lowered and came to rest when clicking against its stopper. Brian said, "Lead the way."

The two moved quickly down the steps to the lowest level of the home, tucked behind the garage. Dexter noticed that the door leading to the parking area was slightly open and took it upon himself to shut it securely. His father stopped in front of his workbench and gave Dexter a nod, as if allowing permission to place the laptop down on the row of perfectly aligned video monitors situated behind the bench.

The black screens stood out against the rows of computers lining the back corner, connected by a long electronic wire mold that stretched along the twenty-foot-long bench. This was no ordinary garage workshop; Brian was no ordinary father. In addition to a section filled with mechanical tools for car repairs and small home projects, he had built an enormous lab into their house fifteen years ago.

Dexter strode confidently toward the large, high-tech workbench in his father's lab He carefully selected the necessary cables from a row of neatly organized computers and began connecting his laptop to his father's impressive system on his workstation.

"I'm going to transfer the design to your central bank," he informed his father. "That way, we have a backup of all the revisions in a safe spot. Your firewall is the best I've ever seen."

Brian looked pleased by Dexter's proposal, and with a slight blush of pride, he activated a section of his computer system and pulled out a keyboard. A monitor in front of him displayed each level of entry as he skillfully navigated through the system. Moving down the bench, he retrieved another keyboard and activated yet another screen.

Dexter watched intently as his father located the secure folder where his previous work remained behind an advanced firewall. With both men now ready to proceed, Dexter quickly typed away on his laptop while the distinct sound of clicking keys filled the air above the sophisticated air conditioning system that maintained the room's perfect temperature. He glanced at the light blue walls he'd painted with his mother after she commented that the rooms was too stark.

After a few moments of intense concentration, Dexter looked up at the large central monitor with a satisfied smile. Walking over to his exact copy of a father, he placed a hand on his shoulder and asked him to look closely. The two men stood tall and identical in their casual blue jeans and golf shirts, but their minds were uniquely different –Dexter was more defiant and risk-taking while his father was more calculating and precise. Dexter asked, "Do you notice anything in the chip?"

Brian moved closer to the screen, his eyes darting across the vast array of colorful circuits spread out on the very large monitor. He scratched his scruffy chin in thought before glancing at the mouse and taking hold of it to move the design to the right a bit. Then he held down the button and zoomed in on one section. "What is going on here in this segmented portion of the design?"

Dexter's smile widened as he replied, "That's the machine-learning section."

"Why is it cordoned off? Why not embed it with the rest of the decision matrix?"

Dexter grabbed the mouse and deftly moved in on a specific section. He pointed to the large video monitor and began explaining the intricacies of the decision-making process. "This is where the AI can determine if the decision should be sent to the cloud or kept resident on the chip. I call it AI PC design, which is a combination of artificial intelligence and personal computer technology."

Brian let the complexity of the design sink in and replied, "That would speed up the decisions, machine learning, as well as personalization of the intelligence."

Dexter's fingers flew over the touchpoints on the screen, his eyes focused and determined. With each tap, he revealed hidden copyright information. His father studied it intently, with a proud smile spreading across his face.

"Unless you know the sequence of the touchpoints, the copyright is impossible to find," Dexter explained. "If anyone steals my design, I can easily prove it by punching in this code."

His father leaned in closer, a conspiratorial gleam in his eye. He whispered while leaning in even closer to the screen, "This could be even better than a patent. You've created an embedded patent."

"That's exactly what Brad called it," Dexter said. He went on to describe how he and Brad Baumers had come up with the idea and worked out the bugs at their San Francisco apartment.

"How's he doing on his master's degree?" Brian asked, knowing that Brad was just as brilliant as his two parents but lacked discipline.

"Oh, he's doing fine," Dexter replied quickly, though a slight sideways glance betrayed some hidden knowledge about Brad's involvement in some shenanigans at school. No need to explain his friend's quirks or shortcomings to his understanding father. He would graduate in two years —only four years younger than Dexter.

Father and son, both immersed in their passion for technology, spent countless hours poring over every detail of their design. After a while, Dexter took a break to grab some beers for them to enjoy while they continued their work. His mother would often interrupt their intense lab sessions to remind them to take breaks and maintain a healthy balance between work and personal life. She expressed concern that their dedication could strain their relationships with others. Occasionally, they would follow her advice and take a breather upstairs.

"When do you start at MAST?" Brian inquired.

"I actually started last week," Dexter replied, having already accepted the position. He described his role and first assignment, which consisted of working on an inferior design compared to the one he had created and displayed on the video screen before them. "I showed it to one of my colleagues there."

"I'm not sure if that was a wise move," Brian commented, studying Dexter's face.

Dexter looked away and answered, "She's brilliant, Dad. Her name is Jyoti, and she's also working on AI chips."

"Jyoti Bandla?" Brian asked with a raised eyebrow, turning to his son, who seemed surprised by his father's knowledge.

"How do you know about her?" Dexter asked, taken aback.

Brian moved a keyboard aside and leaned against the workbench. "Sam Thomas is an old friend of mine who has been at MAST since day one. He mentioned this young prodigy named Jyoti. He says she's the best chip designer he'd ever seen –until now that is."

CHAPTER 34

A promise kept to continue old ways,
Generations entwined through countless days.

With a delicate touch, Jiewen carefully adjusted the position of Yu Chen Li's portrait behind the checkout counter at Li's Family Market. The portrait stood out among the older portraits with a modern metal frame she had chosen to honor her grandmother after her death only a few years ago. Jiewen vowed to replace all of the other older wooden frames holding the portraits of her ancestors who had run the market over the past eighty years.

Jiewen glanced down at the counter below and then began moving little figurines around to ensure that each row of grab items was neatly arranged for the customers. Her gaze then fell upon a row of lucky Maneko-Neko cats on display near the cash register. With their vibrant colors and waving paws, they were a symbol of good luck and prosperity. Jiewen found it ironic that these cats originated in Japan, not China. Despite this error, the little cat figures were incredibly popular among visitors to Chinatown from all over the world.

Unlike most Western cultures that view the cat's gesture as a wave, in Chinese culture, it is interpreted as beckoning someone with its palm facing forward and fingers pointed downwards. But for Jiewen, all that mattered was that she could sell these lucky cats like hotcakes to eager customers seeking some extra luck in their lives. The atmosphere of the market buzzed with energy as people browsed through the rows of products and mementos, drawn in by the rich history and deep-rooted traditions that filled every corner of the store.

A middle-aged woman with dark hair and a thick accent strolled past the colorful display of lucky cat figurines and said something undiscernible to

Jiewen. The woman's fingers grazed over each little cat as she made her way to the checkout counter, where Jiewen was waiting with a warm smile. The woman spoke slowly, her accent hinting at a possible Middle Eastern heritage. She picked up one of the lucky cats and handed it to Jiewen.

Jiewen used an equally measured voice as she assisted the customer with her purchases and demonstrated how to use the Apple checkout system when it came time to pay. As they finished the transaction, Jiewen noticed the imprint of an old cash register on the very spot where her grandfather used to collect payments for goods using a machine that sat there for twenty years. Shadows of the past, she thought as she ran her fingers over the subtle grooves on the wooden counter.

As the woman left with her bag of purchases, Jiewen looked up toward the top of the stairs and saw her father, Wei Guo, keeping watch over the store from his vantage point. She waved affectionately at him before turning back to tend to her duties.

"I'll be right up with some soup, Father," Jiewen called out before continuing her work with a sense of pride and nostalgia for the family business passed down for generations. It had been a tough decision to give up her banking career and take over the Li's Family Market, but this way she could keep the business in operation now that her parents had retired.

Wei Guo's gentle smile faded into a deep, raspy cough as he retreated to his room above the creaky stairs that led to the living quarters above Li's Family Market. Jiewen's expression revealed concern as she watched him depart. As she turned back to the store, she spotted Jay Baumers emerging from under the back staircase, wiping sweat from his brow and wincing with strain from lifting heavy boxes. He wore his usual attire of worn blue jeans and a short-sleeved dress shirt, remnants of his high-tech job before retirement.

Now in his sixties, Jay had faced discrimination due to his age at each new job he took, leading to frequent changes. But he had saved up enough money over the years to buy the neighboring building and now ran a bustling shipping department for Li's Family Market. The sales from online orders far surpassed those of in-person shoppers. But the bricks and mortar building provided legitimacy to the Chinese online business.

Jay's lips brushed against Jiewen's cheek in a loving gesture, but her worries consumed her thoughts. As they talked, Jiewen expressed her concern about her father's health, especially with the news of a new virus spreading rapidly.

"He's been coughing more lately," she confided to Jay, her voice filled with anxiety. His strong hands on her shoulders offered support, but Jiewen could not shake off the rising tide of fear within her.

"Try not to worry," Jay said confidently, his voice steady with conviction. "It's just a winter cold. Your father is strong, and he'll fight through this."

Jiewen's heart pounded in her chest as she voiced her fears, the words heavy with dread. "What if it's that new virus?" Her voice shook with fear as she imagined the worst. "People are dying from it in the hospitals."

Jay's face grew grim with worry, his mind racing as he considered the possibility. But then, a glimmer of hope appeared on his features as he revealed a secret plan. "I've been preparing for this," he confessed, determination evident in his voice. "I have an oxygen generator and filtration system ready if anyone gets infected. It just arrived at the warehouse."

A wave of relief washed over Jiewen as she realized Jay had already thought ahead and had a chance to protect them all, offering a glimmer of hope in a time when at-capacity hospitals were turning people away —with people dying in the parking lots awaiting admission.

With gratitude shining in her eyes, she reached out to squeeze his hand and pulled him in, her warm embrace conveying her appreciation. "Thank you," she whispered, her voice thick with emotion and her lips touching his ear. "Thank you for being here and looking out for us."

Just then, their son Bradley burst into the room carrying a large box, a smile lighting up his face as he caught his parents embracing behind the checkout counter. "Hey, get a room," he teased playfully.

Jay released his wife and poked Brad in the arm as Brad set the box on the counter. Jay took a knife and cut the top of the cardboard box, then peeled open the lid and the plastic wrapping of a brown, rectangular item that he gently lifted from the box. He nudged the item and shook it gently to release the plastic that tried to cling to it as he extracted the item clear of the cardboard box. Brad reached inside the box and retrieved a bag full of hoses and instructions as they explained the workings of the oxygen generator.

"This will only provide two cubic feet per minute of oxygen to the room, so we have to make the room airtight," Brad explained as he scanned the instructions quickly. He and his father had been working on the design of the safe room just as a precaution if someone started developing symptoms of the virus. They could quickly isolate somebody to keep it from spreading to the others. The safe room offered a similar environment to the hospitals, so if they had to wait for a hospital room, at least they would have an easier time breathing in an oxygen-rich isolation room in their own home.

Later up in the isolation room, Jay and Jiewen scrubbed the surfaces with a sense of urgency, their hands gripping the scrubbing pads and disinfectant spray bottle tightly until their knuckles turned white from the cleaner. Meanwhile, Brad huffed and puffed as he lugged boxes up the steep stairs, trying to keep up with his parents, who were racing against time. They knew Wei Guo had been displaying symptoms of COVID-19 and was scheduled for another round of testing. When Jiewen gently used a cotton swab to take a sample from deep inside her father's sinuses, they all shared a laugh as he joked about it feeling like she was scratching the back of his eyeball.

The tension in the air was unmistakable as they anxiously awaited the results, constantly checking the time and praying for a negative outcome. Luckily only the blue line of the control strip was all that showed up. Jiewen looked deep into the test section, double-checking to make sure they did not miss even the faintest of a taunting blue line that would reveal an infection.

Jay looked concerned as he double-checked the supplies in all the boxes that Brad delivered to the isolation room. "Did the filtration system arrive yet?" he asked Brad while passing by with another box, his voice echoing with a hint of anxiety.

Brad shook his head as he kept traveling up the stairs, his arms laden with more boxes. He saw his mother standing at the top of the stairs. "Not yet, Dad."

Jay went to the top of the stairs to embrace Jiewen, offering her a reassuring hug. His voice remained steady despite the uncertainty that lingered in the air. "It's going to be alright, Jiewen,"

She leaned into her husband's embrace, finding solace in his strong presence. "Let's get the room ready then, just in case," she murmured, her voice tinged with determination.

And so, they worked tirelessly, unpacking boxes and assembling the components of the isolation room according to Jay's extensive research. They used whatever supplies they could find, relying on Jay's connections with high-tech companies for testing kits and protective gear and Jiewen's resourcefulness in procuring essential building materials from neighboring businesses. They felt almost secretive while building a room they hoped they never needed.

Together, they meticulously sealed every crack, duct, and vent that could potentially allow the virus to spread, ensuring that the isolation room remained airtight. They installed the air exchanger that finally arrived in another shipment of supplies. It had a fresh air intake and exhaust system strategically positioned to minimize the risk of contamination while changing the air in the room eight times per hour.

In the anteroom they built in front of the isolation room, they carefully planned for the needs of whoever might be assisting the person in isolation, equipping it with disposable smocks, double masks, and face shields to prevent transmission of the virus. The person requiring assistance would not want their helper to get sick too. The stories they heard about entire families getting sick hung in the air like a fog.

Their preparation was thorough, a testament to their dedication and love for their parents, Wei Guo and Meiyu Li. As they added the final touches to the isolation room, a sense of grim determination settled over them with the thought of both of them getting sick and with only one isolation room. They knew the risks involved but were willing to do whatever it took to ensure the safety of their family. The news spoke about the hospitals filling up quickly and people waiting for two days to receive treatment, often dying in the hallways while the doctors and nurses scrambled to save as many as they could.

Once everything was in place, Jay and Jiewen stood back to survey their work, a mix of exhaustion and worry etched on their faces. Jiewen reached out to grasp Jay's hand, her eyes reflecting both fear and resilience. "We've done all we can," she said quietly, her voice unwavering. "Now we wait and hope nobody gets it."

Brad came into the isolation room and grinned at his parents. He walked over to the oxygen generator. "Let's start it up and see how she runs."

"Let'er rip," Jay replied and walked over to the rectangular box with a small water reservoir on the side. He bent down to look inside the plastic water tank and flicked his finger against the side to make the water inside move. He motioned for Brad to flip the switch and the box started a low rumble that vibrated the surface of the water, forming little waves across its top. At one end of the box, a small tube stuck out the end and a stream of highly oxygenated air pointed out into the room. Brad leaned down to the tube and inhaled, then stood up smiling.

DAVID LEE LUEDTKE

CHAPTER 35

Tension vibrates as people meet that night,
Two families, passing the torch with might.

The tension in the air was unmistakable as Yuze Li sat across from Jimmy Baumers in the dimly lit room above the bar serving as their meeting place. Jimmy dressed for the occasion with a golf shirt and jeans, while Yuze wore a business suit purchased for the occasion. This was a big event for him and his son.

Yuze's fingers drummed a nervous beat on the polished wooden table, his eyes darting around the space he had come to know so well over thirty years of working at the Top of the Tunnel bar. He couldn't believe that he and his son, Lawrence, were about to become the new owners, taking over from Jimmy who had purchased the bar three decades ago from its previous owner, Frank Renado.

For weeks now, Yuze and Jimmy had been discussing every detail of the transfer, poring over documents and negotiating terms. But tonight was different –tonight, they would finalize everything and officially pass the torch from one dedicated bartender to another. As they sipped on their drinks in silence, Yuze could feel his heart racing with both excitement and anxiety.

Breaking the silence, Jimmy finally spoke up. "I'll be honest with you, Yuze. This bar means everything to me. I've poured my heart and soul into it for thirty years, and I want to make sure that whoever takes it over will do the same." He fixed Yuze with a serious gaze. "Is Lawrence ready for that kind of commitment?"

Yuze met Jimmy's gaze confidently. "We both are," he replied firmly. "We promise to honor the legacy of this bar and carry on the traditions that Frank and you have established."

As they went over the details of the purchase, Jiewen Li Baumers, dressed in a gorgeous blue suit, quietly entered the room and took a seat at the table much as she had done when Jimmy bought the bar from Frank Renado. She pulled out a laptop and fondly recalled using a paper ledger last time. The screen came alive and revealed columns upon columns of numbers. Her long wool skirt swished against her calves as she walked, giving glimpses of her long and elegant boots. At age 59, she looked just as sexy as she had when she married Jimmy's brother. Now, she must help both of her families make this transition of ownership.

"Which pieces of equipment need replacing now?" Jiewen asked as she scanned through the columns from January 2019 to 2023 while forecasting the equipment purchases for the next four years. Yuze felt grateful for her help, knowing that her sharp mind and keen eye for detail would be invaluable in running the finances for the bar over the next four years.

They started with the refrigerators, which ran quietly in the corner of the kitchen. Then came the grills, clean as a whistle after Yuze kept vigilant in cleaning the continuous buildup of layers of grease and grime from the last ten years of use. Next were the dishwashing machines, their hoses leaking water onto the already wet tile floor.

But as they reached the end of the list, Jiewen paused before mentioning the walk-in refrigerator. It was by far the most expensive item on the list, but also the most crucial for keeping the bar up to health code standards. Yuze held his breath as he waited for Jiewen's and Jimmy's reaction.

Jimmy said, "This one is twenty-five years old and may be good for another ten years if you replace the compressors."

After much discussion and guidance from Jiewen, Yuze had saved up sixty percent of the sales price through hard work and living frugally. And his parents had given him a bit of their inheritance from Yu Chen Li's estate.

Jiewen and Yuze made their way through the dark, musty rooms of the Top of the Tunnel bar, laptop in hand. Yuze's eyes scanned every inch of the space, while Jiewen jotted down notes about each piece of furniture, fixture, or equipment they saw. Although Jiewen was happy the bar would stay in the family, she knew it was a difficult decision for Jimmy to sell the place.

Jimmy sat at the old kitchen table upstairs, overseeing the inventory process with trust. The room was small, with a single bed tucked into one corner and a small kitchen off to the side. He looked as if he recalled sitting in the opposite position all those years ago.

Jiewen and Yuze made their way to the main area of the bar, with Yuze carefully measuring each item with his eyes and verbally noting its value.

Shelves lined the walls, filled with odd trinkets and curiosities. A narrow hallway led to more rooms including restrooms, a pool room, and a storage space. In the back was a forgotten pile of memorabilia that was never put back up on display after the big earthquake in 1989.

Yuze and Jiewen retraced their steps, inspecting every inch of the bar area with keen eyes. The first floor was filled with natural wood fixtures, carefully crafted and stained to a deep mahogany hue. Jimmy and Yuze had personally refinished the bar top a decade ago, and the rich wood still gleamed under the soft lights. However, upon closer inspection, they noticed fresh nicks and scratches adorning the edges of the bar, evidence of a new generation of customers leaving their mark with their daily use. As they approached the dishwashing station at the rear of the bar, they saw a man diligently stacking glasses in the machine with intense focus. Without hesitation, Yuze playfully grabbed a bar towel and snapped it on the man's rear end, causing him to jump in shock. Jiewen looked on disapprovingly as her brother laughed loudly.

Young Lawrence Li frowned at his father and smiled at Jiewen. "Hi Aunt Jiewen." He bore a striking resemblance to Yuze, but his skin was lighter like his mother's. His hair was a lighter shade as well.

Lawrence turned to his father and gave him a knowing smirk. He rubbed his rear end lightly from the sting and said with amusement, "Real funny, Dad."

Feeling slightly guilty for going too far with his joke, Yuze went over to Lawrence and pulled him into a hug. The young man seemed satisfied with this show of affection from his father before returning to his task at hand. He was a little taller than his father and wore tight jeans that accentuated his athletic build. Already nearly thirty years old, Lawrence had been working with his father and gradually took over more and more of the managerial duties at the bar.

Yuze added, "You are never too old for a hug from your father."

Later while continuing the inventory, Yuze's dress shirt stuck to his back with sweat as he walked back into the break area upstairs again. Jimmy sat at the main table by himself, looking over old inventory logs on a laptop as Yuze and Jiewen joined him.

"I think we got everything now," Yuze said as he offered a chair to Jiewen. She set the laptop on the table for everyone to see and slid gracefully into the chair. She moved the ledger for Jimmy to see the total at the bottom.

"Thirty years," Jimmy said and turned with a smile to Jiewen. "Just like you said, this place tripled in value."

"This was a great investment, Jimmy," Jiewen replied and smiled kindly while pointing at some numbers on the laptop. She looked over at Yuze and said flatly, "If you handle it well, this will triple again by 2050."

"If I can just get through the first few years, I think I can make it work, then I will turn it over to Lawrence to run." Yuze patted Jimmy on the shoulder and stood up to retrieve a tea just delivered by one of the new bartenders.

"I'll help you just like Frank helped me," Jimmy said in return. "Plus, Lawrence does half of your job already."

Jiewen stood up and kissed Jimmy on the cheek. "I'll get all this entered into the spreadsheet at the bank and have the loan agent finish drawing up the papers tomorrow."

Yuze stood in a chivalrous way as Jiewen left the table. He thanked her and said, "I appreciate what you are doing for your family."

Jiewen smiled and patted her heart as she locked eyes with her younger brother. "For our families."

The noise from the TV downstairs grew louder and more urgent, interrupting their conversation. The newscaster's voice echoed throughout the house, announcing an imminent broadcast from the Center for Disease Control, the CDC. The name Dr. Fauci was on everyone's lips as the three of them moved downstairs and gathered around the television, anticipating the announcement about the looming pandemic.

As they listened to the familiar voice of the newscaster, they exchanged worried glances in silence. Dr. Fauci urged people to start wearing masks in public places and spoke with a sense of urgency that conveyed the seriousness of the situation. This was not just another flu season; this was something far more sinister.

The word "pandemic" hung heavy in the air, causing a collective shiver among those listening. As Dr. Fauci spoke to the nation about the growing situation, the severity of it became painfully clear. It was like a punch to the gut when they heard that COVID-19 was quickly spreading across the globe. They were facing a crisis unlike any other.

Yuze suggested buying masks for protection and wondered why the CDC had decided to add the number, "19" to the virus's name, as if there would be more versions of it and keeping track of names and the year of its discovery would become increasingly necessary.

CHAPTER 36

Once bustling, now still, each night and each day;
Friends meet, yet remain apart in dismay.

The once bustling Top of the Tunnel bar now seemed abandoned. A few lone customers occupied tables scattered throughout the space, all following the six-foot distancing rule recommended by the CDC. Despite it being a Saturday night, many had chosen to stay at home instead. Tonight, it was Lawrence Li running the bar in place of Yuze, who finally had a rare evening off. Yuze had gone to visit his family's home in Chinatown to spend time with his parents and sister Jiewen. As Lawrence wiped down the counter with a smile, he felt grateful for this moment —his first time managing the bar alone since officially taking over ownership with his father from Jimmy Baumers on February 28, 2020, just a few weeks prior.

The sun had already set, casting a dim light through the windows of the front of the bar. Daniel Kim, still sharp and stylish at sixty, arrived first and took a seat at the back table, polished with a new wooden top. He wore his signature ensemble of blue jeans, a golf shirt, and a blue sport jacket —a throwback to his successful days as a hip executive in the 90s. Retirement from Sequoia Capital hadn't slowed him down; he now spent his time casually investing in local startups. One of which had already hit the billion-dollar mark in just one year.

Daniel's eyes widened as he caught sight of Charles Kang, his oldest friend from the early days, walking toward him from the far end of the quiet bar. He smiled and stood up to greet him warmly with a strong handshake. After exchanging pleasantries, they both waved at Lawrence, who was busy mixing drinks behind the counter.

As they settled in at a table near the window, Daniel gestured for his usual drink –a smooth bourbon on the rocks. Despite their jam-packed schedules, Daniel and his wife, Suzan Bolstock, remained a strong and ambitious couple who constantly researched new investments and opportunities to grow their wealth. They often traveled together for both business and pleasure, but due to the looming pandemic, their plans were now on hold temporarily. "Suzan wanted me to pass along her regards," Daniel mentioned casually as he picked up a coaster to fiddle with while waiting for his drink. "She thought it would be nice for us guys to have a night out on our own."

Charles let out a hearty chuckle, "Well, someone certainly takes orders well."

Unlike Daniel, Charles had never been married and still maintained a fit physique that resembled that of a Polynesian gym rat. He even added Polynesian tattoos on both forearms. His success in the software industry, along with smart investments, allowed him to live a life of luxury by himself. He enjoyed his alone time and cherished moments spent with only a select few friends.

"At least I manage to leave my cave every once in a while," Daniel playfully retorted, causing Charles to laugh even harder. Daniel patted Charles on his shoulder. "What? Getting groceries and hanging out here is your life now?"

"Sometimes I go see Jorge too," Charles added and laughed more. "And that's about all these days."

"What a life," Daniel surmised and asked about the welfare of their friend Jorge, who had moved back to the Central Valley after retiring from his job at the cable car company. The two men chatted and drank their cocktails for a while when the remaining two members of the group came in. Jay Baumers approached first, looking tall and thin with his hair cropped closely. Brian Lomax followed, wearing his standard blue jeans and golf shirt. He also wore a blue surgeon's mask that covered his nose and mouth. Daniel and Charles looked at Brian and stared at the mask.

Jay went to the bar and said hello to his nephew, Lawrence, and asked how he was doing and how his father was doing. Jay kept an eye out for his friends at the table in the corner. Brian walked directly to the table where Charles and Daniel sat. Charles leaned back in his chair, taking a sip of his beer. "Why are you wearing that?" he asked Brian, eyeing the mask on his face.

"Just a precaution," Brian replied. He adjusted the nose piece that contained a small piece of metal to cinch across the nose for a tighter fit, and then he pulled at the straps to adjust the uncomfortable mask. "The CDC recommends we all start wearing the masks in public places now."

Daniel nodded while setting down his drink. "Looks like they're closing down non-essential businesses, too."

Charles added, "Just as long as they don't close the bars. Otherwise, I'll never get out of the house."

As they surrounded the table, their initial light-hearted chatter quickly shifted to more serious discussions. The looming threat of the pandemic hung heavily in the air, casting a shadow over their normally carefree conversations. Despite their efforts to keep the conversation on lighter topics, thoughts of the growing crisis continued to creep into their minds and words.

"Joanne has me wiping down our groceries before bringing them inside," Brian added, his voice tinged with urgency. "I have a table and all the cleaning equipment set up in my garage."

"It's unbelievable," Jay mused, "that we have to be afraid of touching things that other people may have touched."

"And wearing gloves everywhere, too?" Charles shook his head in disbelief. "This is all so bizarre."

The group fell into a hushed conversation, their voices betraying their anxiety as they discussed the current situation and the possibility of an extended lockdown. Brian's expression grew somber as he shared news from the hospital. "Joanne had more deaths at the hospital yesterday," he said quietly, causing everyone to pause and take a deep breath. "She said that patients are fighting the virus until their bodies just give out. Even with oxygen pumped into their masks."

A weight settled over the group as they all looked down at their drinks, unable to shake off the heaviness of reality. They wondered how long this nightmare would continue and if there was any hope for an end in sight.

Jay looked at his best friend and asked, "Aren't you afraid of Joanne catching the virus?"

Brian replied, "Of course I am. But Joanne said she is very careful and wearing double masks and a face shield." He remained quiet as the others listened intently. "I'm surprised she can even breathe in all that gear."

The front door of the bar opened and in walked Greet and Liz, who saw the men sitting together and walked directly toward them. Greet carried a large plastic turtle to add to their growing menagerie on their front porch. They exchanged pleasantries, and Brian pulled up two more chairs to sit around the table with his friends.

"This one reminds me of the one I had in Belgium," Greet explained while Liz rolled her eyes and smiled. Greet noticed the silent gesture and added, "It will fit with the others, I promise."

Liz chuckled and replied, "Only if we move Deery to the living room."

The men all laughed and shared stories of which plastic animal was their favorite. The last time everyone got together in Liz and Greet's new apartment on Nob Hill in San Francisco, the drinks and camaraderie ended up with a race around the expansive deck with each person pretending to ride one of her plastic pets. A little duct tape and some glue repaired the only injury when a collision occurred during a sharp turn in the race track.

Greet held on to her new turtle dearly and pointed her finger at each of the men. "Nobody is riding my turtle, is that clear, everyone?"

CHAPTER 37

Isolated and alone, locked away,
No more meetings or work, just home to stay.

Sturdy table legs and a worn plastic surface bore the weight of a spray bottle of antiseptic, a roll of heavy-duty paper towels, and a box of disposable gloves at the entrance of Brian's garage. He had one chair pushed in under the table and one chair set off to the side of the driveway in case anyone came by to visit and could still maintain the proper social distancing space as recommended by the health department. The air was thick with the sharp scent of disinfectant as he carefully donned a mask and blue latex gloves, preparing to extract the groceries from the open trunk of his sleek Tesla.

Each item received its own individual treatment, a thorough spray and wipe down before being set on the side table to dry. The Center for Disease Control guidelines recommended waiting at least two hours before bringing any items into the house, but Brian still felt overly paranoid and careful. As he stood straight to stretch his back, he caught sight of his neighbor doing the same routine at his house across the street. They exchanged tired waves, a shared understanding born out of both camaraderie and fear in these uncertain times.

Brian toiled at the laborious spraying, wiping, and setting aside each item to dry. Out of the corner of his eye, he caught sight of Dexter's luminous blue jeep coming up the steep road leading to the driveway. The jeep no longer had a thunderous roar to its engine, so when Brian glanced at the jeep moving in silence, he felt like he was watching a silent film. The jeep pulled to a stop at the bottom of the driveway and Dexter climbed down from the tall vehicle and stepped foot on the ground where he stood and stretched his tall and muscular body —evidently weary from a long drive.

"Hey, Dad," Dexter yelled out through a mask he just fitted over his face. He walked up the steep driveway and stopped ten feet short of his father where he pantomimed a hug. His father returned the air hug and smiled through his own face mask. Dexter asked, "How are you, father?"

"Amazed," Brian replied and pointed at the jeep. "You got some work done, I see. That is a stunning transformation."

"Nothing else to do during the lockdown," Dexter explained and described in detail how he replaced the large combustion engine with the motor from a crashed Tesla he was able to buy for cheap. It took him two weeks every night after work. "The hard part was running the controls to a new computer interface I've been working on with Jyoti and Brad."

"Jyoti is helping you, too?" Brian inquired, suspecting there was more to the story.

"I just dropped her off at the airport. She's going to stay with her parents in Bangalore until this is all over." Dexter had a look of worry on his face and tried to behave nonchalantly after delivering the news.

Brian realized his son had fallen head over heels in love with Jyoti in the past two months, but what he didn't know was that they were really a couple now. Brian asked if she would still be able to work remotely while in India.

"Yes, she is going to work nights there, so she is on the same time zone as here," Dexter explained as he moved toward the chair set to the side. He sat down and looked awkwardly at his father who was carefully spraying down each of the grocery items. They discussed the pandemic as most everyone did these days now that the State had ordered all non-essential services closed. People began to feel more and more isolated –and more people died with the hospitals at full capacity and seemingly no cure for the virus. Dexter asked, "How's Mom doing?"

"She's exhausted," Brian replied promptly with a worried look on his face. He explained how she felt in danger of jeopardizing his own life so she now stayed in the guest room so she could remain isolated from him and not spread any potential sickness to him. He also explained how the life seemed to be draining away from deep inside her. She looked sad and lonely, and there was nothing he could do about it. The hours were incredibly long.

"She should get out of there, Dad," Dexter exclaimed forcefully. "She's risking her own life!"

Brian thought about that statement and went back to work spraying down the plastic on a loaf of sliced bread. "I already suggested that, but she said she has a responsibility to all of those people lying there and suffering all alone."

Dexter protested and threatened to call his mother and tell her so, but then another car pulled up behind Dexter's jeep and out popped Brad Baumers with a black briefcase. He wore shorts and a tee shirt as if he had just finished a workout.

"Hello, Mr. Lomax!" Brad called out as he walked up the driveway. He called out to Dexter, too, and marched up the driveway toward the other two men at the cleaning table. He stopped about six feet short of Dexter and gently tossed him the briefcase. "Here ya go. The first sample chips from MAST."

Dexter's eyes went wide, and he eagerly flipped open the briefcase by pushing both releases at the same time. Brian stopped what he was doing and moved a little closer while Dexter retrieved a bright white plastic container about two inches long. Barely visible through its translucent cover, a very small black square stood out in contrast to its white background.

Dexter held it up and showed it to his father. "This is the first AI chip with memory stored inside the chip with a multi-directional output. This baby can decide if it should send its machine learning to the cloud or keep it resident on the computer."

Brian asked question after question about the workings of the chip. Brad added some color to the answers when it came to the manufacturing process, which seemed to be a bright spot in Brad's interests. While Dexter focused on the designs of the chips, Brad figured out a way to make them. His recent employment at MAST already showcased his talents.

"I'm going to try this out in my jeep as a test case," Dexter explained as he unconsciously walked some of the way toward the jeep as he explained his strategy. "This is called an AI PC chip because most of the machine learning is held on its own motherboard instead of translating to the internet and then back to the chip after logging the learnings."

Brad looked at Brian Lomax as if he were a father figure and added to the plans for the jeep. "That way, whatever traffic and roads the jeep learns will be stored in the jeep instead of the cloud –and it will match exactly to how Dexter drives. Jyoti helped with the transition language we used in the design. I did the manufacturing run to create one wafer full of these chips. We got fifteen chips off the first wafer."

Brian stopped what he was doing and asked a few questions about how MAST was managing this side project. He knew the costs of making such a test wafer were staggering and he knew that it would not be done without senior management approvals. "How did you get the funding?"

"Sam Thomas," Dexter stated flatly.

"Of course," Brian replied. "He's a risk-taker."

"He said any son of Brian Lomax was like a son to him, so he personally spearheaded the funding for us."

Brad watched with pride and added one more piece of news. "And DARPA funded the whole thing."

Brian looked at both of the young men as they explained how the whole funding and approvals process went. He listened to how the president of the company himself wanted to review the design and how the project became the center of attention. Brian waited for the men to finish the story. He looked at them and said, "Let me guess. The man from DARPA. His name is Dr. Phillip Burnett, right?"

The men exchanged glances. Dexter was the first to ask. "How would you know that?"

Brian explained how the same man was involved in several of his own key projects, too. "That man came into my life three times. And all three times I went to a new company at his urging."

Dexter and Brad asked question after question, but Brian had very little information about the mysterious person from DARPA.

"I worked on the 100mm to 300mm wafer projects as I moved from National Semiconductor to Apple Computers. I worked at Apple for five years before we perfected the computer chips."

"How did you get to Tesla then?" Dexter asked his father. The three men stood awkwardly apart in their new normal of social distancing. It looked like three coaches discussing a game strategy at center court.

"Dr. Burnett urged me to work on autonomous driving that Tesla began to develop," Brian explained and went back to spraying his groceries, one piece at a time. He stopped and looked up at the two young men. "You know he also guided the funding, and Daniel Kim followed that money and it made him a rich man."

CHAPTER 38

Inside their homes, the people stand and fight,
Against the illness with all of their might.

Jiewen carefully smoothed the sheets on the bed in their makeshift isolation room, located on the third floor of their family's market. She had just finished setting up the room according to Jay's instructions —a precaution they both agreed on in case anyone in their family started showing symptoms of COVID. It was a scary thought, but Jiewen knew it was better to be prepared.

Jay had researched and read about how quickly the virus could spread within a household, with whole families falling ill one by one. That's why he insisted they have an isolation room ready and equipped with all the necessary supplies. Jiewen shivered at the thought as she gazed out the window, three stories above bustling Chinatown. The world seemed to stand still as she imagined the worst-case scenario. The street below looked nearly abandoned because almost every store on the block remained closed as a non-essential business. Each store tried to sell products from their sidewalk but very few people emerged from their homes in such a dire state of the pandemic.

But Jay had thought of everything —there were wet wipes, paper towels, face masks, and even disposable bunny suits that he had taken from one of his clients at a semiconductor manufacturing business. They also had access to at-home COVID testing kits, although they were uncomfortable and painful. Still, it was better to know if someone had been exposed early on rather than risk infecting the others in the household.

As Jiewen tucked in the final corner of the bed covers, she said a silent prayer that no one in her family would need this room. But if they did, she hoped it would provide them with the early treatment that may be hard to come by at overcrowded hospitals. Her friend Joanne had told her horror stories of bodies lining hospital corridors for hours, with some of them dying there, then being moved to refrigerated trucks in the parking lots, as funeral homes turned away grieving families due to restrictions on gatherings. It was a grim reality that Jiewen hoped she would never have to face.

The room was small but clean, with a large window that let in the warm afternoon sunlight. On the window sill sat the air exchange device. A small table below held the brown oxygen generator with its reservoir of water prepared and ready. The walls were painted a soft yellow, and a colorful quilt hung on the wall opposite the bed. Jiewen had bought the quilt on her last trip to the market down the street, hoping to add some cheerful touches to the otherwise austere room.

She ran her fingers along the edge of the quilt, feeling the intricate stitching and admiring the vibrant colors. A small smile tugged at the corners of her mouth as she thought about how much her mother loved this quilt when she showed it to her before hanging it up. She had always loved bright colors and patterns, and Jiewen had inherited that love from her.

Jiewen walked downstairs to the shop floor and heard Jay in the backroom moving shipping boxes around. They closed the market interior as instructed when the health department decided they were not an essential business because the majority of their income now came from the shipping department with online sales. For those neighbors that still shopped for their daily food at Li's Family Market, Jay had constructed more exterior food bins and even moved several refrigerators outside so they could sell milk and meats curbside. They even set up a tea service and handed out delicious tea in disposable cups they distributed to people standing a safe distance apart in front of the store —normally a practice that people would shun but now embraced.

Jiewen adjusted her face mask and checked the time on her phone before heading upstairs to check the COVID test she had just administered to her father fifteen minutes ago. He had been running a slight fever and had started coughing more frequently, so she decided to use one of their precious testing kits just to be safe. Her father always hated when she gave him the test —the long plastic wand with a cotton swab at the end had to be pushed all the way to the back of his nasal cavity, and then she had to carefully mix the contents with a small pen-shaped syringe. After flicking her finger against the syringe to ensure proper mixing, she then deposited three drops into the designated spot on the testing cartridge and set it on the counter.

As she passed by her father's room, Jiewen greeted him with a simple "hello." The sound of his labored breathing didn't go unnoticed as she made her way to the counter where she placed the test cartridge. Two spots caught her attention on the indicator: one labeled with a capital "C" and a straight blue line, confirming that the cartridge was functioning correctly, and the other marked with a capital "T," representing the test marker. In all of her previous attempts, this second spot remained empty, but not this time. She held the cartridge up to the light to make sure she wasn't imagining anything as the sudden realization set in that her father's life was in jeopardy. She sat down and her shoulders slumped over. Sitting quietly to collect her thoughts, she formulated a plan of action.

Jiewen walked quickly past her father's room and took the stairs two steps at a time. She rounded the corner at the bottom of the steps and practically flew into Jay's arms when she bumped into him as soon as she entered the stockroom. She showed Jay the COVID test and said her father's name.

Jay took the cartridge and held it up to the light to confirm for himself. He thought inwardly for a moment. "We have to get him into isolation right away. Let's get the room ready right now."

"I finished it up a little while ago," Jiewen replied and burst into tears, slumping into Jay's arms while also setting the contaminated cartridge on a nearby counter. Although worried for her father, she also worried for herself, Jay, and Bradley, who all had been in contact with Wei Guo recently. She suddenly thought about her mother, Meiyu Li, who spent nearly every moment with her husband.

First, they must get Wei Guo into the isolation room and turn on the oxygen generator and filtration system. The family must follow strict isolation protocols to keep the virus spreading to the others. And they must watch for signs of deterioration with her father or they would have to get him to the overly crowded hospital where people went to die.

Jiewen and Jay donned their masks and each added a facemask over the whole ensemble. Then Jay unfolded two long bunny suits with a long zipper that closed over their chest. He pulled the zipper open and handed it to Jiewen, who sat down and slid her long slender legs into each bunny suit legging, then she stood up and zipped up the closure, then added blue plastic gloves. Jay followed closely with the same procedure. They paused and looked at each other through their Personal Protective Equipment, or PPE as everyone had become accustomed to calling them.

"I'll take father and you take mother," Jiewen instructed. Both suddenly thought about the possibility that more of the family members had already contracted the deadly disease. They began walking up the stairs and Jiewen instructed Jay to give her mother, Meiyu Li, a COVID test to make sure.

They approached her father's door and Jiewen went inside. Her father looked shocked at seeing a big white alien enter his room. But he instantly recognized Jiewen's eyes through the mask and then looked dejected as he surmised what it meant.

"Does anybody else have it?" Wei Guo asked, more concerned for his family's health than his own. He paused and added, "Meiyu Li?"

"No, father," Jiewen replied and went to help her father up from the bed. He coughed badly as he stood up, with sweat appearing on his forehead. She knew she must remember to begin monitoring his temperature as her friend Joanne suggested. They must get him to the oxygen generator until they figured out what to do.

Meanwhile, Jay escorted his mother-in-law to the other isolation room, although it did not have the air exchange system, an oxygen generator, or the anteroom. They had hoped they would only need one room if someone contracted the disease.

Meiyu Li asked about her husband repeatedly and Jay did not know what to tell her. Finally, she stopped him in the hallway before entering the third-floor stairwell. She held his shoulders through the bunny suit. "Tell me Jay what is wrong with my husband of fifty years."

Jay felt the woman's grip on his arms and realized that someone must tell her sooner or later. He shrugged and she let go.

"Jay. Tell me."

"He has COVID-19. He must go to the isolation room to protect us all."

CHAPTER 39

They gaze upon the bar, once full and bright,
Now cloaked in silence, swallowed by the night.

Yuze Li looked out at the now-empty bar that used to be a vibrant after-work hangout spot. An eerie stillness now replaced the once lively and cheerful atmosphere as the sun set outside. The neon lights that used to cast a bright glow through the windows sat unplugged, a somber contrast to the energy that used to radiate from within.

Beside him stood his son Lawrence, with both of them wearing N-95 masks as protection against the invisible threat that had caused their restaurant to temporarily close its doors. Despite the gloomy scene, a small group of devoted customers had ventured out to support Yuze and Lawrence by ordering take-out food during the mandated lockdown. It was their way of showing support and also a chance to see other people after being confined at home for so long.

Daniel Kim, a regular member of their group, joined the others with a mix of sorrow and determination in his eyes. Despite the challenges they faced, there was a strong sense of solidarity among them, bonded by the shared understanding of the difficulties ahead. They told jokes and tried to make the best of a dire situation while standing on the sidewalk out front.

Liz, now a retired health inspector who used to be an authoritative figure in their world, took comfort in the company of those she had once policed. Standing among them, she served as a reminder of the unprecedented times they were living in. She and Greet chose the Top of the Tunnel bar as a place they would support through however long the pandemic would last.

Together, the regulars stood within marked circles on the sidewalk, carefully measuring out six feet between each other to follow social distancing

193

guidelines. Lawrence moved gracefully among them, ensuring their cups were full and everyone was comfortable, while also keeping a watchful eye for any authorities that could shut down even this small part of their business. With only one LP gas heater, it felt nearly impossible to keep everyone warm. It was like trying to warm the earth with a single heater.

The smell of disinfectant hung heavy in the air as Yuze and his workers moved about, wiping down the front door handles and railings of the walkway that spanned the top of the Stockton Street tunnel. In the kitchen, the sound of exhaust fans hummed overhead, a constant reminder of the need for fresh air in these enclosed spaces. The cooks and dishwashers all wore double masks to keep them alive while trying to support their own families.

But despite the eerie silence of the street, there was an undeniable energy radiating from this makeshift gathering. In the face of adversity, they had found camaraderie and strength, united in their determination to survive.

As night fell and the city lights flickered on in the distance, they continued to share stories and laughter, refusing to let fear control their spirits. For in this moment, they were bound together by resilience and hope, reminding each other that even in the darkest of times, humanity prevails. And so, they lingered outside the bar, talking and snacking on the bar food that Yuze's kitchen prepared. As each person left with a bag of ordered food, they felt a strong bond with their friends.

Daniel stood six feet from Liz and set his plastic cup on the railing of the walkway while he bit into his chicken sandwich. He chewed for a while and then looked at Liz. "I'm going to support Yuze by taking as much of my food orders as I can to this place."

"Me too," said Liz and glanced back to the front door at Lawrence who had just delivered an order to someone else down the street. "They work so hard and I'm afraid it may not be enough."

CHAPTER 40

Death's cold grip lingers in each somber space,
As sorrow echoes in this haunting place.

As she moved through the hospital corridors, Joanne's eyes stung from the sharp scent of disinfectant mixed with a hint of fear. She wore wrinkled and stained scrubs with her hair pulled back into a tight bun to keep it out of the way. She wore an N-95 mask over the top of a surgical mask as well as a full clear facemask that covered her entire face. The doctors and nurses felt as if they were in a war zone.

She felt the eerie tension that hung heavy in the air, a constant reminder of the invisible enemy, COVID-19, they were all fighting against. Every room overflowed with patients struggling to breathe, their cries and wheezes creating a haunting symphony that echoed through the halls. A row of the dead lined the hallway while they awaited room in the refrigerated trucks outside in the parking lot. The temporary morgue had become an assembly line of incoming dead that replaced the bodies sent to morgues around the city.

Joanne's face looked determined as she made her rounds, checking on each patient and adjusting IV lines and oxygen masks. But despite her tireless efforts, too many lost their fight against the virus, leaving a trail of heartache in their wake. The sounds in the hallways were so strange. There were no family members, only doctors, nurses, and dying patients.

She knew the risks all too well, but refused to falter in her duty. She had a job to do, and lives to save, even if it meant putting her own life on the line. The camaraderie she felt with the other staff felt as if they were doing battle together. As the days wore on and her exhaustion grew, she pushed forward with unwavering determination –barely finding time to travel to her home and sleep in her lonely bed in the guest room. The risk of contaminating her husband and son was far too great, so she became a ghost in the house and only communicated with her family across large distances.

But one evening, after a particularly grueling shift, Joanne could no longer ignore the weight in her chest or the shortness of breath that troubled every inhale. Her colleagues noticed her worsening condition and gently guided her to a secluded room usually reserved for critically ill patients. They administered a COVID test and that evil second blue line showed that she had contracted the disease.

As the medical team bustled around her, preparing an oxygen tank by her bedside, Joanne's heart sank as she came to the realization that she was now one of them —a patient in her own hospital, battling against the very enemy she had devoted her life to defeating. The fear and uncertainty on the faces of her colleagues were reflected in her own thoughts, as she wondered how long she could fight this relentless illness.

Her mind drifted to Brian, her beloved husband, and the pain she would bring him with news of her condition. She couldn't bear the thought of seeing his worry etched on his face, or the fear that would surely be mirrored in his eyes. She loved him with every fiber of her being, and now she questioned whether it was fair to put him through this ordeal.

As Joanne struggled for each breath, the weight of the virus bore down on her chest like a heavy weight, suffocating and oppressive. It felt as though an invisible hand was squeezing the life out of her with every labored inhale. Her lungs burned with searing pain as if they were being scorched from within.

Fear gripped her heart as she fought against the unrelenting onslaught of symptoms. The once familiar rhythm of her breaths had been disrupted by harsh coughing fits, each one feeling like a violent attack on her already weakened body. Sweat drenched her brow and mingled with tears streaming down her face as she grappled with the terrifying reality of what was happening.

Every movement became an ordeal, as her body grew weaker with every passing moment. Simple tasks such as lifting an arm felt like moving a heavy weight, while her muscles protested with every effort. Nausea churned in the pit of her stomach, threatening to overwhelm her as waves of dizziness washed over her.

But still, she fought on. Her will to survive burned bright within her, fueled by the hope that somehow, someway, she would emerge victorious from this battle. Yet, as time passed and her body continued to betray her, a nagging fear crept into her mind —what if this was a fight she couldn't win?

Through all of the pain and struggle, Joanne refused to give up. Even as her body began to shut down, her spirit remained unbroken. With every ounce of determination she could muster, she pushed forward, refusing to surrender to the darkness that threatened to consume her. For in the depths of her struggle, she found a glimmer of hope, a flicker of light that reminded her that even in her darkest hour, she was not alone.

With a heavy heart, Joanne resolved to find the strength to have this difficult conversation with Brian. But for now, she focused on drawing in each precious breath, holding on to the hope that somehow, someway, she would emerge from this battle victorious. Each breath was difficult but she knew it was a marathon, not a sprint.

DAVID LEE LUEDTKE

CHAPTER 41

Amid turmoil and some people's health dire,
They soldier on for what customers desire.

Jay and Jiewen worked tirelessly day and night, their days merging into nights as they urgently shipped products from Li's Family Market to maintain some form of income in order to support their family. They also had the added responsibility of caring for both of her parents isolated on the third floor of their market.

Despite the chaos of the outside world and their father's illness, they continued to run their food stand at the market with firm dedication. They were proud to see their regular customers continue to support their struggling business. There was a slight increase in online orders as more people stayed home due to the pandemic, but it hardly made up for the loss of in-person sales at the market. With COVID-19 present in their household, they could not risk exposing their remaining employees to the virus. It fell upon Jay and Jiewen, along with occasional help from their son Brad, to manage both their home and business.

But upstairs, Jiewen demanded that Meiyu Li and her husband Wei Guo remain separate in isolation rooms that they had hastily constructed. Wei Guo's condition deteriorated with each passing day, his struggle for air becoming more desperate despite the help of an oxygen generator. His once strong body was now frail and weakened by the relentless virus. The coughing was endless and his fever began climbing.

Meiyu Li could only watch helplessly from the doorway as her husband's fever spiked, tears streaming down her face with each labored breath he took. She longed to hold him close, but fear of the deadly virus kept them apart. Wei Guo could only shout for her to stay away, terrified of infecting her too. She occasionally smocked up in one of the bunny suits, wore two face masks and a face shield, and entered the room despite his protests. He was not too weak to be in control of his situation.

Jiewen became their caregiver, dressing in a full cleanroom suit with an N-95 mask and face shield to tend to her father. Her hands shook with love and desperation as she tried to ease his suffering.

Desperate and frantic, their pleas for help fell upon deaf ears as they tried to reach out to their friend Joanne Lomax, a dedicated nurse at the hospital in the East Bay. For some reason she would not pick up her cell phone calls. They assumed she was too busy in the hospital to take personal calls. They assumed the chaos of an overwhelmed healthcare system swallowed up their calls, leaving them with no guidance amidst the conflicting news reports.

Everywhere they turned, they heard stories of hospitals pushed beyond their limits by the relentless pandemic. They called repeatedly for an ambulance and when finally reaching a dispatcher, they told them it would be two days before one became available.

Left with no other options, they braced themselves for the daunting task of getting Wei Guo to the San Francisco Hospital. After lengthy discussions of how to transport him safely, they chose a delivery van and prepared the back of the van that normally held rows of food and boxes. They removed the storage shelves and erected a plastic barrier between the two rows of seats and the back of the van. They also added a wooden cot where they placed Wei Guo after dragging him like a rag doll down the stairs and out to the awaiting van.

Brad could not convince Meiyu Li to stay in her isolation room, so she sat in the second row of the van as the others helped place her husband into the cot in the rear of the van. She spoke words of comfort to her husband through the curtain. Her voice came through both masks and a face shield that Brad insisted she wear to protect not only herself, but also the others in case she had COVID and still had not tested positive. Finally, all four sat inside the van, looking like a hazardous response team in all their white bunny suits and face shields. They all glanced back at their father struggling to breathe while holding onto the bouncing makeshift bed.

Navigating through empty streets that once bustled with life, tension, and uncertainty riddled their journey. Time seemed to blur together as they pressed on, fueled only by their determination and finding the streets nearly empty of cars and pedestrians. It was almost like some sort of natural disaster wiped all the people from the earth.

Finally arriving at the hospital, a scene straight out of a nightmare greeted them. A line of cars stretched around the block, each one carrying a person fighting for their next breath. Hospital beds lined the emergency room entrance like somber statues, each one occupied by someone battling against the virus. The air was thick with despair and fear, a tangible reminder of the dire situation they faced. They circled the chaos and received threats and warnings from others in their cars not to cut the line.

Horns honked at them, and people gestured wildly at them for driving and pausing as they looked for an opening in the lines of cars. They realized they would have to get to the end of the line of cars and wait. Wei Guo's breaths had become alarmingly labored, prompting the family to consider taking him back to the isolation room at the market where they could at least provide him with oxygen.

A policeman observing them walked their van to the end of the line. He carried flags and riot equipment to signal his authority and directed traffic while speaking into the microphone attached to his lapel. He also carried an assault rifle slung over his shoulder.

After enduring several hours of waiting, they managed to navigate through the chaos and found themselves under the canopy of the emergency room entrance. Two attendants in full protective gear arrived to help them, and unloaded Wei Guo Chu onto a stretcher. They radioed in the status and rattled off the details that Jiewen offered about her father. The attendants seemed inured to the severe status Wei Guo displayed and said some sort of code status to the dispatcher inside, almost like a triage on a battlefield where the first attendants ranked the importance and severity of the incoming victims in order to prioritize the limited resources.

The attendants wheeled Wei Guo inside on a makeshift stretcher —an indication of the shortage of equipment. The entranceway echoed with moans and machines, an eerie symphony of suffering that threatened to crush their spirits. Clinging to each other for support, they watched helplessly as the attendants stopped the family from following them and rolled Wei Guo down a hallway and out of sight of the family. The security officer at the door told them that strict protocols meant their family could not accompany him.

As they stood outside the hospital entrance, hearts heavy with worry and sadness, they could only hope and pray that Wei Guo would receive the care he needed inside. An attendant handed them a piece of paper and told them they must leave instantly to allow others to bring their sick into the hospital.

CHAPTER 42

Father and son, beneath her window stay
Hoping and praying for a better day.

As the third day of their watch was nearly over, Dexter and Brian remained steadfast on the lawn below Joanne's window of the hospital. They kept their eyes fixed on her room, hoping for any sign of improvement or news from the hospital about her condition. Occasionally, someone walked by the window but did not even have time enough to look out the window. The two men sought solace in the only way they knew how and ended up creating a makeshift picnic on the grass as they waited. They laid out a blanket beneath them and used a small table covered with an array of snacks and drinks for any of their friends who stopped by to offer their support.

Despite their efforts, the lack of information from the hospital weighed heavily on their hearts. They could only hope that Joanne could sense their untiring love and support as she fought for her life inside. They phoned several of her associates at the hospital but received no return calls.

Passersby paused and took notice of the unusual scene. Some approached, curious about what was happening. With heavy hearts, Dexter and Brian explained the situation, their voices trembling with worry and fear. As word spread, sympathetic nods and offers of assistance came pouring in from their friends.

Dexter took on the role of runner, darting to the store whenever supplies ran low. He returned with bags filled with more food and water, his determination resolute as he did everything in his power to ensure his father remained comfortable during their vigil. The atmosphere was heavy with emotions, but Dexter refused to let it show –determined to stay strong for both his father sitting next to him and his mother inside a room on the second floor.

With each passing moment, Brian's desperation grew into a gnawing ache in his chest. He yearned to be by Joanne's side, to hold her hand and whisper words of comfort in her ear. Yet, every time he tried to enter the hospital, a stern policeman blocked his way with a unyielding expression. The officer turned away everyone except for hospital staff, tasked with maintaining order amidst the chaos that erupted within the walls.

Frustration boiled within Brian, his emotions threatening to spill over as he pleaded with the authorities to let him through. But their protocols remained unyielding, a necessary measure to prevent frantic loved ones from swarming the ward and overwhelming the hospital.

As the hours stretched into days, Dexter and Brian stood steadfast in their vigil, their unbreakable bond forged through adversity. Though separated by circumstance, their love for Joanne burned fiercely like an eternal flame, a beacon of hope amidst the darkness of uncertainty. And as they gazed up at her window, they silently vowed to never give up, to keep fighting for her until she emerged victorious from the clutches of the merciless disease.

One day, Dexter arrived later than normal to accompany his father and cheerfully revealed he had obtained one of his mother's nursing friend's cell phone numbers. He handed his phone to his father when the nurse answered the phone. Dexter pushed the phone toward Brian.

Brian looked timid but mustered up the courage. "Hello, this is Brian Lomax. Can you give us any information on my wife Joanne?"

The other end was silent as the person then began asking how he got this number and this was a private cell phone.

"Please," Brian asked. "Please tell me what is happening. We have been sitting outside her window for three days now."

The phone was silent again when suddenly, a nurse in full protective gear peered out the window and looked down at Brian and Dexter. They sheepishly waved to her.

"Oh my gosh," the voice said. "I wondered if that was you out there. Hang on just a second."

After a few moments, a familiar voice got on the other end and gasped for air as she tried speaking. Brian recognized the voice but was alarmed at the struggle evident in every breath. "I'm so sorry," Joanne said into the phone. A few heavy breaths later. "I'm so so sorry I let this happen to us."

"My God, Joanne!" Brian replied. "I'm so worried and nobody will give us any information! I didn't even know if you were alive!"

The sobs on both ends of the phone relayed their love and their worry as they poured out their feelings to each other. Dexter began sobbing too as he listened to his father plead. He reached down and picked up a few pebbles that lay around the ground nearby and he gently tossed them at the window some twenty feet higher. The startled nurse who helped them appeared shocked at the sounds of pebbles bouncing against the window. She seemed to understand, and Brian heard her tell Joanne that her husband and son were only a little way away from her.

Joanne began coughing so terribly that she could no longer speak. The phone remained active, and the two men could hear the sounds of attendants trying to help Joanne. Then the phone went dead.

Tears streamed down Brian's face as he clung to the instant hug after the phone call dropped, their bodies trembling with emotion. Across the parking lot, Dexter's electric jeep sat waiting, a symbol of hope in the midst of chaos.

"I can't do this anymore," Dexter choked out between sobs. "I'm done. Follow me. I have a solution."

Brian followed his son but kept asking questions that Dexter would not answer. "We are not leaving!" Brian finally yelled at his son while stopping. He grabbed Dexter's arm to hold him back.

"No, Dad. We're not leaving. We're going inside."

Confusion clouded Brian's expression, but they began walking toward the jeep again.

With a click of a button on his key fob, Dexter opened the front trunk of his jeep. Where once a gasoline engine resided, now lay a spacious storage area.

"But they won't let us in!" Brian exclaimed, frustrated by everything that was going on at the moment.

At that moment, Dexter reached inside the trunk and pulled out two yellow firefighter's jackets and matching bib overalls. He showed them to his father and said, "But they will let in the hazardous response team."

Brian's eyes widened at the sight of the yellow suits. "Where did you get those?" he asked incredulously.

A smile spread across Dexter's face as he pointed at a symbol, ERT, on the suit and replied, "I'm on the Emergency Response Team at MAST. Both Brad and me."

Dexter tossed one of the bib overalls to his father and draped the jackets across the hood of his jeep. They both slipped into the large yellow and black bibs and tightened the straps and adjustments to match their height and weight. Then the jackets and that's when Dexter reached inside the cavernous front trunk and retrieved two oxygen tanks and full breathing apparatuses. He even had the large black waterproof boots, full-sleeved gloves, and the plastic badges that identified them as part of the ERT.

Brian looked at the badges and glanced at Dexter. "But these say MAST Technologies."

Dexter paused for a moment and then reached inside his jeep to take something out of the door pocket. He looked at two business cards from the hospital and slid one of them into his MAST badge that covered the MAST name. He smiled and handed the other card to his father.

Dressed in full firefighting gear, with bulky breathing apparatuses obscuring their faces, the two Emergency Response Team members marched confidently toward the hospital's main entrance. All who witnessed their arrival heard the loud hissing of air through their face shields. As the two men approached the front door, they saw a police officer attempting to manage the chaos of multiple people trying to enter.

Without breaking their stride, Brian and Dexter saluted the officer, a silent but powerful gesture. Dexter spoke only three words as they passed by the officer: "Emergency Response Team."

The officer paused for a moment, taking in the gravity of the situation, before returning the salute. The ERT members continued on their mission without hesitation. Those waiting in line to enter the hospital quickly realized the severity of the situation and stepped back, giving way to Brian and Dexter so they could do their jobs.

The looming danger within the hospital was palpable, causing a sense of unease among those present. But Brian and Dexter remained focused and determined as they entered the building, ready to face whatever lay ahead. Their first bluff was over, so now to the nurse's station where they would repeat the march through until they could get all the way into Joanne's room.

CHAPTER 43

A woman gasps, her eyes fixed on the screen,
Numbers blink death's edge, a sight too well seen.

As Joanne lay there, struggling for each breath, her gaze shifted toward the small oxygen sensor affixed to the side of her bed. The blinking numbers on the monitor revealed near-fatal levels, a hauntingly familiar sight. Over the past few months, she had guided over a dozen people through the same agonizing process, and each journey had ended in death. It was a relentless march toward the inevitable, a cruel reminder of the limits of modern medicine and care. The COVID-19 pandemic had proven unstoppable, a menacing force threatening humanity's very existence unless scientists could invent a miraculous vaccine swiftly.

In her weakened state, Joanne's mind drifted to her husband, Brian, who had spent countless hours sitting in a lawn chair outside her window. Her fellow attendants constantly reassured her that he was still there, offering his undying support. But Joanne longed to see him for herself, to make sure he was truly there. A kind nurse, understanding Joanne's yearning, held up a small handheld mirror so she could catch a glimpse of her husband. When Joanne saw Brian's image, her heart filled with gratitude. The nurse waved at Brian and gave a thumbs up as a sign of reassurance before turning back to Joanne with empathy in her eyes.

Despite her declining state, Joanne mustered a faint smile, grateful for Brian's attempt to connect with her. As she struggled to speak, her chest heaved with another bout of painful coughs. She felt the restraints holding her down on the sterile hospital bed, knowing they were necessary for her own safety. That's when another nurse's phone rang and the woman handed the phone to Joanne, who began sobbing as she spoke to her husband for the first time in days.

Joanne knew her moments of consciousness were few and fleeting, and she desperately tried to take deep breaths in an attempt to fill her failing lungs. She glanced at the nurse, their eyes briefly meeting before a peculiar sound interrupted the somber atmosphere. Small pebbles were bouncing off the window in a rhythmic percussion. The nurse looked down and saw Brian standing by his lawn chair, determined to reach out to his ailing wife in any way possible. She saw Dexter tossing pebbles at the window.

A short while later, Brian and Dexter disappeared from sight as they ran toward the parking lot. The nurse watching out the window found this behavior endearing but also strange; Brian had been coming every day for a several days now. Why would he leave now?

The ruthless COVID-19 virus had ravaged Joane's body, causing her heart to race and fight against itself in a desperate attempt to combat the infection. But it was a losing battle —each moment brought her closer to death as her frail body fought against the unstoppable virus. Her heartbeat quickened as her body attempted to flush out the invading illness, making every breath an immense struggle against suffocation. The once bustling hospital room now felt eerily quiet, save for the steady beeping of machines and hushed voices from outside. Joanne wondered if she had already slipped away into death's embrace.

As the COVID-19 virus took hold of Joanne's body, her heart rate became even more erratic —speeding up in moments of distress and slowing down as her energy faded. At first, her body fought back with a fever, trying to combat the invading infection. But as the disease progressed, her heart struggled to maintain a steady rhythm under the intense stress.

Physically, Joanne exhibited many common symptoms of severe COVID-19 infection. Initially, she experienced chills and body aches as her immune system worked hard to fight off the virus. As it spread, she developed a persistent cough and her lungs became inflamed and congested with fluid. Every breath became a struggle as she fought for air.

As the virus continued to attack her body, Joanne began to feel extreme fatigue and weakness. She became dehydrated as her fever caused sweating and her breathing became labored, making her feel even weaker. Nausea and vomiting also occurred as her body tried to cope with the toxins from the infection.

In the final stages of her illness, Joanne's organs started shutting down under the intensity of the virus. She became confused and disoriented due to the lack of oxygen to her brain. Her skin grew pale and clammy as her circulation slowed down. Throughout this ordeal, Joanne's body sent warning signals through different mechanisms, such as a rapid heart rate and difficulty breathing. The medical staff closely monitored her vital signs which showed unstable blood pressure and low levels of oxygen. Despite their best efforts and despite pumping massive amounts of oxygen into her system, Joanne could not overcome the brutal effects of the virus on her body.

Her mind wandered back to the beginning of the pandemic, when everything suddenly seemed to fall apart. As an experienced nurse, Joanne had faced challenges before, but nothing could have prepared her for this invisible enemy. She remembered the faces of her patients as they succumbed to the virus, a constant reminder of its devastating impact. Despite the fear and uncertainty, she remained dedicated to caring for others, a beacon of hope in dark times. And now it was about to take her life.

As she lay on her deathbed, Joanne's heart ached with sadness and regret. She opened her eyes and saw yellow figures standing beside her bed. She struggled to focus until one of the figures reached out and held her hand in its big black glove. The other black glove covered her hand but then stroked her hair. She felt sweat pouring down from her eyes as another black glove wiped them away.

The second yellow figure leaned in close, and she saw a bright plastic face shield press against her. Inside the face shield, she saw tiny droplets of water begin to puddle inside the shield as it pressed against her forehead. She heard the word, "Mom," several times in a row. The face shield pulled away for a moment, and she recognized her son Dexter inside the layers of protective gear inside the yellow suit.

To the right, she slowly recognized Brian in the other yellow suit. Water droplets also streaked his face shield, and his breaths were almost as loud as her own as he struggled to fight for air inside his hazardous materials suit. He tried a faint smile and then leaned in close to his wife. "Joanne, my love. We are here for you. You must hang on longer."

Joanne smiled briefly between coughing fits. Her body felt lighter knowing the most important people in her life stood by her side right now. At first, she worried about their safety and wondered if the police would arrest them, but then she thought about how intelligent these two men were and realized they had taken every precaution. Her instinct to scold them both withered away into thoughts of happiness they were with her somehow.

She looked her two men over, dressed in HazMat suits, and breathing through oxygen tanks to be by her bedside. She longed to reach out and hold them one last time, but the layers of plastic and rubber created an insurmountable barrier between them. She wondered how they ended up here and why they were just standing there silently with tears streaming down their faces. Even as they touched her arm, it felt like she was watching a silent movie unfold before her eyes. Her heart suddenly began to beat slower and slower.

As Joanne's consciousness faded, a swirling mix of memories and emotions filled her mind. She fondly remembered the simple pleasures of family dinners and outings, moments filled with laughter and love that now seem distant and fleeting. She wondered how her loved ones would cope without her, leaving behind a void that could never be filled.

Despite the overwhelming sadness that threatened to consume her, Joanne took comfort in knowing that she had led a purposeful and meaningful life. As a nurse, she dedicated herself to easing the pain of others, offering compassion and care to those who needed it most. And though her time on earth may be coming to an end, she knew that her legacy would live on as a testament to kindness and resilience in the face of hardship.

As her strength dwindled and her vision faded, Joanne took one last shaky breath, thinking of Brian and Dexter and trying to see them one last time. She longed to express her love and gratitude for them before she went, but the words remained unspoken, lost in the silence between them and her measured breaths.

In the darkness, Joanne felt a sense of peace wash over her, like a gentle wave lapping at the shores of her mind. With her loved ones standing next to her, she found the courage to let go and embrace the inevitable passage of time. And as her spirit soared free, she carried with her the memories of a life well lived, a legacy of love that would endure long after she is gone.

Behind her, she left a broken man and a loving son who must endure without her. She spoke to herself when she asked God to forgive her for what she had done to her family.

CHAPTER 44

With heavy hearts, they trudge back through the square,
Father's battle still heavy in the air.

The trio of Jiewen, Jay, and Meiyu Li treaded back to the market with heavy hearts, the weight of what they had just witnessed still lingering in the air like a thick fog. With each step, the memory of Wei Guo's struggle against the grip of the COVID-19 virus echoed through their minds. The haunting image of him moving away on a stretcher, his labored breaths and desperate gaze etched into their memories, weighed heavily on their souls. Despite shouting words of encouragement, they could not shake off the feeling of helplessness as they watched their father and husband fight for his life.

As they entered the quiet Li's Family Market once again, it seemed almost surreal without Wei Guo's familiar presence and the sight of customers roaming the food bins. His absence left a void that seemed to engulf the entire marketplace. Gone were the sounds of his jovial laughter and warm greetings to customers, replaced by an eerie silence. Gone was the sound of his pleasant whistling that made him and others happy.

Their eyes scanned the stalls out front and saw only a handful of customers stopping by for tea and a few limited items for sale on the curb in front of Wei Guo's now deserted stall. They mainly relied on sales from their online business that Jay ran smoothly from the neighboring warehouse.

Meiyu Li could feel her heartache increase as she thought about how much Wei Guo loved tending to his beloved stall and interacting with customers in person. She retreated back to her room on the second floor and felt the empty place on the bed where Wei Guo normally slept with her before the pandemic.

Jay headed back to work in the stock room, keeping himself occupied amidst the quietness. Jiewen took over preparing tea for any customers who might stop by, trying to bring some semblance of normalcy to their now somber market. But deep down, they all knew that things would never be quite the same without Wei Guo's infectious energy and unwavering spirit driving them forward. They wondered whether he could survive the ordeal and felt helpless to do anything about it. They could not even visit him in the hospital. They could not find out anything about him, as if they had dropped him off at a prison.

Each step up the stairs of their market weighed heavily on Meiyu Li's heart, a reminder of the life she and Wei Guo had built together over the past fifty-five years. She climbed the stairs wearily, her feet dragging with exhaustion and grief as she moved from the second floor to the third floor to look upon the isolation room.

As she reached the top floor, her heavy limbs seemed to collapse under the weight of her sorrow. Entering the isolation room, Meiyu Li moved slowly, almost mechanically, like invisible strings held her up like a puppet. She longed for the comforting presence of her beloved husband and desired to clean up the isolation room for when he returned, and just in case anyone else needed the room. But all she found was emptiness, a void that seemed to swallow her whole. She suited up into one of the bunny suits and donned the face masks and face shields to begin the cleanup.

With trembling hands, Meiyu Lu reached out, searching for any remnant of Wei Guo's warmth in the bed. His familiar touch had always brought her solace through even the toughest of times. But now, as she stood alone in the room, she could only feel his absence like a physical ache in her chest.

Throughout the pandemic, Meiyu Lu and Wei Guo had clung to each other, finding strength and comfort in their unbreakable bond. But now that he was away and in so much danger, she felt lost and uncertain about what tomorrow might bring. Tears welled in her eyes as she whispered silent prayers for his return, her heart heavy with longing and sadness.

The next morning, the sunrise peeked through the curtains, casting a warm glow over Jay and Jiewen as they woke up separately in their own rooms. Jay walked down the hallway and stood at the door of their bedroom on the second floor of the market and said good morning to Jiewen, who slept fitfully by herself so that she and Jay would not transfer the disease that may be consuming their family at that very moment. Sleeping alone became the new norm for people during the pandemic.

"Good morning, Jiewen," Jay said to his wife. "I missed you last night."

"I love you, my husband," Jiewen replied, her voice thick with emotion as she reached for the COVID testing kit on her nightstand, a promise they had made to each other to monitor their health every morning. Fighting back tears, she held up her test cartridge and revealed a negative result. At least for today, she would be safe from the deadly virus.

Jay also held up his test kit, showing the same negative result. They both let out a sigh of relief before looking at each other and shedding tears. In that moment, they longed to embrace each other but knew they must maintain a safe distance. After all, her father lay dying in a hospital because of this terrible disease, and they all were anxiously waiting for any updates on his condition. He would demand that they not let the virus spread to anyone else.

"I can't just sit here and wait for news," Jiewen said determinedly. She grabbed her cell phone and frantically searched for the paperwork they had received when dropping off their father at the emergency room the night before. Finally finding the phone number given by the attending nurse, she pressed the numbers on her cell phone with shaking hands.

Meanwhile, Jay stood helplessly by the doorway, his heart heavy with worry. Jiewen's call went straight to voicemail after a few rings. She left a message reciting their father's name and case number, along with her contact information in hopes of receiving an update soon. As Jiewen finished leaving the message, her heart pounded with anxiety, each second feeling like an eternity as she waited for any sign of a response from the hospital. Meanwhile, Jay could only offer silent support, his own worries mirroring hers as they both grappled with the uncertainty of her father's condition.

"I'll get your mother to take another test," Jay added while trying to keep control of the situation as best as anybody could. He held a blank test kit in his hand and showed it to Jiewen.

"I already tried last night," Jiewen explained and motioned for Jay to give up on that. "She said she doesn't care if she has it or not."

The minutes dragged on like hours, each second thick with tension as they went about their tasks in the quiet market. Jay diligently shipped off two large orders, securing enough income to keep their small business afloat for another few weeks. Meanwhile, Jiewen served tea and fulfilled orders for customers on the sidewalk, her mind racing with worry and stress.

Finally, the phone buzzed with an incoming call, causing Jiewen's heart to flutter nervously. She walked toward a portion of the market where the cell service was best, then answered with trembling hands, her voice barely above a whisper as she listened intently to the voice on the other end.

As the hospital staff delivered the devastating news of Wei Guo's passing, the world seemed to shatter around Jiewen. Tears welled in her eyes, and her body shook with uncontrollable grief. The phone fell from her hand as she sank to the ground, screaming for Jay at the top of her lungs. The few people on the street looked inside the market in amazement at the sound emanating from this small and beautiful woman.

Hearing his wife's cries of anguish, Jay's heart sank, and his own grief threatened to overcome him as he knew the cause of the grief without him even hearing it himself. Screams like that from his wife could only mean one thing. He rushed to Jiewen's side and helped her up from the floor, guiding her into the safety of the back of the market.

But even there, they were not alone; they saw Meiyu Li standing at the top of the stairs, her face already bearing the weight of the loss. She knew only death caused people to scream and cry like she had witnessed taking place at the bottom of the stairs.

Jiewen could hardly believe that her father was gone and felt immense sorrow for her mother, who had lost her husband. Her hands shook relentlessly as she allowed Jay to steer her toward the stairs to begin the climb to help her mother.

With a heavy heart, Jay wrapped his arms around Jiewen one more time and nudged her up the stairs as they both wept for their tremendous loss. He gestured toward Meiyu Li, who stood in shock at the top of the stairs. In that moment, it felt like all the weight of their grief was too much to bear, cutting deep into their souls like a sharp knife.

Meiyu Li collapsed to the floor, barely managing to catch herself to avoid falling down the stairs. Jiewen rushed to her mother and fell down on the floor at the top of the stairs with her mother. The cries and emotions released at that moment had become commonplace among people during the pandemic. And the pandemic was far from over as it spread across the globe.

After the grieving calmed to a point of numbness, Jiewen helped her mother up from the floor and guided her to their marital bedroom. Meiyu Li paused at the door the bedroom she shared for fifty-five years and looked around the room as if it were a foreign place.

Jiewen went back to the arms of her own husband and sobbed like a baby as he held her closely. Jay's own feelings for his father-in-law were very deep. Wei Guo was the first to accept him into the family and behaved like a second father to him. The people of Chinatown slowly accepted him into their community from that point on.

Jay suddenly looked into Jiewen's eyes as he remembered they must now tell their son, Bradley, about the terrible news. The cell phone call went as expected when anyone hears the news about a death in the family. Within 30 minutes, Brad arrived at the store wearing a mask, face shield, and gloves. Jiewen and Jay were a little surprised at the sight of their son in protective gear, but understood that was an intelligent decision. He would not do an "air hug" with his parents as had become the norm. Not on this terrible day for the family. He hugged his mother for as long as they both could hold their breath. Then he spent a little shorter time with his father. They all commented on how maturely Brad behaved and complimented him on his caution. They vowed that nobody else would contract the virus on a day already filled with catastrophe.

Next, Brad went upstairs to search for his grandmother and came upon her in the isolation room as she mechanically cleaned the room in an attempt to distract herself from her grief. She saw her grandson in the antechamber and smiled through her tears at him. She directed him as he began to enter the room. "Stay out there, Sūnzi."

"Yes, Zǔmǔ," he replied using the proper term of respect for his grandmother.

As Meiyu Li tidied up the room, she noticed a small box under the bed. She recognized it as her husband's stash box for little trinkets he always cherished. She bent down to retrieve the box and walked to the anteroom to clean up for her grandchild. She opened the lid and saw her husband's wedding ring, gold watch, numerous seemingly unimportant items, and a neatly folded piece of paper. She glanced at it and immediately recognized Wei Guo's handwriting in a flow of words written in simplified Chinese. There was also a sketch of some kind of table with long legs.

Meiyu Li motioned for Brad to step out of the anteroom so she could remove the contaminated garb and reveal her still-clean clothes underneath. She handed the paper to Brad and he began reading the paper.

"What is it?" Meiyu Li asked as she stepped out of the bunny suit and replaced her mask with a fresh one.

Brad looked confused at first but slowly began to smile. He held the paper up and showed it to his grandmother. "He wants a sky burial."

Meiyu Li was puzzled at first, but then she remembered Wei Guo Chu was part of a family that believed in such traditions –far differently than the Li family who held to more modern concepts. She looked at Brad and grinned. "If my husband wants a sky burial, then he shall have one."

CHAPTER 45

Workers rushed to create a terrace new,
With beams and boards, an inviting view grew.

As the day wore on and prior to the crisp evening air descending upon Top of the Tunnel bar, Yuze, Lawrence, and Daniel Kim sprang into action outside. With a sense of purpose and dedication, they set out to transform their makeshift outdoor dining area in the parking spots outside the front of the bar into a haven of warmth and comfort for their customers that night. The three of them moved in perfect unison, each one knowing exactly what needed to be done to create a safe and enjoyable dining experience amidst the ongoing pandemic.

They constructed the outdoor dining area with sturdy beams carefully arranged and secured to the pavement to form a solid foundation. Lawrence, a budding craftsman with a hobby for wood working, deftly wielded his tools, fastening each remaining floor board with precision across the tops of the foundation boards. Yuze and Daniel joined in the effort, tirelessly hauling supplies and offering assistance whenever needed. Together, they worked as a well-coordinated team, driven by their shared goal of creating an inviting space for their valued customers now that the health department approved their permit for dining outside of the restaurant in the parking spots directly in front of the bar. Yuze thought about how nice the view was from this new outdoor terrace and wondered if he should have done this before the pandemic.

They moved on to building a barrier wall using recycled beer kegs to keep passing traffic well away from the first row of tables. Lawrence lined the kegs up in a row and connected them with thick ropes, creating a charming yet functional divider between the outdoor dining area and the occasional passing traffic. Together, they worked on constructing the platform, carefully placing propane heaters around the edges to keep each table warm. Lawrence made sure to position each heater safely, taking into account both functionality and appearance.

Yuze, Lawrence, and Daniel worked in perfect harmony as they bustled around the makeshift outdoor dining area. Despite the chill in the air, their faces glowed with warmth and resolve, driven by the knowledge that they were providing a much-needed escape for their patrons. When they finished, they took a step back to admire what they had created. The platform extended across the sidewalk and parking spaces, with tables spaced apart according to health department regulations. The atmosphere was comfortable and inviting, with the soft glow of heaters and twinkling lights strung above.

As the sun slowly descended behind the city skyline, the previously empty street outside the Top of the Tunnel bar came to life. Strings of twinkling lights crisscrossed above rows of tables, each one set with flickering candles and small vases of fresh flowers. The air was filled with the irresistible scent of sizzling burgers and crispy fries, drawing in passersby with promises of comfort and indulgence.

As the first guests arrived, bundled up in blankets provided by the bar, Yuze greeted them with a genuine smile and a warm welcome. He took great pride in knowing that every precaution had been taken to ensure their safety and enjoyment, from the carefully spaced tables to the frequent sanitation procedures.

Liz and Greet, regulars at the bar, arrived right on time, their faces lighting up with excitement as they approached their reserved table. Yuze personally attended to them, eager to hear their thoughts on the new outdoor dining experience as he engaged them in lively conversation.

"I cant believe how this looks," Liz said excitedly to Yuze. She resisted the urge to hug him so instead extended her hand for a fist bump —the new handshake widely in use since the start of this pandemic.

"Thank you both for supporting us," Yuze replied and also fist-bumped Greet. He escorted them to a table while explaining all the steps they took to get the permit and build the deck. Although Liz had been retired from her job as a health department inspector years ago, Yuze still sought her advice when building the outdoor dining area.

In the bar area, Lawrence showed off his mastery as he effortlessly crafted cocktails and poured glasses of wine with precision. He served each drink on a gleaming silver tray, showcasing his attention to detail and professionalism. He smiled and exchanged some small talk with Liz and Greet, happy to see more people arriving as the evening wore on.

In the kitchen, two waiters worked tirelessly to keep up with orders for steaming hot plates of food. Despite the chaos of the busy kitchen, there was a sense of camaraderie among the staff as they worked together seamlessly to flip burgers and toss fries. And they were happy they could continue working and provide for their families.

Throughout the evening, laughter and chatter filled the open-air space, accompanied by clinking glasses and music wafting from inside the bar through the open windows. The Top of the Tunnel had transformed into a warm sanctuary of hospitality, a beacon of resilience and hope in the midst of challenging times. The future was uncertain, but for now, they worked together on a solution to keep the business going. Each worker occasionally paused to look out over the bridge and wondered about the health of their loved ones.

CHAPTER 46

With bated breath, they joined the online meet,
Uncertain what to expect from this feat.

Charles Kang clicked the "Join Meeting" button on his laptop screen, and a mixture of excitement and apprehension washed over him. The familiar sound of the Zoom meeting room's notification echoed in the background, marking his entry into the digital world that had become the norm since the pandemic began. He adjusted his glasses and settled back into his chair, anticipating the arrival of his friends as they showed up on small squares on the video screen.

Moments later, Daniel Kim's face appeared in one square on the screen, his salt-and-pepper hair neatly styled and his glasses resting on his nose.

"Hey, Charles! Good to see you," Daniel greeted warmly, his voice filling the small room where he sat alone. Behind him stood a bookshelf filled with thick volumes on economics and finance, a remnant of his previous career as a venture capitalist. He still cherished reading the actual book instead of doing research online.

"Hey, Daniel! Glad you could make it," Charles replied with a smile, grateful for a familiar face in this virtual world. "Just waiting for Jorge now."

As if on cue, Jorge Freeman's video feed came to life, revealing the rugged features of a man who had spent decades tinkering with machines. His gray hair was slightly disheveled, and he nervously fidgeted with his webcam. "Sorry I'm late, guys," Jorge apologized sheepishly, his deep voice tinged with uncertainty. In the background, an organized array of tools hung from a pegboard, a reminder of his days as a repairman. His office was his shop, and his shop was his office.

"No worries, Jorge! We're just getting started," Charles reassured him with encouragement. "Glad you could join us."

Daniel moved a bottle of wine into view of the camera, and attached a corkscrew to the top, and skillfully pulled the cork out, then poured himself a full glass in a large bowl of a wine glass. The glimmer from the burgundy liquid reflected lighting from the side. Charles poured himself a scotch and Jorge popped open the lid on a can of beer. They all made sure the others could see what they were drinking.

"First things first," Charles said solemnly while raising his glass to the camera of his laptop. "We've got to support Brian and Jay in their time of need. We cannot hold a funeral, so we must figure out a way to help them."

Daniel looked into the camera while toasting his video screen. "To Joanne. One of the kindest and most beautiful women I've ever met."

The other two said similar kind words and then toasted and drank silently in her honor. Each of the men choked back tears and reflected on what a wonderful person she was and how terrible this must be on Brian and Dexter.

Next, they moved on to toasting Wei Guo, whom they had seen through the years, and they all looked upon him as a second father. But they knew Jiewen and Jay must be struggling and loved them deeply. They echoed how hard this must be to not hold a funeral. They vowed to help Yuze and Lawrence run the bar during this time of grief.

After honoring the dead, the three men caught up with each other, reminiscing about their pioneering days in the high-tech industry during the dot-com boom. They shared stories of late-night brainstorming sessions, daring business ventures, and the thrill of exploring uncharted territories. Despite the physical separation of the stay-at-home orders, their friendship remained strong, bridging the gap between virtual pixels and reality.

As they delved into their meeting's agenda, navigating virtual communication with a mix of laughter and occasional technical difficulties, Charles felt grateful for technology's ability to connect them across time and distance. In a world filled with uncertainty, their friendship provided a sense of stability, anchoring them amidst the chaos of the pandemic.

Daniel thought of a way to help the families, and the three of them started hatching a plan. If they cannot hold a funeral, there must be some other way to show support for their lifelong friends during their time of sorrow.

CHAPTER 47

The war was won, battles not lost in vain,
Fallen heroes in our hearts remain.

With the experimental artificial intelligence chip implanted into the brains of his luminous blue jeep, Dexter drove with precision and ease. The software he had installed guided the vehicle along the predetermined route set by Brad and his father, Jay Baumers. Daniel Kim and Charles Kang had provided them with a map of the street in front of the Top of the Tunnel bar, where a surprise event awaited them.

As they started in the North Beach area of San Francisco, Dexter's father Brian, remained fixated on the laptop installed into the dashboard. Following closely behind in their delivery van were Jiewen, Jay, and their son Bradley. Behind them were Yuze and his son Lawrence taking up the rear of the caravan in their small car. Though she remained in her third-floor unit at Li's Family Market, Meiyu Li promised to keep an eye out from her balcony as the cars passed by on the predetermined route.

The route outlined on the map began with a turn down a quiet street in North Beach, where Joanne resided in the old Renado apartment building decades earlier. While the Renado family rebuilt the collapsed apartment building after the devastating Loma Prieta earthquake of 1989, it still retained many of its original features and charm. They had eliminated the first floor garage design that had caused the collapse due to its vulnerability during the earthquake, but Frank Renado and his descendants made sure to maintain its overall design and atmosphere. The lower floors housed young residents now, while the upper floors were home to more mature and affluent tenants.

Brian became overwhelmed when he saw the Renado building and recalled how he first fell in love with Joanne when she lived in that building years ago. Dexter drove the jeep slowly with its now silent engine past the building and paused when they got to the entrance of the building where a large group of people sat in chairs at the side of the street.

Dexter slowly drove ahead and realized what this day was about now that he saw the setup. On each side of the street were rows of chairs spread out with the proper six feet of social distancing. In each of the two dozen chairs sat people they knew from the building when Joanne lived there, including Liz Mowbry and her partner Greet. Alongside them was Greet's menagerie of life-sized plastic animals all decorated solemnly.

As they drove by all the people, they noticed that every one of the people in the chairs held up a photo of Joanne in her honor. Some of the people also held up a photo of Wei Guo Chu, who must have also known him and his relation to the family. Brian waved solemnly at each of the people as tears streamed down his face. Similarly, the people in the other two cars began weeping as they realized this was the best their friends and families could do during this time of the pandemic. Brian looked at the funeral urn placed carefully in a safe spot on the console, and thought of Joanne. He reached out and touched the urn with a loving hand.

The next part of the route took them up Stockton Street and led them into the heart of Chinatown. Once again, the organizers maintained the safety protocols and placed the chairs six feet apart from each other in both rows and columns of chairs. About a hundred people lined both sides and held up photos of Wei Guo and Joanne. The people in the chairs and the occupants of the three cars exchanged tearful waves as they drove slowly in the middle of the street. The emotions became nearly heartbreaking to the people in the cars.

As the caravan of cars slowly approached the front of Li's Family Market, they saw that someone had hung up a large banner with both of Joanne and Wei Guo's photos across the front entrance with a twenty-foot-long colorful banner. The cars stopped in front and they all looked up at Meiyu Li standing at the balcony, watching the parade and the well-wishers from the neighborhood. She stood with her hand across her mouth and sobbed deeply. She exchanged knowing glances with the people in the cars as they hung their heads out to look up at her.

Next the three cars traveled through the Stockton Street tunnel and wound past the main hospital, where once again, rows of chairs filled with people spanned the two blocks before and two blocks after the hospital. This time doctors, nurses, ERT members, firefighters, and policemen filled the chairs with people in uniforms who came out between shifts to honor a fallen first-responder. Each of them must have seen dozens of deaths already with no letting up in sight. But this was one of their sisters.

The three cars slowly made their way through the throng of people in the protected lane set just for them. Suddenly, applause rang out and echoed through the street as everyone stood and stared into the windows of the passing vehicles. A fire truck parked at the end of the group let go of its blast of air horn that reverberated through the streets of San Francisco. The caravan went past the hospital finally and moved down a street mainly empty of cars and people. The people in the cars took their time collecting their thoughts and wiping away tears, knowing that next was the parade route past the Top of the Tunnel bar.

The winding road took a turn up a steep road that led the caravan of three cars to the bar. As they made their way up the hill, they saw over a hundred people lining the street in front of the bar on both sides, their faces etched with sorrow, remembrance, and excitement to show their love. At the top of the hill stood the Ritz Hotel looking stoic sitting by itself on its throne while overlooking the scene.

Charles Kang sat in the front row of the first row of chairs, clutching pictures of his lost friends as tears streamed down his face. He looked at each person in the car as they drove ever so slowly past each row of the mourners. Next to Charles, Daniel Kim and Suzan Bolstock held each other's hands tightly, their fingers shaking with emotion as they gazed at the photos in their own trembling hands and then into the cars. Jorge Freeman solemnly rang a bell that he had taken from a cable car, its slow beat adding to the somber atmosphere. Jimmy Baumers placed a hand over his heart and silently wept. Other patrons, friends, and family members filled the street, paying their respects to those they had lost.

As they reached the summit of the hill, two sharply-dressed Ritz hotel attendants approached the line of cars and presented wreaths to each passenger. From a balcony above, a lone bagpiper played a haunting melody that resonated off every building in an eerie harmony. The sound carried across the rolling hills and winding streets, almost as if it were carrying away the souls of their loved ones.

Brian instinctively reached for his son's hand for comfort as they listened to the mournful tune from the bagpipes. Just then, the screen on their AI-powered laptop lit up with a new suggested route and painted a line heading westward. Instead of stopping at the Ritz as planned, this new line extended off toward the Golden Gate Bridge. Brian and Dexter shared a surprised smile through their tears as they followed the suggested path without further thought. Somehow the AI understood what must be done.

In a moment of trust and surrender, Dexter let go of the steering wheel and allowed the car to drive itself along the new route, seemingly guided by the notes of the bagpiper's music and drifting spirits.

The passengers in the other cars looked at each other in confusion as they followed the jeep down the hill past the Ritz. After some phone calls between them, they all agreed to continue following this unexpected path that ended up leading them to Stinson Beach, just north of the Golden Gate Bridge.

Brad, sitting in the second row of Jiewen's delivery van, suggested that Stinson Beach would be a fitting location for a sky burial ceremony. "Mom, Dad," he said excitedly, "We could fulfill Grandpa's final wish there."

Jiewen's eyes flicked to the rearview mirror as Brad explained his plan, intrigued by the unconventional suggestion. She could see the determination in his gaze and nodded in agreement with a slight tilt of her head.

Jay's expression turned skeptical as he rubbed his temples, considering Brad's idea. "It seems a bit...unorthodox," he stated warily.

"But it's what Grandpa wanted," Brad insisted, his voice firm with conviction. "Remember how he used to tell us stories about the sky burial ceremonies in Tibet? He always said he wanted something like that."

Jiewen chimed in, "He did mention it several times. It would be a beautiful way to honor him."

After a moment of contemplation, Jay sighed and gave in. "Alright, let's hear your plan then."

Brad's excitement was palpable as he outlined the details. "We'll find a secluded spot at Stinson Beach, away from prying eyes. Then, we'll lay out a cloth and place Grandpa's urn on it. After that, we'll open the bag of bread and scatter it around the area and then mix in Grandpa."

Jiewen glanced at Jay and then through the mirror at her son, silently feeling like they were about to do something wrong.

"The birds will come, and...well, you know the rest," Brad added and looked at his mother's eyes in the rear-view mirror.

After a moment of consideration, Jay nodded with a small smile. "Alright, let's do it. It's what Wei Guo would have wanted."

With their decision made, the family called Yuze and Lawrence in the next car and continued their journey to Stinson Beach, following along behind Dexter's jeep, each lost in their own thoughts about the unconventional yet meaningful send-off they were about to give to their beloved Grandpa Wei Guo.

Inside the jeep, Brian suggested that Stinson Beach would be the perfect place to put Joanne's ashes into the ocean as she had directed in her will long ago. She wanted her family to know she was part of the ocean, and they could look upon her every time they saw water.

The winding road to the beach went past a favorite restaurant of the Lomax family, a place called the Pelican Inn. Brian looked at the restaurant as they turned into the road that led down to Stinson Beach. He recalled several romantic dining experiences there with Joanne and touched the urn as if there could be some sort of connection. Dexter noticed his father's expression and looked away and straight ahead to the road.

The three cars pulled into a parking area along the beach and they all got out to stretch their legs and exchange thoughts and feelings about what had occurred back along the parade route. Then, they each explained what they were going to do. Brian and Dexter looked at each other, puzzled by the sky burial explanation, but then shrugged and agreed to help.

The group first decided they would honor Joanne and then perform the sky burial ritual later. Brian and Dexter solemnly carried Joanne's urn to the water's edge and paused to find a peaceful spot away from a few others at the beach. The sun had already set by this time so the place was nearly deserted save for a small group down on the other end of the beach. The wind stayed mostly calm and carried a hint of the deeper ocean past the reef. A slight spray filled the air as the winds wafted little clouds of mist in haphazard paths to the small stream that spilled into this part of the beach. Brian studied his son's face, and they silently agreed that this was the right spot. They glanced back at Jay, Jiewen, Yuze, and Lawrence, who all waved somberly at the two men.

"I'm going to wade in a bit," Brian said as he started moving into the first little, flat wave. He didn't care that his dress shoes would get wet so kept walking further in anyway. Dexter waited at first but then followed his father until they stood in gentle waves that splashed above their knees.

"This is good, Dad."

Brian held the urn up and removed the shiny gold cover that sparked with the reflection of a half-moon that appeared behind them. He handed the cover to Dexter, who held it carefully as he watched his father stare into the inside of the urn. The tears that fell into the urn mixed with the dry ashes and formed tiny puddles on the dry surface. At that moment he felt several sets of hands on his shoulders when he realized the other four joined them in the water.

Jiewen leaned her head on Brian's shoulder and said, "I hope you don't mind us being part of this. She was my best friend, you know."

Brian touched her forehead and replied, "Thank you."

Jay also leaned in and placed a strong hand on Brian's and Dexter's shoulders and said in a halting voice, "She was my friend too."

Brian and Dexter expressed thanks to the group and Brian slowly lowered the urn all the way into the water and let the flushing action of the moving water pull Joanne from the urn. A small trail of Joanne formed like a light gray wisp of smoke that drifted off to the sea in a meandering path. Soon the entire contents of the urn emptied into the ocean and Brian turned it upside down in the water to make sure it was completely empty. He stood up and the six of them stayed in a group hug for a few minutes as they looked out into the ocean and remembered their friend, mother, wife, and aunt.

After a few more quiet moments, the group waded back to shore, and Brad quickly ran to the delivery van to retrieve Wei Guo's urn and the large bag of bread he brought along. He took a few moments to gather everything and hurried back to the group who had been busy clearing away a flat section of sand near the water.

The sand squished beneath Brad's shoes as he approached the edge of Stinson Beach near the water again. He paused to take in the vast expanse before him, a sense of reverence washing over him as the sound of gentle waves filled his ears. Jiewen, Yuze, and Lawrence surrounded him, their faces solemn and determined. Brian and Dexter entered the group and stood closely by their friends and relatives.

Brad lowered the bag of bread that weighed heavy in his hands with the significance it carried. This previously ordinary loaf now held a special purpose of delivering a person's soul to the cosmos. Forming a tight circle on the sand, they gathered around the bag, preparing to honor their grandfather's final wish.

Setting the bag down carefully, Brad motioned for his friends to join him with unfolding the blanket. Brad said, "Spread this out and then we'll add Grandpa and mix him in."

Jiewen offered a gentle reprimand to her son while looking him in the eye and smiling. "I'm sure we can phrase that differently."

Yuze interjected with a touch of humor. "Well, technically, that's what we're doing, isn't it?"

A chuckle rippled through the group before they grew serious once more, their thoughts turning to the task at hand. Yuze laid out the blanket on the sand, tucking the edges under to keep it in place against the gentle breeze. Lawrence and Brad approached their grandfather's urn with solemn reverence, their movements slow and deliberate as they then mixed his cremated remains with the bread.

As they worked together to pour the ashes into the bag of bread, Brad felt a sense of peace wash over him. He watched with awe as the grains of ash blended seamlessly with the bread, symbolizing their grandfather's spirit becoming one with nature. They gently shook the bag to mix it all together.

With each pour and shake, the group grew closer to completing their task. Once finished, they gathered around the makeshift altar with joined hands, offering a silent prayer in their hearts. Then, with a final gesture of solidarity, they scattered the mixture of bread and ashes across the blanket and moved away to a safe distance. Brad made sure every piece of bread and Grandpa came out of the bag. He folded the bag neatly.

At first, nothing happened until one seagull bounced across the sand and looked strangely at the altar of bread and body. Then two more birds bounced over and seemed to have a discussion. Then an entire flock swooped in and the entire altar became a ball of seagulls almost boiling as birds flew in and out.

As the birds swooped down to claim their offering, Brad felt a profound sense of closure. Though their modern interpretation of the traditional sky burial ceremony may have deviated from the customs of old, the essence of honoring their grandfather's final wish remained unchanged —a testament to the enduring bond of family and the eternal cycle of life and death.

Slowly, the boiling birds flew off and the last remnants went with them, including the blanket dragged off by two fighting birds that dragged it all the way into the water where it sank out of sight.

In traditional Tibetan sky burial ceremonies, there are often ceremonial words spoken, invoking blessings upon the departed and offering gratitude to the natural world. Brad removed a paper from his pocket and used his flashlight to say the first words of the blessing. "May the winds carry your spirit to the heavens, where it may find peace and serenity."

He handed the paper to his mother who said the next part. "We offer thanks to the birds, guardians of the sky, for their role in this sacred ritual."

Then Yuze: "May the earth embrace your essence, nourishing new life as you journey into the next realm."

Then Lawrence: "Through this act of liberation, may your soul find release from the bonds of earthly existence."

The last verse took some negotiation, but the last three in the group, Jay, Brian, and Dexter, spoke the verse together as if it had some special meaning for them all: "Though we part with your physical form, your memory shall remain etched in our hearts forever."

DAVID LEE LUEDTKE

A Poem In Three Acts

Act 1 – The Year 1989

At tunnel's peak, where paths converge and blend,
A mix of old and new, delights extend.
Paths veer and meet, old college friends in tow,
San Francisco hills steep, car and bike below.

Thinking of creations, only a shell,
Unseen hands craft places for us to dwell.
A woman stirs up dreams of times long past,
Regulars, like kin, remind us what will last.

In sterile rooms where filters guard the air,
And miracles take place with fervent care.
Through banks and Chinatown, her steps resound,
Echoing in the tunnel's dark surround.

Noiseless entrance, clad in woolen thread,
Numbers assured for what lies on ahead.
Their income mirrors dreams and goals aligned,
In turbulent times, love's anchor they find.

Shops fade into a bustling market's call,
A corner stall stands tall, renowned for all.
Through heights they roam, with grace in each step's sway,
Towards North Beach's end, where their hearts will stay.

His ardor firm, though burdens bend his frame,
Yet weary, his spirit remains aflame.
Beyond nature's grasp, at the edge of their home,
Seeking the west coast pulse, why people come.

Their tiny home, a legacy of kin,
Nestled in hearts of the people within.
Walking the marina's brim with grace,
Hearing the city's secrets in shadows' space.

He sifts through rubble, thoughts of loved ones in mind.
His heart beats fast, to those loved he will find.
After the quake, they toil in makeshift inns,
Trading meals for goods, the healing begins.

In Chinatown's streets, smoke and spice abound,
Proud fighters they are, amidst the ruined ground.
More than a ride, with a test in each stride,
And chips that power this unusual glide.

Act 2 - The Year 2002

Years pass by, with new inventions in time,
Unlocking doors, discoveries sublime.
A gamble in mind, he sees cards in view,
Eyes searching for foes, his options are few.

In dot-com rush, he treads a cautious path,
But temptations of quick gains spark his wrath.
Tracking records from a paper to the screen,
A decade gone with a sadness yet unseen.

With confident strides through neon-lit streets,
She turns, skyscrapers shift to old-world meets.
Tech's light beckoned, a manager embraced,
A gateway built, meeting long-craved haste.

As eve drew near, the tech world in suspense,
With a hustling staff and fears immense.
A world paused, breaths held tight and lights aglow,
The millennium went like a vanquished foe.

Friends gather beneath the New Year's bright view
Thinking of fortunes and wishing they knew.
Amid the finance flurry, screens aglow,
A sage plots trades, timing the house cash flow.

Sunset on the city, post-dot-com strife,
They find refuge in friends, safety in life
Together they face their startup's plight,
Born to revolutionize, yet reckless in flight.

In the wild tech world, a manager steers,
His family's ventures online amidst fears.
In a safe place, for hearts that are weary,
the host serves solace, binds friends in theory.

Act 3 - The Year 2020

Years on, sailing hills in electric glides,
A nurse signals new changes in the tides.
A promise kept to continue old ways,
Generations entwined through countless days.

Tension vibrates as people meet that night,
Two families, passing the torch with might.
Once bustling, now still, each night and each day;
Friends meet, yet remain apart in dismay.

Isolated and alone, locked away,
No more meetings or work, just home to stay.
Inside their homes, the people stand and fight,
Against the illness with all of their might.

They gaze upon the bar, once full and bright,
Now cloaked in silence, swallowed by the night.
Death's cold grip lingers in each somber space,
As sorrow echoes in this haunting place.

Amid turmoil and some people's health dire,
They soldier on for what customers desire.
Father and son, beneath her window stay
Hoping and praying for a better day.

A woman gasps, her eyes fixed on the screen,
Numbers blink death's edge, a sight too well seen.
With heavy hearts, they trudge back through the square,
Father's battle still heavy in the air.

Workers rushed to create a terrace new,
With beams and boards, an inviting view grew.
With bated breath, they joined the online meet,
Uncertain what to expect from this feat.

The war was won, battles not lost in vain,
Fallen heroes in our hearts remain.

Tibetan Sky Burial Ceremony

May the winds carry your spirit to the heavens, where it may find peace and serenity.

We offer thanks to the birds, guardians of the sky, for their role in this sacred ritual.

May the earth embrace your essence, nourishing new life as you journey into the next realm.

Through this act of liberation, may your soul find release from the bonds of earthly existence.

Though we part with your physical form, your memory shall remain etched in our hearts forever.

The Beeze Series

Book 1: Last Mile

Book 2: Tales at the Top

Book 3: Critical Paths

Book 4: Rise of the Contros

Book 5: Roots of Mars

Book 1: Last Mile

In a world ruled by Controllers, Dr. Manny Rio, along with young Maggie McKenna and her mother Dr. Rosita McKenna, must search for hope forty years from now. With only a small team of courageous scientists, long-distance haulers, and Beeze AI vehicles as their allies, they fight against the tyrannical control of algorithms. As they travel across the nation in search of a cure for their illness, danger lurks at every turn. They must navigate through multiple pods, constantly evading capture before electronic leashes ensnare them and prevent escape.

Book 2: Tales at the Top

Brian Lomax, a young engineer, had high hopes for success in San Francisco during the rapid growth of Silicon Valley. Despite the booms and crashes of the computer industry in the 1980s and early 2000s, people still held onto dreams of a future filled with advancing technology. When the pandemic hit in 2019, there was a surge in demand for control to save lives, but it soon became clear that algorithms were taking over and controlling people's lives. This sparked the development of artificial intelligence and the emergence of powerful Controllers.

Book 3: Critical Paths

A decade after the devastating 2019 pandemic, Brad Baumers and Dexter Lomax, son of Brian, were employed at MAST Technologies in San Francisco. The company specialized in developing advanced AI computer chips. One of Dexter's inventions was DAVE, a state-of-the-art vehicle powered by artificial intelligence and designed to prevent deadly crashes. Unfortunately, artificial intelligence couldn't save Dexter's wife from a fatal accident years earlier. DAVE became the first of many Beeze vehicles, created to swarm together for maximum efficiency. When Megan Sumners and her cameraman joined forces with Dexter's team to make a TV series on the dangers of excessive AI use, they never expected to uncover a cover-up by the authorities. Determined to reveal the truth, they set out to investigate a catastrophic event that had been swept under the rug.

Book 4: Rise of the Contros

Dexter Lomax's ambitious dream of developing a fleet of self-driving Beeze vehicles was thrown off course by the pandemic of 2050. With his loyal companion, DAVE, at his side, he harnessed the power of AI not only to outsmart the Controllers, but also to improve the functionality of his daughter's prosthetic limbs and manage the growing number of Beeze vehicles. As they navigated this new world defined by powerful AI-driven Controllers, Dexter, Ashlie, and her mother Christi found themselves torn between their own moral beliefs and those enforced by the enigmatic Controllers.

Book 5: Roots of Mars

Despite the challenges of life in 2075, with the lingering effects of the pandemic, technological manipulation, and artificial intelligence, the Controllers maintained a tight grip on society, keeping it in a state of controlled stasis. However, a team consisting of Dr. Manny Rio, Maggie McKenna, Dr. Rosita McKenna, and tech guru Theo Wiggins devised a plan to create a revolutionary vertical farming system that could provide sustenance for its inhabitants without reliance on the Controllers. This story showcases the resilience of the human spirit as these individuals work towards a self-sufficient food production system that has potential to benefit not only Earth but also beyond our planet.

ABOUT THE AUTHOR

David Lee Luedtke, author, inventor, painter, engineer, and traveler, resides in the San Francisco Bay Area. Along with writing the popular book *Last Mile*, the first installment in the *Beeze Series*, he also contributed a weekly column to a local newspaper for many years. With a background in executive positions within the semiconductor industry and the field of robotic surgery, he holds numerous patents for his innovative creations. His passion for developing autonomous driving technology fuels his imagination and provides inspiration for his novels.

www.ingramcontent.com/pod-product-compliance
Lightning Source LLC
Chambersburg PA
CBHW022110240626
47153CB00007B/2314